Wings of CONTRITION

A tale of young men coming of age in the
maelstrom and horror of the world's first air war

Leon Hughes

Copyright © 2013 Leon Hughes
All rights reserved.

ISBN: 1482590247
ISBN-13: 9781482590241
Library of Congress Control Number: 2013903568
CreateSpace Independent Publishing Platform
North Charleston, South Carolina

Rugby School, June 28, 1913

For James Caulfield, speech day was the purgatory that preceded summer. Dreary weskit-clad warriors, with rheumy eyes and complexions borne of scotch and sunshine, took to the stage of Rugby's Temple Speech Room and dealt out the mantra of imperialism with a fervour that rivalled Joseph Chamberlain.

James wriggled on the tiny seat, the starched, cheap cotton of his shirt crackling against the thick wool of his jacket and earning him a reproachful look from Mr. Aldridge, his cadaverous housemaster. Feigning interest with all the incapacity of youth, James sat rigidly, the perfect posture of the young paladin undermined only marginally by the dead eyes of the opium addict.

It was sweltering: six hundred boys and as many parents packed into an oak-panelled oven and toasted gently by the mid-afternoon sun flooding through the high western windows. James watched as a trickle of sweat ran down the neck of the F-block boy in front of him before being hungrily swallowed by the off-white folds of his high collar. Everyone was uncomfortable, and the stench of a thousand damp frock coats permeated the room.

The speaker's exhortations were reaching their height, and the sense of an ending produced a barely restrained excitement in the faces of the tightly packed group of unfortunates in the audience. Major General Cunnicliffe was unperturbed. He had faced the furious charge of the Mahdi's dervishes at Omdurman, and for him, boredom was as British as Bovril. Stabbing a pudgy forefinger over the lectern, he railed against the liberalism permeating British society, the insufferable suffragettes, the ingratitude of "Hardie's mob," and the sinister Teutonic wiles of the kaiser and his navy.

"It is the boys before me that will fight the next great fight. My generation has built you an empire, and with the Lord by your side, you will fight to the last man to defend the gift we have given you. You carry the Christian vision of Dr. Arnold and of this great school, and you shall carry those principles of compassion, charity, and virtue into the darkest corners of the globe. Together, we Britons will bring light where there is darkness, and, as ever, we Rugbeians shall form our country's vanguard. Know that if we are united, we shall always prevail, for we are the best of men!"

Flushed and visibly sweating, the puce-faced veteran of the thin red line signalled the end of his oratory by pulling a rather disreputable handkerchief from his top pocket and wiping his brow. His porcine eyes squinted at the audience, and the thick fur of his cavalry whiskers momentarily lifted in what might have been an approximation of a smile.

The audience gave a tangible sigh of relief, which slowly gave way to a rippling of applause, rolling like a wave from the parents at the back of the hall to the boys and masters seated in the front rows. One or two stalwarts, fathers, perhaps themselves veterans of some vainglorious imperial adventure, took to their feet and clapped loudly. James and his housemates were shamed into action and got to their feet too. Lethargy forgotten, they applauded wildly, lost in the relief that, after nearly two hours, the old boy had finally finished. Three boys down from James, Spencer—the bluff giant of a boy that had been that year's Head of Tudor House—was even moved to shout out, "Bravo! Hear, hear. Floreat Rugbeia!"

The room quietened as the headmaster, Reverend Albert Augustus David, climbed the side stairs to the stage. He vigorously shook Major General Cunnicliffe's hand and took to the lectern while the military man sat on a stool immediately to his right.

Reverend David was a small man with battleship grey hair cut into a severe puritan style. Piercing green eyes were framed by bushy eyebrows, which the smaller boys at the school swore were actually tame caterpillars. His academic gown trailed to the floor and gave him the air of a slightly dishevelled Roman senator, which, together with his middle name, had earned him the soubriquet "little Caesar." He had command though, not least because his earnest Anglicanism was tempered by a ready willingness to punish any infraction with a liberal use of the cane. When he raised his hands, parents, masters, and boys alike took to their seats and closed their mouths.

"Thank you, Major General. I am sure that the redoubtable service you have given your country, as well as your fine words this day, will serve as an example to all the people who have had the good fortune to hear you speak. I especially hope that the boys that leave us for the final time today will carry your words with them into the world and always endeavour to bring a civilising light to those places where darkness reigns. For, as you so rightly said, they are Rugbeians, and they have a duty to uphold the honour of this school wherever their path may take them."

The headmaster inclined his head towards the major, whose face took on a flush of such amethyst lustre that it reminded James of the colour of the Madeira wine his father served at dinner parties.

"And now," the headmaster resumed, "all that remains before we adjourn for the cricket is the school song. Mr. Burgess, if you would be so good."

Somewhere to the right of the stage, the wheezy strains of the school organ began. As one, the audience took to its feet, and as the introduction ended, six hundred pubescent boys raised their chins to the sky and began to shout out the familiar words at top volume.

"Evoe! Laeta requies
Advenit laborum
Fessa vult inducias
Dura gens librorum
Nunc comparata sarcina
Nunc praesto sunt viatica
Nos laeta schola miserit
Nos laeta domus ceperit
Aequales, sodales
Citate, clamate
Floreat, Floreat, Floreat Rugbeia!"

James' mind wandered as he mouthed words so firmly etched in his memory that he was sure he could repeat them in his sleep. Learning the school song was a right of passage for new boys at the school, and he well remembered being dragged from his bed as a thirteen-year-old F-block boy by a group of older prefects for his "Floreat" test. In Tudor house, it was mandatory for all boys to know the song in both Latin and English, and both forwards and backwards. James had spent weeks learning the ancient words and had then been subject to a series of harsh interrogations in the wee hours of the morning. He recalled the sessions in the prefect's room at the top of the house and the endless permutations of the questions.

"What's the third to last word in the first line of the fourth stanza from the end of the Latin version?" The question rapped out by a cane-wielding worthy called Selkirk who, at the time, was at least two feet taller than the younger James and at least twice his weight.

James had passed the tests though, as everybody did in the end, no matter that it might take months to get every question right. He had taken his place as a full-fledged member of Tudor House and had then delighted in inflicting the tests on subsequent generations as he, in time, eventually became a prefect himself.

Now, with the fear of the testing years behind him, James derived a comfortable pleasure from singing the words. His mind emptied, and the catechism of nobility seized his soul. The "Floreat" was a clarion call to the paladins of empire, a litany of strength.

And then the song ended. The final song for James and many like him. The doors of the Temple Speech Room were thrown open, and a thousand sons of privilege streamed into the welcoming arms of the early summer sun.

Cricket on the close. Some thought it a sacrilege to besmirch the birthplace of the game of Rugby with a sport so languid, but it was an undeniably pleasant diversion on a hot day. The crowds gathered around the mound to watch while the sainted first eleven withdrew into the pavilion to change into their whites.

James' rangy frame ambled through the gates of the close as he waited for the game to start, stray strands of jet-black hair escaping his brilliantine-plastered scalp and blowing in the light wind. Tall but somewhat frail, he had a conventionally attractive, if rather thin, face and a severe Roman nose with a broad bridge, an effect softened by prominent cheekbones and warm brown eyes. Shorn now of masters hurrying their charges to morning chapel, the close felt unusually relaxed. James' eyes surveyed the crowd and the buildings, capturing images in a way more permanent in memory than a mere photograph. He realised he had been happy here, and as he did so, he experienced a fleeting sense of imminent loss, the joys of childhood slipping into sepia-tinged recollection.

The close was the epicentre of the school. These fields had created the game of Rugby, inspired the founder of the modern Olympics, and witnessed a school revolution that had seen a group of Georgian schoolboys blow the door off the headmaster's house with the imprudent use of cannon. The turf was hallowed by tradition, and only masters and the all-powerful "levée," the collective term for the head boys of each boarding house, were allowed to cut across it on their way to the schoolrooms of the new and old quadrangles. With a stab of regret, James realised he had never "cut the close." He'd been a house prefect, but the heady heights of the levée had eluded him, most probably because he was hopeless at team games, the true measure of leadership in Rugby's sport-dominated curriculum.

In his first year at the school in 1909, James had watched the then-king, Edward VII, plant an oak tree, predictably called now the "King's Oak," which served to mark the spot where the head boy of the school stood on cold mornings, chivvying the boys as they snaked their way to lessons. The king himself had been a disappointment to the young James. Bloated and unable to stand for any length of time, he had struggled with the ceremonial spade and then proceeded to make a speech so insipid and incomprehensible that it had confounded all present. Still, he had been a king, and, for James, that compensated for the rumoured indiscretions with actresses and even for the appalling beard that seemed more suited to a socialist agitator than the emperor of India.

Behind the oak stood the greying stone edifice of School House, with its vast windows, complete with battlements, and topped off with a small clock tower that chimed the hours of the school day. The clock wouldn't last much longer though. The tower would remain, but Reverend David had announced that he had commissioned a new three-ton bell for the school chapel, which was to be installed over the school holidays. This new device would be used to call the weary to morning service and to sound the start and end of lessons. Even before a single peal had sounded, the boys had already christened it "the boomer."

Ruefully, James glanced at the turreted tower that sat at the corner of School House. The tower housed the office of the headmaster, and, since Dr. Arnold's time, the door was always open during the school day. Nominally, this was so that boys could access spiritual and pastoral guidance at any time, but, more pragmatically, this made it so that pupils on their way for corporal punishment need not trouble the housekeeper to open the door. James had climbed that turret on two occasions. The first had been during his second year at the school for the relatively minor offence of making a terrible hash of a Latin conjugation during a public recitation. The second had only happened a few weeks earlier and was for the much more serious indiscretion of being caught with a pint of ale at a pub in the village of Dunchurch. He had nearly been ignominiously expelled for that, but it had been so close to the end of the school year that Reverend David had relented and instead opted for the ever-trusty cane.

Unconsciously, James rubbed at the still healing scar on his right hand, and then felt a hand on his shoulder

"Hallo, old chap. You look miles away. Mind if I walk with you?"

Elliot Pearson was nearly nineteen, but he still looked pretty much as he had five years previously when he'd joined Tudor House at the same time as James. At five foot five, he was a good five inches shorter and considerably rounder than his friend, and his untidy mop of reddish hair lent him an elfin quality that was both impertinent and inquisitive. He'd struggled at the school initially, a target both for bullies because of his small frame and for masters because of his utter inability to remain silent in class. Garrulous, playful, and obsessed with the mechanisms of the modern world, he had finally achieved a measure of popularity through sheer perseverance and an absolute refusal to let other people get him down.

"Of course," said James. "The game will be starting soon. We should head to the mound."

The two boys linked arms and strolled purposefully to the small swell of ground immediately next to the cricket pavilion, already full of parents and boys settling in to watch the game. The mound was actually an ancient

Bronze Age burial mound, but that venerable legacy had been supplanted in the group consciousness of the school by the fact those revolutionaries of old had made this mound their last stand following their abortive revolution in 1797. It had taken the local militia, armed with pikes, to break down their barricades and crush the spirit of the school-aged Robespierres. Even after more than a century, the boys who had led that attempt were still venerated by the current crop of boarders, not least of all because several of them had gone on to have senior military commands in the various small wars that had characterised the era of gunboat diplomacy.

The mound was full with spectators, so the two boys walked past it towards the pink-bricked School Field house. They found a space under the elms and managed to procure a jug of ginger ale and two glasses from a diminutive little fellow from Whitelaw House, too in awe of the older boys to protest that the drinks were for guests of the school.

"Want one of these?" said Elliot, opening a sliver-plated cigarette case and taking out a Turkish blend.

Two hours ago, the boys would have been expelled for smoking, but now that the speeches were concluded, they were officially young gentlemen and able to indulge in a vice ordinarily reserved for the head boy alone.

With an unconscious furtive glance towards the watching eyes of the mound, James accepted, fumbling in the inner pocket of his jacket for a box of matches.

"Allow me," smiled Elliot, producing a splendid storm lighter from the depths of his trouser pocket, flicking it, and producing an outrageously high flame that threatened to singe James' eyebrows as he leaned forward to light his cigarette.

Coughing, James asked, "Where on earth did you get that monstrosity?"

"Oh, Father sent it over from India. Apparently, it's made from a shell casing from the Russo-Japanese show a few years ago. Lords knows where he found it, but it was a present for leaving this place."

Puffing gently and taking slow sips of ginger ale, the boys paused to join the applause as the two team captains emerged from the cricket pavilion and took their places on the field of play. Resplendent in gleaming white flannels and wearing their school colours, they met in the centre of the wicket and shook hands first with each other and then the umpire, the rather frail Mr. Aldridge.

He looked ill at ease in a shabby white coat that hung loosely off his shoulder like an opera cape.

"I'm not sure he'll last the game, you know," mumbled James in between drags.

"I don't know. That skeletal physique has a surprising strength, old man. I should know. The blighter beat me bloody when I got caught climbing through the window of the billiard room that time. I'd say he is immune to death's embrace, in any case. He's so stringy, even the grim reaper would spit him out."

James chuckled as he watched the Rugby captain win the toss and elect to field. Moments later, the opening batsmen from the Lawrence Sheriff school team emerged from the pavilion to a rather muted reception. The school had been founded some thirty years earlier, as a grammar school, to provide an education to the boys of the local town. This also had been the original purpose of Lawrence Sheriff himself when he founded Rugby School back in 1567. The patrician sensibilities of Rugby's pupils and their parents were still somewhat offended by the idea of playing any sport against a grammar school, even one based in the town. Lawrence Sheriff boys were academics, selected on the basis of examination, not wealth or family. In the parlance of the older public school, they were "oiks," closer to the peasants in the field than to the gentlemen of Rugby.

As if on cue, a small voice somewhere in the sea of hats on the mound, shouted out, "Smash the oiks, Rugby!"

There were some titters, and several ladies pressed gloved hands to their mouths, lest they betray their upbringing with an unseemly display of mirth. Within seconds, a master emerged from the crowd on the mound, pulling a small boy by his ear in the direction of School Field House and the certain ministrations of the cane. A smattering of supportive applause came from a few of the younger fellows congregating at the edge of the close near the Barby Road.

"They never learn, do they?" laughed James, stubbing out his cigarette on the grass at his side.

"We were like that once, old chap," mused Elliot. "Vim, vigour, and 'damn yer eyes, Sir.'"

"I suppose so," agreed James, "although it is a little unfair to ridicule a chap for his background, wouldn't you say?"

"Basic Darwin, Comrade Caulfield, like those eugenics chaps say—Bell and Churchill and those coves. A man is poor because he is predisposed to be. Intermarriage between the classes, consorting with foreigners, that sort of thing corrupts the blood."

James waved a languid hand in the direction of the Lawrence Sheriff batsmen. "Yes, but a man can raise himself up surely? At some point, we must have all been grubbing in the fields or whatever beastliness these fellows get up to. And yet, here we are now. Like my mother says, a man should be measured by his achievements, not by his background."

"Careful, old chap, you'll be singing the red flag if you're not careful, and bear in mind your mother has rather colonial leanings," replied Elliot. "Oh, I say, well bowled, Sir, well bowled."

The first wicket had fallen to a wicked piece of seam bowling from Templeton, the best of Rugby's bowlers. With no score on the board, the sorry batsman wended his way back to the pavilion with head held down. Desultory applause accompanied him, more patronising than purposeful.

"Cricket," sighed Elliot, "is evidently a gentlemen's game, despite being so unforgivably tedious."

The Three Horse Shoes was lively that evening. Although most boys and parents had decamped by train immediately after the cricket, a few of the boys leaving had elected to take rooms in the hotel opposite School House. Now it was closing on 11:00 p.m., and the air was thick with an acrid fug of tobacco and the sharp smell of hops. Boys and the odd recalcitrant father clustered in groups around the saloon bar of the hotel. From the public bar, a badly played piano could be faintly heard over the drunken braying of the more intrepid Rugby men and the occasional protestation from a local drinker.

"Engineering, that's the ticket," opined Elliot, sipping from an evil-looking brew with several discernable chunks of solid matter floating on its surface. Known as "old growler," it was considered to be virtually undrinkable.

"The things they are doing with planes down at Farnborough," he continued, "will change the face of the world."

"Balderdash," said Andrew Oakes, a bespectacled Latin whizz with thinning blonde hair, late of School Field House. "The bally things keep falling out of the skies. A man would be insane to get in such a contraption."

"Oh ye of little faith, Oakes," replied Elliot. "What of the BE2? Ten thousand feet that reached. The test chappie said he could reach out his hand and almost touch the stars."

"Yes, and what was the fellow called! Hereward!" Oakes laughed.

"Really?" interrupted Shotton, a pimple faced product of Kilbracken House. With still a year to go at Rugby, he nursed a pint of porter that was in flagrant breach of school rules. "Like Hereward the Wake?"

"Exactly," said Oakes. "A bally outlaw, and this Hereward de Havilland is no better, flouncing around the skies in a kite. Mark my words: a sticky end beckons for friend Hereward."

"A man's name is of no account," said James. His head was aching after quaffing a brackish claret with his beef and potatoes, and he was in no mood to broker a spat between friends.

"It's his brother Geoffrey that's the brains, in any case," James continued. "The fellow had some pluck, building his own plane, with his own money—borrowed against his inheritance I heard."

"Exactly, Comrade Caulfield, and he didn't let a silly thing like piling the crate into the Lichfield valley worry him a jot! Just brushed down his trousers and set off again. A true Englishman."

The group laughed, and the rather inebriated Oakes was sufficiently mollified to place his arm round Elliot's shoulder.

"So, are you really going to skip out on Oxford then? Swap the dreaming spires for some dreary factory?"

Elliot's face took on an unusually serious expression. "It is the *Royal* Aircraft Factory. It's not exactly a cotton mill, old chap, unless of course King George is really letting standards slip. I won't be spinning a jenny or joining the worshipful company of weavers. Maths mainly, a spot of drawing, paternalistic oversight of the building chaps, and, one day, up there with the birds." He pointed his finger at the ceiling to emphasise his point.

"Still a factory though," grumbled Shotton. "The old paterfamilias won't be too pleased."

"I wouldn't know. I've not asked him yet," admitted Elliot. "I'm sure the old chap would rather I became some sort of merchant prince, but I just cannot see myself as a sweltering Sahib. If you've ever been to India, you'd appreciate a factory in Farnborough has its attractions. India has a certain beauty, but it is so frightfully hot it makes your head boil."

Shotton asked, "Do you have to wear a uniform or anything? Like a proper solider?"

"I imagine there may be the occasional sartorial inconvenience," said Elliot. "I understand that overalls are somewhat à la mode in Farnborough this season. I'm a civilian though, and after my experience in the cadets at this place, I'm not sure I'm quite cut out for the military."

James smiled at this, recalling Elliot's notorious behaviour at the 1912 Combined Cadet Force Review. A bigwig from the admiralty had come to inspect the school's army and navy cadets. Ensign Elliot Pearson, impeccably turned out in navy whites, had ruined the display during a prolonged period of standing to attention while the elderly admiral walked the lines. He had suddenly yelped, swatted his own face, and then proceeded to jump up and down like a madman. He later claimed a wasp had landed on his face and crawled down his neck and into his uniform via his collar. No trace of said wasp could later be found, and Reverend David had taken a close personal interest in correcting Elliot's militaristic pretensions. The review the following year had seen Ensign Pearson safely confined to barracks.

"What about you, James?" asked Oakes, waving his hands as if massaging a crystal ball. "Any plans for the future, or will father be giving you a London allowance?"

"No such luck. He is a stickler for education," sighed James. "A veritable martinet. It's Cambridge for me, Corpus by choice. I'll sit the exams in October and go up the following year. In the meantime, I suppose I shall sow my wild oats in the metropolis, assuming I can find fertile ground."

"English, I assume?" said Oakes.

"Probably," agreed James. "'In brief, Sir, study what you most affect.'"

"Bloody Shakespeare," growled Elliot. "The bane of my life. Who was that French fellow who called him a drunken savage? Sensible chap whoever he was."

"Voltaire, hardly a study in temperance himself and French to boot," laughed James.

"Stop it, Caulfield. I only asked from a misplaced sense of curiosity," said Oakes. "I really couldn't care less what you read. It's all punting and port as an undergraduate anyway. I don't think they expect you to actually learn anything."

"Touché, Oakes," said Elliot. "I suspect we have all had our fill of actual education. Let us raise a glass to our escape from the clutches of beaks, masters, marshals, and any other bugger determined to make us read Cicero."

The four clinked tankards and took a generous swill of beer, Oakes spluttering slightly as the liquid took a wrong turn. The saloon bar was noticeably emptying now, with several men swaying good-naturedly off to their rooms. One unfortunate grey-haired gentleman slipped on the beer-sodden floor and rolled into a table, raising a walking stick in alarm as he did so. The stick swept across the table, bringing down a crash of empty bottles, ashtrays, and candles onto the wooden floor. The furious proprietor leapt athletically over the bar and began remonstrating with the unfortunate prone gentlemen, demanding compensation for breakage in a forceful tone.

"Time, gentlemen, please," said Elliot, rising to his feet and gesturing at the others to follow.

Sweeping his arm in the direction of the arguing landlord and still prone customer, he muttered, "If you can keep your head, while all around you are losing theirs, you'll be a man my son."

London the following afternoon seemed to echo James' mood. Dark skies spewed forth a relentless, unseasonable rain, and the throbbing hum of Euston station did nothing for his hangover.

He had left Rugby early that same morning, still sufficiently drunk to have managed a hearty breakfast of devilled kidneys and too much Worcestershire sauce, a feast of some regret to him now. He had shared a cab with Elliot and Oakes, the indolent Shotton having resolutely refused to rise and turning green at the prospect of breakfast. The three had negotiated the platitudes of parting amidst an army of porters weighed down with the trunks and detritus of returning Rugbeians. The strange finality of the moment weighed on them all. Handshakes were awkward, farewells were too florid, and eyes shined just a fraction more than they should in the weak morning sun. For those on the cusp of manhood, the bright morning of future does not always eclipse the remembrance of sunsets past.

They had taken different trains, Oakes to some desultory border estate near Carlisle, where Elliot claimed he would be busily engaged in rustling Scottish cattle and vigorously enforcing *jus primae noctis* with the daughters of the local serfs. Elliot had returned to what he called his "ancestral seat," the rather ordinary redbrick home of his elderly aunt in Chester, there to await the return of his parents from India and the difficult task of persuading them to consent to a career as a flight engineer.

James had taken the fast train to London, the unmistakeable fire of a claret headache fanned by the prattle of an earnest young parson keen to share his experiences working with the orphans of the east end. A strategy of impatient grunts and noncommittal responses made no inroads, and he had soon been forced to buy a copy of the *Times* from the train guard and hide his face behind the paper shield. Even then, he had been exposed to a prolonged discourse on the implications of the Greek-Serbian alliance and the risk of the Ottoman Empire being dragged into the second Balkan conflict. Despite not realising that there had been a first Balkan conflict and having only the vaguest idea where Serbia actually was, James struggled manfully until the grey terraces of Harrow hove into view outside the train window. Their soot-covered conformity gave him the perfect excuse to sort his belongings, check the underground timetable, and generally busy himself sufficiently to avoid further conversation.

His mood was bleak as he stepped onto platform 4 at Euston Station, the steam from the train engine billowing over the departing passengers, who were busily engaged in raising brollies, adjusting hats, and preparing for the unexpected chill of the capital on the first day of July. He flagged down a walrus-moustached porter, passed him a shilling, and waited in the lee of the train, avoiding the sizeable drops of rain from the holes in the iron girder and glass roof of the station. When he saw his school trunk, bearing the legend "JHC," approaching on a trolley pushed by the porter, he beckoned to the man and strode purposefully towards the gate at the end of the platform. Passing out of the station and stepping into the deluge of Euston Road, he regretted dressing so hastily that morning. The tweed travel suit was unsuitable for all but the most moderate of summer showers, and the protection of his straw boater lasted only seconds before he could feel his hair slicken and the moisture run down into his collar.

He queued with a number of other first-class passengers for the dubious delight of passage in one of London's new Unic motor-powered taxis, his luggage left by the porter at the head of the queue. James would have preferred an old-fashioned horse and trap, as was still used in Rugby, but advances in engineering meant that those were slowly disappearing from London's streets. Elliot had been a firm advocate of this particular advance, extolling the virtues of the L-head four-cylinder engine capable of speeds of more than twenty miles per hour.

Watching the infernal machines as he moved up the queue, James thought them ugly, with the hand crank protruding like a poked tongue from the front of the engine and the stretched chasse built to accommodate passengers behind the driver's seat. In rain, they weren't too comfortable either, as the tarpaulin that covered the passenger wasn't sealed, as it would have been in an old-fashioned hansom. Wind and especially rain could leak in the gaps, freezing a passenger ensconced in the back. They were French-made, and they had eclipsed all of their British rivals over the previous ten years, so he supposed there must be something to them. He missed the elegant luxury and relative quiet of the older style traps, and he had long admired the skill it took to drive them. The fact that the Unic drivers considered themselves skilled workers was an affront, as was the fact that, earlier that year, they had brought London to a virtual standstill by striking over fares. They'd won too, a case of inconvenience trumping traditionalism and what James considered to be good political sense.

The stately English pastime of queuing reached its eventual conclusion, and James arrived at the front of the queue to be met by a small clean-shaven man in a cloth cap and a cheap wool suit, sporting some sort of trade union badge on the lapel. James pointed out his luggage and climbed into the back of the red-painted Unic while the man loaded James' trunk next to himself in the driver's area.

"Where to, mate?" asked the driver, in the broad vowel sounds of the born cockney.

"It's 'Sir' to you, and Cavendish Square," muttered James.

"Yes *Sir,*" the man said, with tangible irony, and accelerated off into the chaos of Euston Road.

A few minutes later, as they were rounding the corner by Tottenham Court Road underground station into the shopping area of Oxford Street, the taxi came to a standstill before a crowd of people blocking the road. The group numbered around fifty or so, and all were women. Two well-dressed ladies stood facing the crowd, holding up a rain-sodden banner that read, "The hand that rocks the cradle rules the world." The remainder of the women, their backs to the taxi and considerably less well dressed, were singing some sort of hymn that James could barely hear over the sound of the idling engine.

The taxi driver turned to James. "Bloody suffragettes. You'd 'fink they'd 've 'ad their fill at the Derby. What do you want me to do, chief? Sir, I mean."

A few weeks earlier, Emily Davison, a militant suffragette who'd once been imprisoned for violently attacking a man she'd mistaken for David Lloyd George, had thrown herself in front of the king's horse at the Derby. The nation was still undecided as to whether this was a deliberate attempt at martyrdom or an accident that had occurred whilst attempting to secure a banner to the bridle or saddle of the moving horse. Either way, Miss Davison had died of her injuries a few days later, and the male-owned and -dominated newspapers had been universal in their excoriation of what they called her terrorist act. James vaguely sympathised with the cause but had been appalled by the tactics of the more extreme suffragettes. He had read accounts of how the jockey, one Herbert Jones, was haunted by the woman's death, and an attack on the king's horse bordered on *lèse majesté*. More than an inconvenience, these women could be dangerous.

"I'll get out," decided James. "Take my things to number 16 Cavendish Square. I'll walk."

He hopped out of the taxi, gave the driver four shillings, and approached the group of protestors. Behind him, there was a cacophony of horns as the taxi turned around in the crowded street and drove off to find another route.

The women were plum centre in the middle of the street, and the pavements on either side were relatively free. Behind the women with the homemade banner, James could see a long buildup of traffic, omnibuses, taxis, the odd private motor-car, and a few horse and carts. The mood was ugly, and several men were shouting at the suffragettes to clear the road. On the pavement, various idlers lounged in shop doorways smoking, laughing, and generally enjoying the street theatre.

The protestors had stopped singing now, and one of the women with the banner was addressing the group before her. Up close, James could see that the main body of the crowd was largely made up of women of the lower orders. Shop girls, housemaids, and factory workers, judging by the array of uniforms and cheaply dyed fabrics on display, although one or two of the participants had the respectable look of the middle orders—at least they were wearing hats. They were all soaking wet, and some of them were glancing nervously at the buildup of increasingly irate men behind the speaker.

James was intrigued, despite his irritation, and paused under the striped awning of the John Lewis draper's shop to listen to the speaker and to get some respite from the rain. She was quite a striking woman, around twenty-five, tall, and with tightly curled brunette hair under a wide-brimmed hat secured with a rainproof hood. She wore a long, black coat that reached past her knees and an ankle-length dress in a deep burgundy colour that, at a dinner party, might have been intended to complement her hair. On her feet, she wore stout leather boots, mud-splashed but certainly more elegant than the rough clogs of most of those listening to her. Her voice was nasal, high-pitched, and well-spoken, although it didn't carry well, and James strained to hear her.

"...Please understand that what I mean by this is nothing less than revolution. If the men of our country had a grievance and that grievance were laid before their legislature and then ignored, I ask you, what action would they take? The answer is that they would simply vote down that legislature at the next opportunity." She paused, taking in the rapt faces of the women before her and studiously ignoring the catcalls and boos of the men congregating behind.

"We cannot vote them down for they, in their ignorance, do not afford us that luxury. We are accused of being irrational in our campaign. How do we help ourselves by breaking windows, by causing inconvenience to respectable people," here she gestured with a wave of her free hand to the traffic behind her, "by being imprisoned, even by giving our lives to this cause? We benefit because we keep our grievance in the minds of legislators, and we show that we are true revolutionaries, equal to those men who brought the vote to the working classes forty years ago. We are defined by our actions, and we must fight for our rights if we are not to be patronised and sent back to the nursery. Only through action will we be triumphant."

The shivering women in the crowd gave a ragged cheer and began to sing again. There was no accompaniment, but the crowd all seemed to know the words and sang heartily:

"She walketh veiled and sleeping,

For she knoweth not her power;

She obeyeth but the pleading

Of her heart, and the high leading

Of her soul, unto this hour.

Slow advancing, halting, creeping,

Comes the Woman to the hour!—

She walketh veiled and sleeping,

For she knoweth not her power."

The outbreak of song was the final straw for the men congregating behind the speaker. Perhaps hoping that the women would move of their own volition after the speech, they had held off until now. The onset of the second verse was a stretch too far though, and a group of six or seven working men, clad in caps and wool jackets, moved towards the two women carrying the banner. They were surprisingly gentle, but two of them lifted the two ladies off their feet and carried them to the side of the pavement, while their fellows moved threateningly towards the main body of the crowd. The singing faltered as a few of the more timid souls cut and run. The remainder stood their ground though, and the men, nonplussed, hesitated for a minute until they, with James, spotted a group of policemen rounding the corner of Tottenham Court Road.

Deciding prudence was the better part of valour, James strolled off down Oxford Street, occasionally glancing over his shoulder to watch the women being dispersed by the police. The two banner holders were being arrested and placed in the back of an old-fashioned, horse-drawn Black Maria. The rest of the women were simply being pushed by the police to the side of the road, some more vigorously than James would have liked.

As he walked in the late afternoon drizzle, the rain washing away the last residue of his hangover, he thought on the brunette woman's words. There was a point there of sorts, he considered. In a democracy, the vote was a privilege that should be afforded to those with a stake in the system. James was conservative enough to understand that stake in monetary terms, as a qualification of property, but there were obviously women who met that criterion. The problem was that property rights passed to the husband on marriage, and that served to disenfranchise women in both a material and political sense. Not for the first time, James considered whether this might be wrong. A secondary issue was educational. It was a truism that women were the weaker sex, physically and intellectually, but recent years had seen women qualify from universities, and there had been a plethora of great female writers. If literacy were no bar to a man voting, could the alleged inferiority of the female brain be cited as a reason not to give women the vote? James wasn't so sure.

A few minutes after his encounter with the suffragettes, he arrived at Cavendish Square. It was untouched by the nearby fracas, and he paused for a moment in the small park at its centre, appreciating the almost complete silence after the noise and bustle of nearby Oxford Street. A few hardy couples ambulated around the periphery of the park, immaculate in their late afternoon finery. James, still wearing his sodden straw boater and the now rather soiled tweed travelling suit, felt momentarily out of place.

He crossed the square and came to his house, the imposing five-storey Georgian edifice of 16 Cavendish Square. The square had risen in reputation in recent years, ever since Herbert Asquith had taken the house at number 20 some years previously. It had always had a certain cache, but the nearby trade of Oxford Street and the cesspit of Soho rather tarnished it for the traditionalists of Knightsbridge, Bloomsbury, and Mayfair. Politics might be considered a tawdry business to some of London's upper echelons, but proximity to the residence of the Prime Minister and First Lord of the Treasury was still a thing to be sought.

To James' father, the highly conservative Godfrey Caulfield, Asquith's proximity was a source of some irritation and occasional embarrassment. Not only was the man a liberal, but at the last election in 1910 he had clung onto power with the aid of Catholic Irish MPs. There had been a price for that cooperation, and Asquith had paid with the introduction of the third Irish home rule bill, which was intended to provide devolved government to Ireland and, eventually, full dominion status. The act was passed against loud Tory opposition but would not come into force until 1914. Predictably, the bill had provoked a storm amongst English conservatives, who saw it is an assault on the very principle of empire and a betrayal of the loyal Protestant minority in Northern Ireland. To Godfrey Caulfield, Asquith was an incompetent, a libertine, and a philanderer, who indulged himself writing romantic missives to a succession of society beauties, despite a long-lasting marriage. Having a mistress was to be expected, but indiscretion was unforgivable in a man in such a public position. The Asquiths were never invited to dinner and barely merited a curt nod when seen in the square or about town.

James arrived at the house at number 16 and rang the sonorous doorbell. The door was opened by the butler, Harper, who momentarily dropped his ever-inscrutable expression and deigned to smile briefly before ushering him inside. Harper had been with the family for more than thirty years, rising from junior footman at the Caulfield's country residence to his present lofty perch. He was somehow ageless and could be anywhere between forty-five and seventy, with a short, spare frame and receding grey hair that he grew long and swept over his crown in an attempt to stave off the impression of baldness.

"Welcome back, Master James. I hope your journey was not too arduous?"

"Fair to middling, Harper, although there was some bad business with the women's rights shower over in Oxford Street," James replied.

"I'm sorry to hear that, Sir. It is a sorry day when ladies behave with such disregard for decorum," said Harper, with an expression that indicated that such indignity would never be allowed on his watch.

James stepped into the marble-faceted hall, removed his hat and jacket, and handed them to Harper.

"Sir would like to change, I'm sure. Dinner will be served in two hours; your parents instructed me to inform you that they will be home shortly and that your usual rooms have been prepared," Harper said, with only the briefest glance of distaste at James' rather sorry attire.

Two hours later, bathed and dressed in a conservatively cut dinner jacket by an unfamiliar valet, James entered the library. His father stood gazing out of the window overlooking the square, glass in hand. A neglected cigarette curled smoke in the cut glass ashtray on an occasional table by the window seat. He turned from the window as a footman, stationed by the door, closed it behind James.

Godfrey Caulfield was a handsome man, close on six feet, with high prominent cheekbones and the familial aquiline nose, which James had clearly inherited. His jaw was squared, and he was more heavyset than his son, with just the slightest hint of a developing paunch, hidden artfully by his cummerbund. Long black hair streaked with grey was brushed back away from a forehead that showed hints of encroaching recession at the temples. The third son of a baronet and therefore landless, he had made his own way in the world. Against the wishes of his father, who abhorred the idea of trade, he had begun securing patents for the early editions of the Lee Enfield rifle, produced by the Birmingham Small Arms Company. When the rifle was commissioned for use by the British army in the early twentieth century, Godfrey had made a considerable fortune when he secured a lucrative government supply contract. He had bought the house in Cavendish Square, together with a countryseat in Berkshire, and had then taken his place as the Tory MP for Berkhamsted in the same 1906 election that had seen his near neighbour rise to the office of prime minister. After seven years in Parliament, he was respected by his peers as a patriot and monarchist, but considered unlikely ever to rise to high office.

"Welcome home, my boy. Did your final term pass pleasantly?"

"Yes, Sir, it did, thank you."

"No mishaps or misdemeanours to report?"

James hesitated briefly, wondering whether Reverend David may have written to his father about the incident in the pub in Dunchurch. His hand tickled where the scars of his caning had healed, and he involuntarily closed his fist.

His father laughed, exposing irregular tobacco stained teeth. "It's all right, my boy, no need to have an apoplexy. A man is entitled to the occasional drink, although why you'd choose to do so in some yokel hostelry is beyond me."

On cue, one of the two footmen, stationed on either side of the library door, approached James with a tray of drinks, and handed him a glass of yellow Chartreuse. The footman glided silently back to his spot.

"It was the only place I could think of that wouldn't have any beaks, Sir," replied James, sipping the sweet concoction.

"You were wrong there. As I remember it, the Masters at Rugby could always smell out a would-be miscreant. Boys will be boys, after all." Godfrey's eyes twinkled, perhaps recalling some ancient prank from his own time at the school.

"Now," he continued, "before your mother gets here, tell me your plans for the future."

James outlined his intention to sit the Cambridge entrance exam the following October and to then read English at Corpus Christi College.

His father pursed his lips thoughtfully, recovered the cigarette burning in the ashtray, tapped it off, and smoked the last few inches while he talked.

"English, eh? I suppose all learning is a valuable thing, but what do you intend to do with it once you've left Cambridge?"

"I don't know Sir, perhaps take up writing? A position on the *Times* perhaps?"

James was well aware of his father's views on "scribblers," as he called them, and the *Times*, due to a combination of its longevity and political views, was the only journalistic institution that wasn't subject to his complete contempt.

"I suppose that might do. I know Northcliffe rather well, and I'm sure I could prevail on him to offer you a position. Sound chap in the main, Irish I believe, although, to his credit, you wouldn't know it. At least he had the good sense to rid the place of that blasted notion of impartiality that dragged it down under Buckle. A paper should say what it means, and at least he's clear what a danger Asquith and that confounded Welshman are to the country."

James, who rather liked the enigmatic if somewhat notorious David Lloyd George, was sufficiently prudent not to question his father's prejudices. He kept his counsel.

The door opened again, and James' mother, Sylvia, entered the room. She was a small woman, barely topping five feet, with a thin, boyish frame, corseted to give the illusion of curves. She had an oval-shaped, delicate face with fine bone structure, a slightly protruding nose, and warm, dark brown eyes. She was dressed in a voluminous purple frock, complete with a rather antiquated bustle, which carried to the floor and entirely covered her feet. Around her neck she wore a pearl choker inlaid with tiny diamonds, an object of such studied vulgarity that James wondered whether it was placed there consciously in an attempt to advertise her nationality. Sylvia was an American and proud of it.

She had met her husband some twenty years previously, while he was engaged on a short-lived business venture with the Colt Manufacturing Company in Hartford, Connecticut, for the planned importation of the New Service Double Action revolver. The venture had come to nothing, but Godfrey had attended a ball given in his honour in a marquee built especially in the grounds of Trinity College. He had been immediately entranced by the delicate eighteen-year-old Sylvia Master and became even more interested when he discovered that she was the sole heir to a fortune estimated to run to millions of dollars. Godfrey had lingered in the States until he had managed to persuade Sylvia's elderly father to grant him his daughter's hand. They had married in the spring of 1894 at the recently completed Catholic cathedral of St. Joseph. Despite profound differences of opinion in matters of politics and religion, the marriage had largely been happy, though it was a matter of regret to both Godfrey and Sylvia that James had been their only surviving issue.

With her customary disregard for the conventions of etiquette, Sylvia took James into her arms and planted a chaste kiss on his cheek. She smiled broadly, and the effect was dazzling, lifting her features and providing a window onto her more youthful beauty.

Godfrey coughed. "Not in front of the servants, my dear," he muttered, glancing towards the frozen basilisk stares of the two footmen at the door.

"I'm sorry, Godfrey. I quite forgot myself. It is not every day that my son returns from that draughty prison you Englishmen call a school," she replied demurely, extricating herself from James' embrace and taking a proffered glass of Chartreuse from the tray. Her accent was anglicised, with just a trace of an American drawl on the vowels.

"So, my dear child, will you be gracing us with your presence for long?" she asked James, sipping from the drink.

"I hope so, mother. The summer at least, and perhaps until I go up to Cambridge next year."

"How delightful," Sylvia replied. "Your father is quite the Philistine when it comes to literature, and I had so hoped to see what you made of Mr. Conan Doyle's *Lost World.* I thought it quite frightful, but doubtless it offers something more to the masculine reader."

Before he could reply, a gong sounded somewhere in the recesses of the house, and a moment later, with perfectly honed precision, the door opened, and Harper announced that dinner was being served in the small dining room.

Dinner in Cavendish Square was an epicurean affair, distinguished by the quantity and quality of the dishes and the quasi-military movements of the serving staff. Conversation was stilted while the three members of the family ate, confined to the occasional general comment on the quality of the repast and Mrs. Caulfield's observations on the activities of several families of prominence. A brief attempt by Godfrey to interest the table in his views on the expansion of the German navy was dismissed by Sylvia as "anathema to good digestion." After an hour, James was bored, gloomily contemplating the remains of a disappointing blancmange, and enduring a lengthy maternal soliloquy on the inevitable moral decline that would accompany any performance of Stravinsky's modernist ballet, *The Rite of Spring,* in London. From the jaded, browbeaten look on his father's face, James guessed that this had been a popular dinner table topic since it had premiered in Paris the previous month, bringing riots in its wake.

To the obvious relief of the male diners, the cheese course was quickly consumed, and Sylvia departed, leaving them to partake in the ritual of port and cigars in relative peace. Unencumbered by the social constraints imposed by his wife, Godfrey puffed contentedly on an outlandish Corona and poured James a port from the decanter on the round teak table.

"So, my boy, where do you stand on the Serbian question?" asked Godfrey, fixing James with a piercing gaze.

James, thinking back to the young parson on the train, managed to approximate an answer. "I think the current conflict is potentially destabilising, father, but it is surely a local issue, of little interest to the major powers."

"Mmm, I disagree. I think we can assume that the old Ottoman Empire is shot, and whatever crumbs from the table they manage to gobble up in this conflict will do them no good in the long term," said Godfrey, gesturing with his cigar.

"Those dolts in Bulgaria have violated the treaty of London and attacked Serbia and Greece. Individually they simply can't win, and I fully expect the Greeks and the Serbs to trounce them. The problem is, if they do, and I'm sure they will, Bulgaria will be chastened, and Russia will be left with only one ally in the region—Serbia. "

"Now, my boy, if I mention Austria at this point, where would that take us?" Godfrey asked with a mischievous twinkle in his eye.

James racked his brains. Austria was acknowledged as the weakest of the great powers, its autocratic monarchy at odds with various emerging nationalist movements across its empire. A strong Serbia, shored up with Russian support, might be a threat to them.

"If Austria were to assert its imperial rights over its subject peoples," he ventured, "that might antagonise the Serbs?"

"Precisely, my boy. We may make a politician out of you yet."

God forbid, thought James, as his father continued.

"And if something sparked a conflict between Austria and Serbia?"

"Then Russia fights for Serbia, and Austria fights Russia. Germany fights for Austria. France and potentially the British would be dragged in under the terms of the Triple Entente?" he asked.

"Indeed. The balance is delicate, you see. A shift in power, even in a backward region like the Balkans, can be a tinderbox. The bloody kaiser doesn't help."

"We'd win though, wouldn't we, Sir?" asked James

"Oh, of course, though it might not be as easy as we think, and we would gain little by the effort," said Godfrey, easing back in his chair and blowing a lazy smoke ring into the air. "The question is: do you think it worth sacrificing a single Englishman for some dubious notion of Serbian honour? I don't, and I hope to God it'll never come to that."

Hendon Aerodrome, June 12, 1914

The station hotel was packed, even by the standards of an English Saturday afternoon. James met Elliot in the maelstrom of the back bar. They secured a small table and watched as impromptu bookies accepted the wagers of the ostensible gentlemen around them. The third Hendon aerial derby clearly meant something to the sporting crowd.

"Read this, it'll make sense then," said Elliot, thrusting a well-thumbed, cheaply printed magazine into James' hand.

An erratic typeface proclaimed: *Flight, A journal devoted to the interests, practice, and progress of aerial locomotion and transport.* It had been printed that morning.

"Did the cat get at it?" asked James, holding up the tattered magazine

"No. Everyone reads it. We all buy our own, but this one arrives first thing at the factory and gets passed around."

"'Testing the Langley,'" said James, reading aloud from the cover page. "'The flying machine from an engineering standpoint'. Hardly the stuff of dreams."

"Read the editorial. I'll get the pints," said Elliot, standing and manoeuvring his way through the throng towards the bar.

With a sigh, James applied himself to the rather pompous musings of Mr. Stanley Spooner, editor of the august publication. Elliot had provided though, and the tickets to the show were free, so he supposed he owed this small kindness to his friend.

The essence was this: how could one prepare for a future conflict in a world where innovation was the status quo? The answer, according to Spooner, lay in aircraft.

The Anglo-German naval arms race had focused on the mass building of ever-larger battleships and dreadnoughts, but their impregnability was threatened by the advent of the submarine. The submarine was still in its infancy, and it was severely limited by its slow speed, the paucity of its weaponry, and its regular need to surface. When submerged though, and in the midst of a fleet, it could potentially cause havoc. The threat from the unseen enemy below was beginning to be taken seriously by the naval authorities.

But, argued Spooner, wasn't the potential threat even greater from above? Everything could be attacked from the skies, not just ships, but infantry, artillery, even cities. Flyers armed with bombs could reach any target and could easily go where cavalry could not. The aeroplane could enhance the modern army, but at sea its worth would be incalculable. It could compensate for the frailties of both battleship and submarine. It could protect a surfaced vessel; it could seek out the telltale trail of a submerged submarine. It could attack shipping from the air, moving too quickly for the massive naval gunnery to respond. The aeroplane was a game changer.

And in the vanguard of this new kind of warfare would be the pilot. An individual struggle, one man pitted against the might of dreadnoughts and regiments, a fury from the skies. Not since the days of chivalry had war been this individualised. Pilots would soon be eulogised as the new knights. Knights of the skies.

James was intrigued by the argument, although he had his doubts whether the frail canvas and wire planes he had seen were quite capable of the feats that Spooner outlined. The idea of a personal conflict appealed though. At Rugby, he had only ever excelled at individual sports. He had won the gruelling Crick cross-country run twice, but he had never even played for his house at any team sport, never mind his school. A knight was made through his own deeds, he considered, not those of his fellows.

When Elliot returned carrying two battered pewter tankards, he smiled when he caught the expression on James' face.

"Do you understand now?" he asked.

"Yes," said James simply. "I think I'm starting to."

A pleasant summer morning day had turned to mist and rain by the time they arrived at the aerodrome. The English summer was ever a fickle thing, and thick clouds swirled over the ramshackle buildings strewn haphazardly around a large field. A fence of sorts surrounded the area, but the gaps were so prominent as to render the possession of an entrance ticket entirely optional. Small groups of officials, wearing Royal Aerodrome armbands, attempted to bring some order to the chaos, but the crowd was simply too big, and people streamed into the airfield from all sides, many ignoring the entreaties of the beleaguered officials.

"How many people are here, do you think?" James asked Elliot

"I've no idea, old man, but the first show a few years ago had about forty-five thousand in the 'drome, with a couple of million people watching it from various spots around the town. Of course, that was when most people had never seen a plane, so you won't get so many today, but they could probably fill the place two or three times over, I suspect," Elliot replied. He seemed skittish, his face and movement betraying the sort of nervous excitement normally seen in a bridegroom on his wedding day.

They passed through the main entrance, disdaining the various gaps in the fence through which funnelled the more opportunistic sorts. They flashed their tickets at the harassed-looking official vainly attempting to stem the tide of humanity and entered the aerodrome proper. Inside the fence, James had a better view of the buildings and could see that most were elongated sheds, built from wood, with corrugated iron roofs and housing numerous different types of planes in various states of repair. Mechanics swarmed over the planes, and, outside each hangar, small groups of people watched them and discussed the relative merits of each design.

Nodding towards the nearest hangar, where a plane sat with only one wing intact, James said, "I hope they don't intend to fly that one. I might not know much about flying, but I imagine two wings would be a help."

Elliot laughed. "That's an old Bleriot. It broke all sorts of records a few years ago over the pond. It won't be going up today. I doubt any of the ones in the hangars will. They're mainly private planes, owned by members of the club—serious men who don't tend to go in for the derbies—too public, you see."

"Not really," said James. "I'd have thought you'd want to show off a little, if you've got something you'd built to fly."

"I suppose it was like that in the beginning," mused Elliot, "but it's all developing so fast now that the better maverick engineers steer clear of these events in case their ideas are pinched."

"So we get to see the also-rans, is that the size of it?" said James.

"Not quite," said Elliot, with a small shake of his head. "It'll mainly be the factory-produced planes that you see today, the ones that chaps have bought, although there'll be the odd one or two built in a barn somewhere."

"Anything from your lot?" asked James.

"A couple of BE2s, Geoffrey de Havilland and his brother will be taking them up," replied Elliot, a smug proprietary smile flashing briefly across his face.

"All for the love of the sport, I suppose?" speculated James.

To his surprise, Elliot burst into peals of laughter. "Sometimes," he said, "your naivety is astonishing! For the sport, he says!" He shook his head. "All of the flyers are here for the money, dear fellow. Big crowds get big gate receipts, and the newspapers lap this sort of thing up and positively chuck money at events like this. There is a five-thousand-pound cash prize for the winner of the air race, a few thousand for the stunt flying, and even the award for the cleanest landing can net a few hundred for a chap. You can build a lot of planes for the sort of cash on offer here today. Come on, you young innocent, let's check on the models."

James followed Elliot, absorbing the growing sense of excitement emanating from the crowd, thinking that it was a long time since he had looked forward to something with this level of anticipation. In truth, the last year had been tedious. The summer had been consumed with reading, everything from Chaucer to Wells, as he prepared for the Cambridge entrance exam. He had taken and narrowly passed the exam in October and then visited Corpus Christi College for interviews with the English literature fellow and the master of the college. They had been relaxed affairs, with none of the expected formality or incisive academic interrogation. The fellow was an old Rugbeian, well disposed to students from his alma mater and more concerned with questioning James on the fortunes of the school's First XV than he was about his knowledge of Milton or Marlowe. The master was a venerable, port-soaked former politician who owed his preferment more to the quality of his connections than any established academic record. Evidently drunk at James' early afternoon interview, he had contented himself with reminiscing about the governments of Lord Salisbury and Arthur Balfour, repeating the popular perception that Balfour had only succeeded Salisbury as prime minister because he was his nephew. The transfer of power had led to the press coining the phrase "Bob's your Uncle," Salisbury's Christian name being Robert. This made for a source of considerable amusement to the master, who clearly held some soft of grudge against Balfour. James had smiled politely throughout the monologue and was then offered a place.

Admission to university duly secured, James had thought to relax a little, possibly do a little travelling on the continent, and generally loaf his way through the year. Godfrey had put a stop to that though, telling James that he would only provide him with an allowance if he prepared the ground for his planned future career as a journalist. He procured a private tutor, a retired civil servant, who gave James a crash course in politics and the mechanics of government and world affairs to a point where he could now discourse convincingly on most aspects of the news agenda. He was accepted as a member to White's gentlemen's club and began the torturous process of a staggered introduction to London society. Most evenings were spent with the animated Godfrey dispensing pearls of political wisdom and ruminating about the ever-shifting European balance of power. Finally, in April, when he felt James was as prepared as he could be, he invited the press baron Lord Northcliffe to a small dinner party at Cavendish Square, placed James on his right-hand side, and steered the conversation in such a way that James had every opportunity to showcase his newfound erudition on the minutiae of politics. The *Times* was in the bag by the cheese course, with Northcliffe asking James to call on him when he completed his studies.

The invitation from Elliot to attend the air show had therefore come at a time when James was feeling the acute claustrophobia of prolonged exposure to his family, and the event represented a rare opportunity to cut loose a little with a friend without a careerist ulterior motive or the unwelcome scrutiny of his father.

Now, walking with his friend, he felt a contentment that had all but deserted him since he had left Rugby. In some senses, he guessed he was resentfully clinging onto his boyhood, resisting his father's obvious attempts to speed him on his journey to manhood. Elliot offered a glimpse of the past, his boyish love for the mechanical translating seamlessly into the tangible examples of innovation dotted around the field before them. He supposed that, for all the brash modernity of the planes before them, for him they were a link to his past. They recalled stolen moments at school, toasting crumpets over a fire in Elliot's study while he expounded on the latest thrilling achievement of Europe's new aviators.

The planes were parked in the very centre of the aerodrome on a long strip of grass cut very short and resembling an oversized cricket wicket. Ten models sat on display, and here at least, there was some attempt at security in the form of a waist-high barbed-wire fence fixed with hand-daubed posters warning of the dangers of smoking in close proximity to aircraft fuel. Given that a good proportion of the crowd was smoking at any given moment, this was quite an effective deterrent, and people paused in their hundreds at the barrier, looking on at the planes, some with the studied nonchalance of the veteran air aficionado, others with the undisguised glee of the aeronautical virgin. Sketchbooks abounded, and here and there, fixed tripods topped with thick black cloth betrayed the positions of professional photographers.

James and Elliot pushed their way through the good-natured throng and secured a position so close to the barbed wire that the wool of their suit trousers snagged if they attempted too hasty a turn. Elliot took out a slim silver case, wordlessly passed James a cigarette, and took one himself before lighting both with the bastardised shell-case lighter that had been a gift from his father. He gestured with the cigarette towards a pair of biplanes parked at the end of the field.

"There, that's the BE2," he said with a faint smile.

James looked at the pair of planes and wasn't overly impressed. They were flimsy looking things and astonishingly small. Approximately thirty feet in length and perhaps ten or eleven feet in height, they appeared curiously imbalanced and incredibly fragile. James could see them from the rear, and the upper wing of the biplane looked markedly longer than the lower wing, with the engine and a four-pronged propeller at the front. Its two seats were dug out of the fuselage of the plane and exposed to the elements, giving the impression of a primitive hollowed-out log. One seat was set back, with the other set between the two wings, partially hidden by a mess of wooden struts and wire. The body of the plane was a light green-painted wood, with the wings made from some sort of wire-strengthened canvas. Numbers were painted on the tail fins of both planes, but they had no other distinguishing marks of note. Affixed to the front by simple wooden poles were a pair of skis, protruding from the front wheels and angled upwards so that they poked up into the air a few feet from the ground. *If the future was the undiscovered country*, thought James, *then it might be better that it was mapped from the ground.*

He was more circumspect with Elliot though, sensitive to his evident pride in the machines.

"Why have two seats?" he asked, half-turning towards his friend and cursing mildly as his trousers snared on the wire.

"Well, this is a military plane, old chap. It's intended for reconnaissance use over a battlefield. The seat at the back," he gestured, "is for the pilot. The one at the front is for his spotter, although in the corps they call them observers."

"But surely they can hardly see a thing?" said James, looking at the mess of wires and struts that surrounded the forward position.

"I wouldn't know. I've not had a chance to fly as an observer yet," said Elliot with a hint of petulance. "Although, you have to keep in mind that, in the air, you'd be looking around at all angles forward and back, and not just straight down. The chaps at Farnborough seem to think it suits, although I imagine it causes a bit of a pain in the neck after a while."

"Where are the weapons?" asked James, scrutinising the plane and seeing nothing that might be considered even faintly martial.

"It's a reconnaissance plane. No need for weapons really, although, at a pinch, the observer could probably carry a rifle or a pistol or something," said Elliot. Then, with a semblance of smugness, he added, "We don't think that gentlemen flyers would stoop to shooting at each other. The bally things are too bloody dangerous to risk having a pop at another chap in the air. It wouldn't be cricket."

"I suppose so," said James doubtfully. Privately, he was thinking about the recent South African war and the way that the mechanisation of war had quickly seen off any notions of fair play. "What about the skis? What are they for?" he asked.

Elliot chucked softly, expelling smoke as he did so. "Well, the whole thing's so new that, with one or two exceptions, most chaps can't fly too well. They come in too quickly and too steeply, and if the plane is angled too far forward," he held out hand at a steep forward angle to demonstrate, "when the wheels hit terra firma, the whole bally thing tips forward, crushing the flyer. Damn nuisance really but the skis help."

James glanced at the other models on display, some of which had small teams of men busily tinkering with engines and preparing the machines. Most looked like pared-down, single-seat versions of the BE2, with frames constructed of sparse metal struts rather than wood and, in one case, simply an upholstered chair surmounting a primitive-looking wire frame. Two planes at the opposite end of the field from James caught his eye for the simple reason that they were monoplanes, with two wings rather than the more usual four. One of the planes looked particularly unusual, and James stared at it until he realised that it was because a roof covered the whole pilot bay. The legend "AVRO" was stencilled in large, black letters along its length.

Pointing into the distance, James asked, "What are those things? All the planes I've seen in the papers have had four wings."

"Ah," said Elliot, dropping his cigarette and crushing it under his leatherbooted foot. "That's a monoplane, a thing of wonderment to the French and to the odd maverick over here, but an object of some derision back at Farnborough. The thing is, they don't fly too well. The lift is appalling in comparison to the biplane, and weight is a major issue. You recall Santos Dumont?"

James nodded. Alberto Santos Dumont had been one of the most famous people in the world a few years earlier, having been involved in some of the first European powered flights, including one in which he had famously circled the Eifel tower in full view of the delirious press. Brazilian by birth, he had become quite a name in French aviation.

"Well," Elliot continued, "he believes that monoplanes have the *potential* to be quicker than the biplane, due to there being less resistance against two wings than there is against four. In *theory*, he is probably right, but you have to get the thing off the ground first. Dumont solved it by using flyweight pilots, chaps like that Roland Garos cove. Rather like a jockey on horseback. Admittedly, some of the recent Bleriot models have been a bit better, but the chaps at the factory believe that the lift you get in a biplane is far more advantageous. You need less ground to get up to lift speed for one thing, and pretty much anyone can fly them if they have the talent, even the beefier fellows."

"I see," said James, quietly impressed with Elliot's understanding. "What about the roofed one, the AVRO?"

"Even the English breed the occasional madman," smiled Elliot. "Mr. A. V. Roe, secretary of this little place, the Royal Aero Club—you could probably find him over there somewhere. He is never far from a plane." He paused, peering through the rain with his hand shielding his eyes as if to locate the elusive Mr. Roe.

"Roe had the idea that a chap might like a more comfortable ride when flying. Apparently, it can get rather cold up there, and he built a plane with a lightweight roof, the type F. That plane over there."

"Sound thinking," said James. "I've travelled in a few open-top cars, and the wind is rather a bore."

"Well, for comfort, yes, I suppose it is a good idea, but the thing would be useless as a military plane. The pilot can't see much out of the side windows, and the front view is pretty obscured too. No room for an observer either. Roe is a splendid fellow but can be something of a crackpot. The design was rejected at the military trials a few years back, and efforts focused on the BE2."

James thought that rather premature, but his thoughts were interrupted by a sudden flurry of activity on the field before him. As if in anticipation, the large crowd pressed forward, and James was briefly forced against the barbed wire fencing until he fixed a hand onto a post and steadied himself.

Teams of men were busy dragging planes to the side of the field, clearing a path for take-off. Most were wearing overalls, although the team around the BE2 sported green khaki uniforms, complete with a device of either one or two gold wings over the left breast. In the centre of the field, a gentleman, rather incongruously attired in a rubberised fabric Mackintosh and a fabulously antiquated top hat, strode to the centre of the field wielding an enormous megaphone. Arms aloft, he waved his hands, beckoning for silence, and then placed the megaphone to his lips.

"Ladies and gentlemen, we will shortly be commencing the 1914 Hendon aerodrome speed trials, for which we have four competitors," he announced. "The trial will consist of five circuits of the outer ring of the airfield and will be timed from the moment the engine is switched on until the wheels touch on landing. The first pilot will be Mr. Geoffrey de Havilland, flying a Bleriot Experimental Mark 2, or BE2, an aircraft of his own design."

Adjacent to the plane, James noticed a figure in goggles wearing a short leather jacket with a white silk scarf around his neck. The figure paused by the BE2, waved briefly to the crowd, eliciting a short round of applause, and then clambered into the rear seat. The other seat remained empty. At the front of the plane, a man wearing overalls over a khaki uniform, presumably a mechanic, took a firm grip of the propeller. A reverent hush took over the field, and momentarily James could feel his heart pumping quickly in his chest. In the absolute silence, the words of the mechanic and pilot were clear.

"Switches off!" instructed the mechanic.

"Switches off," confirmed the pilot.

"Fuel on!"

"Fuel on."

"Air in."

"Air in."

"Contact!" shouted the mechanic, rapidly pushing down on the propeller and leaping to the side in one continuous, precise movement as the pilot repeated the final command.

The engine rumbled into life, spluttering in a cloud of dense, black smoke that, for a moment, completely obscured the plane from view. Somewhere at the periphery of the field, the top-hatted gentleman could be faintly heard shouting, "Start the clock!" but all eyes were on de Havilland as the mechanic pulled on a rope and removed the two wooden blocks, which had been jammed under the wheels of the BE2. The plane moved slowly forward, the engine keening in a high-pitched tone as it picked up speed. It rolled down the cut grass of the field, bouncing up and down with every dip and divot of the turf. As it moved forward, the crowd around James began to crane their necks, following every inch of the plane's progress. Then, when the machine was three-quarters of the way down the half mile of the field, the engine tone gave an unpleasant squeal, and the plane tottered hesitatingly into the air, its wings waggling in the wind, as if reluctant to embrace the inclement skies. The crowd applauded, although there seemed to be almost an air of disappointment to it, as if the take-off was rather too prosaic and merited a more dramatic show. The chap was flying, surely that deserved some fireworks!

James craned his neck with the rest, watching as de Havilland climbed to a few hundred feet and then began to trace the outskirts of the aerodrome in a series of sharp, left-banking turns. The machine was quick, he thought, but not quite as fast as he'd have imagined. The BE2 didn't flash overhead in a sudden rush of wind. Instead, it seemed somewhat sedentary, like a steam train approaching from a distance and seen from a bridge.

Suddenly, halfway through the second circuit, the low rumble of the engine gave way to a growling, asthmatic cough, the plane visibly shuddered, and then silence followed overhead. Immediately, the plane began to lose height, and there was an audible intake of breath from the crowd. At the edge of the crowd, one or two people of more nervous dispositions began to run towards the wooden hangars, although most stood their ground, eyes glued to the sky.

"What's happening?" James asked Elliot, unconsciously repeating the question that flitted about the field.

"The crate's stalled, the engine's cut out, and he'll have to bring the thing back in," replied Elliot, obviously piqued at the poor mechanical showing. "It's probably the weather. Rain never helps," he added.

Overhead, the plane had ceased its banking manoeuvres and was straightening out. In the strange, eerie silence, it flew once more above the crowd, losing altitude all of the time, and then disappeared out of sight, over the edge of the aerodrome proper.

"Why doesn't he land?" questioned James

"It'd probably kill him," said Elliot bluntly. "He can't bank sharply because, without power, he can't straighten the plane properly. He'd risk landing on a wing or, worse, going into an unrecoverable spin. The only thing to do is to fly level and straight and land it where you can. Let's hope he can find a suitable field or something."

"Is he in danger?" said James

Elliot laughed. "Of course he is. As are the local residents until he gets that thing back on the ground. Still, de Havilland is a capable fellow, I'm sure he'll be all right."

James was quietly worried, but as the minutes passed, mercifully free of the sound of a distant explosion, he assumed that de Havilland had managed to land safely somewhere in the town, doubtless startling some unwary locals.

The other three competitors, a Cody biplane, a Bleriot monoplane, and the roofed AVRO were more fortunate and managed to complete the course. The Cody seemed significantly slower than the BE2, but although both monoplanes needed a far longer run-up to get in the air, they had a significantly quicker airspeed. The Bleriot was deemed to be the fastest by the master of ceremonies, and a beaming and remarkably young pilot of around sixteen was awarded a small silver cup together with an oversized cheque emblazoned with the sigil of the *Daily Mail*. James was bemused to note that the young man's face was completely plastered in black spots until Elliot explained that the spots were due to the engine oil flying into the face of the pilot as he flew.

The afternoon raced by in a haze of engine noise, the twin aromas of aviation fuel and cigarette smoke, and, for James, an increasingly strained neck. The second BE2 fared rather better than the first, taking the prize for the best landing for Hereward de Havilland and serving to cheer up the rather dejected Elliot.

The aeronautical display closed the show, and James was delighted as several planes took to the air simultaneously, each conducting a series of rolls and loops to the roars and applause of the crowd. With his unprofessional eye, James thought the biplanes looked more versatile when engaged in manoeuvres that involved sudden climbs or descent but that the monoplanes had a clear edge when it came to speed and turning. Perhaps the situation wasn't quite as clear-cut as Elliot had intimated, thought James. The last demonstration of the day was from Hereward de Havilland in the BE2, which proceeded to climb to a height of several thousand feet, flitting in and out of view behind the thick clouds as he did so. Elliot gripped James' arm as he then began to descend rapidly in the direction of the airfield.

"Watch this, it's a bloody marvel," he whispered, his eyes fixed on the heavens.

The plane began to spin, like a top, rolling around in ever-faster, tight circles as it plummeted several thousand feet towards the ground. There were worried glances from some in the crowd, but Elliot remained holding onto James' arm, saying in an awed tone, "He's in a flat spin. Until recently, it was thought impossible to get out of that. A death sentence."

Suddenly, only a few hundred feet above the field, the plane pulled upwards, straightened out, and flew level. Wild applause and shouts of "bravo" erupted from the crowd as the pilot began a slow descent towards the airfield.

"It was a navy chap, from the Royal Navy Air Service, who worked out how to do that," said Elliot, as they watched Hereward de Havilland approaching his landing. "Chap called Wilfred Parke. He went into a spin during a test flight. Apparently the instinct is to try to pull the plane up, pulling back the stick like so—" he gesticulated pulling a lever tightly into his chest, "—but that just makes it worse. What Parke had the courage to try was the very opposite. Pushing the stick forward and engaging the rudder so it is in the opposite position to the direction you are spinning. Completely counterintuitive, and apparently he tried it at about fifty feet off the ground. He straightened out and lived to tell the tale. A lot of chaps owe their lives to that discovery. Brave fellow, Parke."

"Now," Elliot continued, shivering slightly, "without a plane to keep me occupied, I've noticed how bloody cold I am. I prescribe a warm fire, a pint, perchance a pie, and a short period of contemplation. Come, Comrade Caulfield, the bright lights of Hendon await us."

In the drizzling rain of the late afternoon, the two friends trudged, stooped, and tired alongside the thousands exiting the aerodrome. As soon as they were able, they deviated off the main road to the station and began a hurried search of the miserable back streets of the suburb, looking for a suitable public house in which to warm their sodden clothes. Their spirits were high despite the cloying damp, and each recounted highlights from the air show, occasionally supplementing their recollections with boyish gestures and sound effects.

They eventually settled on a pub at the corner of two dilapidated Victorian terrace streets, rejoicing in the unlikely name of "Colonel Pride's Rest." The pub was like thousands across London, a converted front room of a corner terrace property with a short bar wedged into the corner, policed by a portly middle-aged man with luxuriant, greying side-whiskers. Six or seven tables filled the cramped floor space. A handful of grim-looking men, all wearing caps and the shabby suits of the manual worker, sat in ones and twos around the room, nursing pints of heavy-looking beer, smoking cigarettes, and staring with various degrees of hostility at the well-dressed interlopers disturbing their repose.

Elliot rose to the challenge, doffing his trilby and smiling round at the drinkers.

"God save all here," he announced grandly. "A cold day requires stern measures, so if any of you gentlemen require a refill, please make yourself known to the barkeep and I shall gladly stand the round." Hostility gave way to startled surprise and even one or two smiles. Elliot and James settled on opposite sides of a table, as close to the weak fire as they were able, and ordered two pints of bitter. Food was unavailable, however, and the two friends politely rejected the landlord's offer to nip to the chip shop a few doors down, instead making plans to find a restaurant on their return to town.

When the beer had arrived and the mollified locals had received their share, Elliot lit two cigarettes, passing one to James.

"I confess to being rather taken with these places," he said in a quiet tone to avoid being overheard in the cramped space. "The retreat of the working man, the calm before the storm of domesticity, the idler's fancy."

"I think it rather an affectation," said James. "An expensive one too, if you have to buy six pints for every one you drink."

"There is that," agreed Elliot, "but the insight it provides into the lives of my fellow man is more than worth the expense. I'm afraid I rather scandalised some of the RFC officers at Farnborough by standing a round for some of the mechanic chaps. Solid fellows in the main—tedium personified though, unless they are talking about planes."

"Anyway, Comrade Caulfield," continued Elliot, "despite the boundless joy of seeing my old school pal once again, I have something of an ulterior motive for inviting you here today."

James, who had sensed something in the tone of Elliot's initial written invitation, didn't register any surprise.

"You see, although aircraft design is rather an interesting experience, a free spirit such as mine does not thrive when chained to a draughtsman's desk. My soul yearns for creative expression. I believe that Marx chap, who so incites the lower orders, would call it 'owning my means of production.'"

"You want to build planes?" said James, his face confused.

"Good lord, no," said Elliot, exhaling a cloudburst of smoke. "I might understand how to build a plane, but the actual building is best left to these fellows," he said waving his arm at the drinkers sat around the pub.

"No," he went on. "I don't want to draw them, nor build them, nor work on the blasted physics of the things. I simply want to fly them. "

"Won't they teach you at the Royal Aircraft Factory?" asked James.

"I'm afraid not. We may be affiliated to the Royal Flying Corps, but to my utter astonishment, they don't actually train new pilots," said Elliot, shaking his head at the flagrant idiocy of the British Army.

"So where do the pilots come from, then?" asked James reasonably.

"From here, old chap. Not this pub, obviously," he said with a discrete smile, "but from Hendon, from the aerodrome, or, more specifically, from the Royal Aeronautical Society."

Elliot sipped at his beer, wincing with exaggerated effect, as he took a swallow. "Rough work, slumming it," he mumbled.

"You see, to qualify as a flyer, you need to take your ticket," he continued. "That means training with someone who is a member of the society and qualified to judge when you are considered capable of not immediately plummeting to your doom when cut loose on your own. At that point, you get a license from the society, and then you *might* be able to join the RFC or at least become a test pilot at one of the manufacturers."

"I understand," said James equably, "but I don't understand where I come in."

"Well," said Elliot, suddenly slightly sheepish, "I'm rather in need of your financial assistance."

"Don't they pay you at the factory?" asked James, taking a long draught of his drink, tasting the bitter decay of slightly off beer and empathising with Elliot's earlier comment.

"Of course they do," replied Elliot sharply, "although I don't think Andrew Carnegie will be quaking in his boots at my bank balance. You see, old chap, the training and license are rather expensive, and my father took such a dislike to my choice of career that he completely cut my allowance when I joined the factory. You see before you an impecunious Pearson. I have barely a bean to my name."

Even given his earlier imprudent generosity, James was still uncomfortable at Elliot's obvious embarrassment and was anxious to provide some sort of resolution. His own allowance was generous, and he had managed to amass some considerable savings over the last few months, being nearly always in the company of his father. He could therefore loan Elliot the money against his future earnings; he could even offer it as a gift. The only problem was that his outgoings were carefully scrutinised by Godfrey, who might take a dim view of an old school fellow tapping him for a loan. He had no wish to expose Elliot's situation to his father, who tended to view wealth as the external stigmata of inner morality. Thinking on the events of the day and to the empty summer stretching ahead of him, he had a flash of inspiration.

"I'll come too. We can train together. My father won't mind, and it'll give me something to occupy me until I go up to Cambridge. I can pay for both of us, and you can pay me back whenever you can," he said, eyes widening in surprise at his own impetuosity, a broad smile playing across his face.

Elliot looked relieved, his face flushing under his red hair. Reflecting back James' smile and raising his glass in salute, he said, "You, Sir, are a prince amongst men, a veritable Samaritan of the air. You have my everlasting thanks."

The two clinked glasses and raised a toast to the gentlemen of the air. The other drinkers looked at the laughing pair and wondered if their good cheer might hold the promise of another round. In fact, it delivered several, and it was almost time for the last train to town by the time the two friends staggered off into the night air, arms wrapped around each other's shoulders, humming *La Marseillaise*.

Weybridge, June 15, 1914

Three days later, James sat smoking alone on the terrace of a hotel in Surrey, contemplating his imminent first meeting with his flight instructor. The late afternoon sun played over the grounds of the hotel, reflecting off a carp pond and streaming patchily through a small, well-tended copse of Elm trees.

His father had been remarkably sanguine about the flying idea. Having secured the patronage of Lord Northcliffe, he was content to let James pursue whatever follies he chose until he went up to Cambridge, providing of course that they were commensurate with his station. James' mother was much less impressed, citing the incredible danger of air flight and suggesting instead that he take up shooting. With Godfrey's permission secured though, there was little she could do, and, when James explained through the fog of a shattering hangover that flying was now attracting people like Lord Brabazon of Tara and others with titles, she soon gave way, content to consider it merely an extension of the gentleman's club. There had been no quibbling over expense either, and if they thought the £60 it had cost to secure the two sets of lessons was an extravagance, nothing had been said. Only Harper, the butler, had voiced any doubts, and they were entirely concerned with what a young gentleman might wear at an airfield. He had been rather scandalised when James had informed him that a leather coat was the norm, rather than the three-piece suit he had initially proffered.

Elliot, to his credit, had moved fast, contacting the Royal Aero Club by telephone from Farnborough the morning after their session in the pub and ascertaining the process. Pilot qualification, like everything connected with flying, was rather ramshackle, a reaction to the plethora of deaths that had occurred in the early part of the century as amateurs built planes in barns and sheds and then proceeded to take them into the air without any formal instruction. The Royal Aero Club had devised the ticketing system to provide a form of licensing to pilots in an attempt to impose some order on the chaos. It had served to professionalise the manufacturers and the two air arms of the military, giving them access to a pool of prequalified pilots with at least some guarantee that they were capable of flying solo. The impact on the amateur community had been limited, however, as, without the threat of any punitive sanctions people in possession of their own planes could wilfully ignore the process and continue as before.

The mechanics were simple, owing more to the idea that flying was a hobby rather than a regulated vocation. There were no dedicated or trained instructors. Instead, any of the several thousand men or handful of women who had successfully taken their ticket could instruct a potential pilot and then make a subjective judgement as to when their pupil could be regarded as qualified. In practice, very few actually did instruct others because most did not need the money sufficiently to merit taking the risk. Most new flyers were reliant on friends and relatives as instructors, although there had been a few hardy, financially challenged souls who had formed a core at Hendon and were made available at the discretion of the club secretary, usually working as subcontractors for one of the several flight schools that were springing up around the London area.

Elliot, as a member of staff at the Royal Aircraft Factory, had been considered a priority by Secretary Roe and had quickly been assigned the services of a Mr. Benjamin Vaughan, who worked for the Hewlett and Blondeau flying school based in Surrey. Following a brief telephone conversation between the two, Mr. Vaughan had gracefully also agreed to teach James, with the caveat that his initially proposed fee of £30 was doubled. Arrangements had been made, and James had duly despatched a grumbling Harper to the shops of Oxford Street, where he had obtained a knee-length brown leather coat, thick, fur-lined leather gloves, and a pair of oversized skiing goggles. Thus equipped, he had taken the train to Weybridge in Surrey, where he secured a room at the Hand and Spear Hotel, adjacent to the station and about a mile's walk from the famous Brooklands race track and airfield. Elliot arrived later that same evening, having taken a leave of absence from Farnborough. It was only two days since he had petitioned James for his help, a period that had left them both dizzy with anticipation and nearly overcome with nervous excitement.

They had agreed to meet Mr. Vaughan for dinner in the restaurant of the Hand and Spear, a crumbling, redbrick, Victorian edifice that had once served as the Baron of Ockham's summer residence. The hotel had obviously had a formidable aristocratic grandeur at its height, with oak-panelled communal areas, large chandeliers, and pleasant, airy private rooms with three-quarter-length sash windows and their own bathrooms. It had served as a hotel for several decades, but the opening of the Brooklands track in 1907 had significantly boosted visitor numbers, and the owners had tried to capitalise on the sporting theme by filling the walls with numerous photographs and sketches of racing cars, supplemented with the occasional shot of an airplane. The hotel showed hints of decline, though. Some of the panelling was visibly rotting, and the provision of electricity was only partial, confined to the bar area and the hotel's reception. The restaurant, like the bedrooms, was served by a combination of oil lamps and candles. In the absence of a race meeting, the place was quiet, with two or three guests served by at least three times as many staff. The manager had obviously been grateful that James and Elliot had booked in for an initial period of a week, with the possibility of an extension beyond that.

The sun was starting to wane as Mr. Vaughan arrived at the hotel. He met Elliot and James in the reception area, made a curt introduction, and perfunctorily took them through to the gloomy restaurant without waiting on the usual aperitif and leaving a frustrated barman in his wake. The restaurant was a long, cavernous room, with high windows letting in a minimum of evening sunlight, and the dark oppressive nature of the wooden panelling was only partially offset by the tabletop candles being incrementally lit by the serving staff. There were perhaps twenty tables, but the only other diners were an elderly couple, resplendent in full evening dress, tucking into a tureen of soup at the far end of the room.

Mr. Vaughan, with a familiarity that spoke eloquently of the frequency of his visits, greeted the maître d'hôtel by name, gave him his rather tattered trilby and light overcoat, and then selected a table near to the door of the restaurant, as far away from the other diners as possible. Taking his seat, he gestured impatiently for James and Elliot to sit down. In the half-light of the room, he looked a young man, perhaps in his early thirties, although deep lines around his eyes marked him as possibly much older, an impression lent weight by the luxuriant blonde moustache, peppered with grey, that he wore on his top lip. Thinning blonde hair, imperfectly cut, was swept inelegantly to one side, occasionally falling in front of his eyes and causing him to periodically brush it back over his ears with the back of his hand. Keen blue eyes appraised Elliot and James, holding their gaze for an uncomfortably long time. James was conscious that the cut of Vaughan's clothes was a few years out of date, and the suit he was wearing on his slender frame had evidently been patched on more than one occasion. Propriety in dress was clearly not one of Mr. Vaughan's strengths, and neither, it seemed, was conversation.

"We're delighted to make your acquaintance, Sir," ventured Elliot, smiling politely at the near-catatonic Vaughan.

Without taking his gaze off Elliot, Vaughan replied in a surprisingly soft, West Country burr, "I'm sure you are, but whether your delight will be reciprocated remains to be seen."

The uncomfortable silence resumed, until briefly interrupted by the arrival of the sommelier. Vaughan smiled disarmingly at the man and ordered two bottles of house claret and three glasses, without deigning to enquire what his companions required. The waiter, clearly used to Vaughan's idiosyncrasies, didn't linger, retreating back to the bar with a murmured, "Very good, Sir."

Hostilities resumed at the table, and Vaughan continued to look James and Elliot in the eye, maintaining an increasingly tense silence as he did so. After perhaps a minute of this scrutiny, James' notions of propriety got the better of him, and he cracked.

"I say, would you mind not doing that? It's rather disconcerting," he said in a feeble, almost childish whine.

"I dare say it is, young man," said Vaughan evenly, "but I need to take the measure of a man before I risk my life for him."

Sensing an opportunity to break the deadlock, James asked, "And? What does your second sight tell you about us?"

Vaughan's mouth smiled, showing even, white teeth, although his eyes showed no sign of humour, retaining the same narrow, inhuman focus. The effect was curiously cruel on his narrow, bony face, and James repressed a shudder.

"It tells me," began Vaughan, "that you are a couple of well-meaning idiots who will only realise that flying is not the lark you think it to be when you are trapped in a burning plane with no hope of escape. It's not your fault. You read the magazines, you see the pictures, and you see a selection of all-conquering modern heroes, but you don't see the drudgery, the sheer monotony of constant attention to detail, or the skill and courage it takes to fly."

"I know a little more than that," said Elliot brusquely. "I have been designing aircraft for most of the last year."

"Designing is not flying," snapped Vaughan. "You must start with Socrates. Know that you know nothing, and we might have a chance."

"Well," said James, in a placatory tone, "we are here to learn. Perhaps you can make a start on relieving us of our abject ignorance?"

Nodding, Vaughan paused as the sommelier returned with the claret, uncorked both bottles, and settled them on the table, intending to let them breathe. To the man's surprise, Vaughan picked up one of the bottles, poured a large glass, and then proceeded to quaff more than half of it in one huge swallow.

Elliot caught James' eye, as clearly nonplussed by the indecorous behaviour of this madman as his friend. The appalled sommelier beat a hasty retreat, muttering a vague promise to send a waiter to their table in a few moments.

Waving a hand towards the bottles, Vaughan said, "Help yourselves, gentlemen; there's no use in standing on ceremony if we are to work together."

Elliot poured two glasses, and James noticed a slight tremor in his hand as he returned the bottle to the table. Vaughan, too, was looking at the hand and was again wearing his strange, joyless grin.

"Good. If I frighten you, that's a start. You might even listen to me, which will mean that we may all survive the next week or two."

Elliot, his pale skin flushing in the shadow of the candlelight, started to say something, thought better of it, and instead flashed an angry look at Vaughan.

The older man ignored it, took another huge swallow of his wine, drained the glass, and then poured himself the rest of the first bottle.

"Rule one," he said, extending his index finger, "if your engine fails on take-off, never turn back. Fly straight, and land where you can."

James opened his mouth to speak, but was cut off by Vaughan with a terse wave of his hand.

"Rule two," he continued, "we fly only at dawn or in early evening, and then only if there is no significant wind and no rain. At this time of year, we should be able to get in five to ten hours a week."

He sipped at his wine and held up a third finger.

"Rule three," he said, "my word is to be immediately obeyed. In the air or on the ground, you do *exactly* what I tell you, when I tell you, until such a time as you are qualified. Do not pester me to allow you to go solo. I will judge when you are ready, and I will also determine when you have reached an acceptable standard to be issued with your ticket, should that eventuality come to pass."

He drank the remainder of his wine and suddenly stood up.

"I have another engagement in the village, so I will leave you gentlemen to your dinner. Ask for me at the main office at Brooklands shortly before first light, and be sober. Excessive consumption of alcohol is a luxury preserved entirely for the experienced flyer." He looked pointedly at the open bottle perched on the end of the table.

"Now," he continued, "about my fee."

A stunned James removed his wallet from his jacket pocket, unfolded twelve crisp, new, white five-pound notes, and, in a daze, handed them to Vaughan. Smiling broadly for the first time since they had met him, the older man shoved the notes roughly into the trouser pocket of his suit and stalked out of the restaurant without a farewell, calling loudly for his coat and hat and attracting the critical gaze of the couple at the opposite end of the restaurant.

The two friends sat in silence for a few moments, emotionally battered by the whirlwind encounter. James felt a sense of shame at his own timidity coupled with a vague sense of elation that he had passed some sort of test.

Eventually, Elliot recovered some semblance of self, took a sip of wine, and said, "I'm sorry, old man. I had no idea that the chap was quite such a brute. He's worse than the beaks at school. Shabbier too, and clearly rather fond of the demon drink."

"Oh don't worry about it," smiled James. "If eccentricity is any measure of the quality of a flyer, he could be just what we need."

The greyish-purple light of predawn was trickling over Weybridge common as Elliot and James set out on foot for the Brooklands racetrack. There had been a staccato rainfall during the early hours, which had briefly threatened the day's flying, but it had passed quickly, and although the ground was damp, the skies were clear enough to see the fading light of a number of stars. A light breeze blew in from the south, but unless it ratcheted up a few notches, it wouldn't trouble them.

Weybridge, like many small towns and villages at the edge of London, was changing rapidly, James reflected, as he trudged along the dirt surface of the Brooklands road. People were already up and about on this early Tuesday morning. Dressed in formal office wear, they were doubtless heading for the station and the trains that would take them to the industry of London. Along the Brooklands road and silhouetted across the top of St. George's hill, new houses stood in various stages of creation, built to accommodate the workers relocating to the suburbs and getting away from the grime and pollution of the capital. The old villages of London's outskirts were slowly dying, replaced by a uniform array of discrete villas and terraces. Civic dormitories were replacing the older hubs of agricultural life. Inexorable progress certainly had its price, thought James. And, if flight was a component part of that progress, where would that lead? Which aspects of cultural history would fade away with the rise of the airplane? The planet would be a smaller place from here on in: that was for certain.

Mildly amused by the irony of potentially becoming an airborne Luddite, James was about to communicate his thoughts to his companion when he saw Elliot's face and realised that now was not the time. Elliot had slept badly, equally excited and intimidated by the prospect of the morning to come. Now, unfortified by his usual gargantuan breakfast, he was a picture of misery, his shoulders slumped and his long leather coat flapping lazily in the slight breeze. A palpable tension hung about him, as if he were off to a place of execution rather than a morning's jaunt in a new plaything. But then, thought James, that was the difference between them, wasn't it? For Elliot this was more than a passion, more than a hobby to fill the time until more serious ventures beckoned. This was the fulfilment of a long-held dream, the pinnacle of all ambition. Fear of failure must weigh heavily on his friend, and James felt a pang of sympathy as he realised that he himself had much less to lose.

The Brooklands track and aerodrome was impressive. Built as a home for British motor racing a few years prior, it was a three-mile-long, concrete-covered banked oval, allowing cars and motorbikes to attain incredible speeds in both testing and race conditions. Indeed, the previous year, a racer called Percy Lambert had achieved international fame by being the first man to drive more than a hundred miles in a single hour. Spectators flocked to the various meets arranged at the track, and purpose-built grandstands surrounded the track on a scale unknown in any other popular sport, save perhaps the odd football ground.

In the early morning light, the stadium looked like a monstrous anachronism, looming out of the darkness of the quiet countryside like a Roman amphitheatre left in the middle of nowhere. Recalling the chaos of Hendon, James was impressed that the scale of the place had not diminished its solidity. Wired fencing ran around the whole of the perimeter, occasionally punctuated by ticket offices and turnstile gates. The stands were equally impressive; massive, roofed wooden constructions dwarfed the fencing and looked like they could comfortably accommodate thousands. Scattered on the walls of the stand, garish coloured posters advertised the delights of the racing calendar, complete with idealised images of cars speeding like bullets around the ramped track.

They quickly located the main office because it was the only building on the outside of the fencing that had any light showing in its windows. A befuddled and sleepy old man dozed in a chair behind a large empty desk, on which the sole item was a hand-carved sign reading "Caretaker." Although disgruntled to be awoken by Elliot gently shaking his shoulder and asking for Mr. Vaughan, he soon leapt into action. Seeing the clothes of the two visitors in the electric light of the office, he motioned for them to follow him through a second door on the back wall.

The group tramped down two flights of stairs and emerged into an underground tunnel, weakly lit by occasional lamps at ceiling height. The tunnel was scattered with the detritus of racing support: empty petrol drums, lengths of tubing, and more personal items such as battered helmets, pendants, and vests in team colours.

"The buggers just 'frow everything in here after a race," the old man muttered. "I'm always cleaning up after 'em. At least you gentlemen take your rubbish with you."

The tunnel had a steep incline at its end, and the group emerged into the growing light of dawn to behold a huge field steaming with evaporating dew and neatly bisected by a long concrete strip. James realised they must have walked under the track and were now standing in the centre ground of the racetrack itself. Looking around, he could see rudimentary fencing bordering the track itself and, on the opposite side, the massive structures of the main stand. Ahead of him, on either side of the concrete strip, were six parked planes. A couple had men with toolboxes working underneath them. James recognised a BE2, but the rest were unfamiliar to him. Plumb centre on the strip sat a peculiar-looking contraption, which resembled an enormous Chinese kite. James could just make out Vaughan in the half-light, kneeling under the midsection of the plane, a spanner silhouetted in his hand.

They said their good-byes to the caretaker, who shuffled off back down the tunnel with an instruction to come back the way they had come. Walking towards Vaughan, James got a closer look at the plane under which their flight instructor was tinkering. There was no doubt now—it was a kite, bearing a strong familial resemblance to the photographs of the Wright Brothers' *Kitty Hawk*. Around forty feet long, it had an exposed, wire-braced wooden frame, with stiffened canvas covering the four wings and forming a hollowed box at the tail. There was a long, upholstered bench at the juncture of the wings and the fuselage, and some sort of perfunctory control system protruded from the frame in front of it. Immediately ahead of that, there was a metal bar, presumably some sort of footrest for the flyer. Behind the pilot bay sat the propeller, seemingly strapped to the back of the seating area itself. All of it rested on the now-familiar skis and a series of wooden struts, which linked the frame to the tiny pram like wheels. To James, it looked like a toy or the ancient doodling of some renaissance master. There could be no conceivable way such a thing could fly, unless there was a very strong wind.

From the corner of his mouth, Elliot whispered, "Bristol Boxkite. Damn good plane. Slow but stable."

Under the plane, Vaughan had spotted them, setting down his tools and wiping his hands on the washed-out blue overalls he was wearing.

"I see you look the part," he said, nodding at their coats and the goggles strung round their necks. He seemed strangely cordial in comparison to the previous evening, somehow calmer, and there was the ghost of a genuine smile playing across his face.

"Right, onwards and forwards. Pearson, isn't it?" he said, looking to Elliot.

"Yes Sir," replied Elliot.

"I am assuming that you managed to pick up something at Farnborough and know the rudiments of an aircraft's control system?" asked Vaughan.

"Yes Sir, I've drawn enough of them," said Elliot.

"In that case, I suggest you sit over there," Vaughan pointed at a section of seating adjacent to the track fencing, "and consider, ruminate, ponder—do whatever it is you do when you have an idle moment—while I fill in your colleague here."

"Yes Sir," said Elliot, retreating to the barrier. He picked up a wooden seat, turned it around, and sat down to keep an eye on the proceedings.

"Oh, and Pearson?" shouted Vaughan, as Elliot produced a cigarette from the pocket of his coat. "You don't call me 'Sir.' Mr. Vaughan will suffice, and you don't bloody well smoke! The whole place is soaked in petrol!"

Chastised, Elliot packed away his cigarette case, rested his elbows on his knees, and prepared to settle in.

"Now then, Caulfield," said Vaughan, turning his attention to James. "Have you ever handled a boat?"

James, who had been a reluctant regular at Cowes since infancy, answered that he had.

"In that case," Vaughan continued, "you will know that a rudder allows a boat to turn to port or starboard when it has forward momentum. You will also know that the speed of that movement is dictated by the speed at which the boat is travelling."

Taking James' arm, he pulled him around to the rear of the aircraft. Pointing at the boxed canvas tail fin of the plane, he said, "This is the plane's rudder, and the principle is exactly the same as on a boat. In the air or at speed on the ground, the rudder will allow you to control the yaw of the craft in the vertical axis. Or, in English, it will determine which way the nose of the plane is pointing. The major difference is that, in most aircraft, the rudder is not operated by hand but instead manipulated by a bar, generally placed by the feet and depressed by the pilot when he wishes to bank left or right. Different manufacturers vary the placement of the bar, with some being controlled by attached stirrups and others directly by pedals. This primitive little beauty is controlled by applying pressure on the bar itself. "

Without waiting for an acknowledgement, he steered James along the fuselage of the plane to the pilot bay area at the juncture of the fuselage and the wing.

"This bar," he said pointing to what James had thought to be a footrest.

"Obviously," Vaughan continued. "This is where we sit. It is a little cosy for my tastes, but unless you eat your way to gout, two people can usually fit. My point is that there is only one bar. If I tell you to, lift your feet away and let me take control."

James nodded acquiescence, and Vaughan was satisfied enough to continue.

"This," he said, pointing at the device immediately in front of the pilot seat, "is the stick, the little beauty that turns this thing into a plane. Pull back and you lift, push forward and you descend. Have you got that?"

"Yes Sir. I mean, Mr. Vaughan," said James hesitatingly.

"Good. The other handle is the throttle, which controls your speed. The rest of this stuff," Vaughan said, waving his hand at the series of switches to the left of the pilot's area, "is all to do with fuel and when you can start the propeller. We'll cover that in a moment, but you already have enough to fly. Ready?"

Vaughan fixed James with a teasing, malevolent glare that made him forget the questions he had been carefully formulating for the last few minutes. This was a challenge, and James was suddenly determined that this dishevelled drunkard would not get the better of him.

"Yes," he said mildly. "I'm ready."

Ten minutes later, perched on the precarious seat in the pilot bay of the Boxkite, James fully appreciated how he had been manipulated into this show of bravado. *Too late now*, he thought. He couldn't back out with any degree of pride. And besides, Elliot was still watching from the sidelines, tobacco tetchy and impatient for his own turn. With his goggles and coat, at least he looked like a pilot. Even Vaughan had said that. A display of confidence and sangfroid would see him through.

Vaughan, politely oblivious to the visible nerves of his pupil, clambered up the frame and sat down next to James.

"First thing, take the bloody goggles off!" said Vaughan good-naturedly. "In this machine, the engine is behind us, the risk of being blinded by oil is therefore minimal, and we will not be going more than a few feet off the ground."

James slipped the goggles off his face and down to his neck. Vaughan nodded in approval and busied himself with the switches to his left: simple metal protrusions, like slightly bulbous tines of a fork, with "on" and "off" written in what looked like crayon above and below them.

"And so to the litany, Mr. Caulfield," said Vaughan. "The engines on all aircraft must be started manually, mainly because designers like Mr. Pearson over there like to make things difficult for us and have yet to come up with a way to switch on from the pilot bay."

He turned to the propeller behind the seat. "Propellers usually have four spokes on biplanes," he continued, "two on monoplanes. They can be made of metal, but because of the weight differential, wood is usually considered a better alternative. Regardless of type, when started, the propeller on any plane rotates at a ferocious speed, and it is absolutely imperative that there is no one in the vicinity when it kicks into life. Many a man who has failed to heed that warning has lost a hand or even his life. So, to ensure things move smoothly, we deploy a technique known as the litany, words that precede any flight and are there to ensure the safety of you, your mechanic, and the plane itself."

James nodded as Vaughan pointed to the small bank of switches.

"As you can see, every switch is currently in the 'off' position. From left to right, these control the flow of fuel, the flow of air, and lastly the master switch for power to the engine itself." Vaughan paused and looked at James, assessing whether the information had been absorbed. Giving a small nod, he continued.

"The mechanic, or in this case you, will position himself by the propeller." James moved to climb out of the pilot bay, but Vaughan restrained him with a hand on his shoulder. "Patience—you need to see the order of the switches first," he added.

"The mechanic will then say, 'switch off.' At this point, the pilot will check that all the switches are in the off position. Even if you know this is the case, you will always make a visual check." He glanced at the switch panel with an exaggerated swivel of his head, confirming everything was in the correct position.

"The mechanic will then brace a hand against a spoke of the propeller and give the instruction, 'fuel on.' The pilot will then move this switch to the upward position and confirm 'fuel on,'" Vaughan said, pointing to the left of the panel. "Following me so far?"

"I think so," said James.

"Not good enough," said Vaughan angrily. "Do you understand what I have said?"

"Yes, I do, Mr. Vaughan."

"Good. Do not think. Always know. If you don't know, ask. Got that?"

"Yes," said James meekly

Satisfied, Vaughan continued. "Next comes the air, which will mix with the fuel to create combustion when the engine is powered. Again, the mechanic will shout 'air on,' and the pilot will repeat the command and then move the switch to the upwards position."

"Finally," said Vaughan, "the mechanic will give the order 'contact,' and the pilot will throw the final switch. The mechanic will swing the propeller downwards as vigorously as he is able, and then he will get the hell out of the way. The engine will hopefully kick into life, but if it doesn't, and often it doesn't, the whole process begins again. Now, assuming you have the brains to have mastered that, we'll start the aircraft. For now, you'll be the mechanic," he said, waving James out of the pilot bay.

James clambered out of the seat and rounded the wing of the plane, taking an awkward position sideways on to the propeller. At the edge of the field, he could see that Elliot had stood to watch, his hand shading his eyes against the glare of the rising sun.

It took him three attempts to get the engine of the plane to start. The propeller was heavy and stiff, and the angle at which he was trying to access it gave him insufficient purchase to bring all his strength to the task. Eventually, an exasperated Vaughan told him to use both hands at the tip of the propeller spoke, and in this way the engine caught and the plane rumbled into life. He re-joined Vaughan and took his place on the second seat of the pilot bay.

"A poor show, Mr. Caulfield, but we got there in the end. Now strap in and we shall begin your practical lesson with a series of straights. Ignore the rudder for this exercise. I can't have you veering all over the field, so you will just be using this," he said, indicating the metal handle of the throttle, "and the stick."

"When I say so, push the throttle gently forward in a continuous motion, until it is fully open," Vaughan said. "The plane will begin to speed up, and within a few hundred feet you will have reached the heady maximum speed, which on this crate is about forty miles per hour. At that point, you will gently pull back on the stick and the plane will begin to rise gently. When you are fully off the ground, you will then carefully push the stick forwards, as slowly as possible, until you feel the wheels hit the concrete. At that point, pull back the throttle until the plane slows and comes to a complete standstill. You will then cut the engine and place all switches into the off position. We'll jump out, turn the plane around, and go again. Got that?"

"Yes," said James, feeling slightly sick.

"No time like the present. *Carpe diem* and all that," said Vaughan

James pushed the throttle and felt the plane jolt forward. Even on a concrete base, the vibration of the plane was appalling. Every rumble of the engine could be felt through the seat of his trousers and down his legs. The shaking affected his hand movement, and he had to concentrate in order to get a tight grip of the instruments. Even at low speed, the wind whipped into his face, bringing tears to his eyes and making him wish he had defied Vaughan and retained his goggles. Slowly at first, the plane edged forward on the concrete. In the corner of his vision, he could see Elliot applauding but could hear nothing over the frightful noise of the engine immediately behind him. The stench of petrol was dreadful, and James was conscious of a billowing cloud of smoke trailing in his wake and being whipped by the gentle wind into a continuous stream.

The plane bumped its way along the concrete strip, getting faster and faster, until James realised that the throttle was fully forward. He switched his left hand to the stick and pulled back. The stick was incredibly sensitive, perhaps overly oiled, and he pulled it back much more sharply than he had intended. The plane jumped into the air, the engine stuttered, James panicked, and Vaughan suddenly reached across him, roughly pushing his hand to one side and taking over the control. He made a subtle correction, and the engine noise stabilised. Placing James' hand back on the stick, he said something that couldn't be heard over the noise of the engine, accompanying the words with a level movement of his hand, followed by a sharp downward motion.

James held the stick steady and realised with sudden clarity that he was actually flying. The plane was about ten feet off the ground and level. The dull grey concrete underneath the plane was flashing past at an incredible speed, and he was utterly elated. That was short-lived though, as Vaughan tapped him on the shoulder, pointed forwards, and then gestured at his eyes. James realised that he was running out of concrete and that he could see the edge of the field approaching a few hundred feet away. He pushed the stick forward as gently and carefully as he could, and the nose of the plane began to dip. His touch was still marginally too heavy, and the plane bounced twice on the concrete before settling on the surface. James cut the throttle and watched anxiously as the plane began to slow. It stopped with around twenty feet of concrete to spare to the barrier of the racetrack. Relieved, he cut the engine and set the switches to the off position. The sudden silence was overwhelming, and he turned nervously to Vaughan.

"Not bad, my boy, not bad," beamed the instructor. "Ham-fisted on the stick going up, and you very nearly stalled, but you learned your lesson on the way back down. I've seen much worse on the first time out, believe me. Hop out and we'll go again."

They climbed out of the aircraft, spun her round from the tail, and set off again. After four more straights, James had mastered the movement of the stick and could take off without risking a stall and land without bouncing or tipping the plane over. Pleased with the morning's work and with Vaughan's faint praise, he was content to swap places with Elliot and watched as his friend went through the same routine. James was amused to see that, despite Elliot's greater exposure to planes, he took several more straights to master the controls. James counted at least two full stalls, followed by undignified bounced landings, with the plane rocking forward on its skis before settling back into a stable position. When they finally left the plane, both Vaughan and Elliot looked pale and rattled.

Vaughan walked them to the entrance of the trackside tunnel, chatting briefly to a group of newly arrived pilots who were congregating around the parked BE2. He explained that wind was forecast for late in the afternoon and that flying was likely to be impossible that evening. They arranged to meet at dawn the following day, and Elliot and James departed, startling the old caretaker again as they exited the racetrack through his office.

As they set off on the Brooklands road back to Weybridge, the colour began to return to Elliot's cheeks, and he turned to James.

"I'd suggest a hearty breakfast, old chap, but my stomach is turning somersaults, and I'm not sure I could keep it down. I'm for a bath, bed, and perhaps a late luncheon at the hotel."

"A sound plan," said James, the exhaustion of the early start now getting better of the elated excitement of the last couple of hours. "It's more tiring than you'd think, this flying lark," he added.

"Indeed," said Elliot, rubbing his eyes, "and a damned sight more difficult."

Just under two weeks later, on the morning of the twenty-ninth of June, Elliot and James were completing a late breakfast on the terrace of the Weybridge hotel when they first heard the news that would send shockwaves across Europe. Their waiter, a deferential young man with a threadbare, set down a silver tray with the pair's pot of coffee and offered them both a copy of the *Times*.

He said quietly, "I believe you gentlemen may find this of interest."

They sipped their coffee, and silence reigned as they devoured the news. The previous day, the heir presumptive to the crown of the Austro-Hungarian Empire, Archduke Franz Ferdinand and his wife, Duchess Sophie of Hohenburg, had been brutally assassinated by gunshot while inspecting Imperial Army manoeuvres in Sarajevo, Bosnia. The *Times* reported that the attack had been coordinated by a group of conspirators who had planted themselves along the route of the archduke's progress and had made several unsuccessful attempts at killing him before finally succeeding with pistol shots fired into the car at close range. In all, there were seven full pages of comment and analysis in the paper, covering the immediate arrest of the majority of the conspirators and detailing their failed attempt to commit suicide with cyanide. The successful assassin was a nineteen-year-old Bosnian-Serb, Gavrilo Princip, who was now in the custody of the Austrian military. The event was made even more tragic by a report that claimed that Duchess Sophie had only been in attendance at the military review because it was her only chance to appear in public with her husband. The disparity in rank between husband and wife prevented them from appearing together except in circumstances where the archduke was performing a military duty. Franz Ferdinand, unusually for a senior royal, was known to dearly love his wife and had apparently seized on the opportunity to appear at the review by her side. Love, it seemed, had led them both to their deaths.

It was some time before either friend spoke. James thought back to the conversation he had had with his father the day he returned from Rugby. Speculating feverishly, he wondered if this could be the pebble that started the avalanche. The *Times*, and indeed the British, bore no love for the Austro-Hungarian Empire, but surely nobody could condone the cold-blooded assassination of a crowned head? Serbia, too, with all of its militaristic pretensions and its practice of irredentism in Austrian territories, would find it hard to find friends amongst the British hierarchy, but the vagaries of international politics were too complex for James to judge objectively. This might be dismissed as an unpleasant event in a tumultuous part of Europe, or it could be the catalyst for full-scale continental war. As if in echo to his thoughts, Elliot broke the prolonged silence.

"Frightful thing to happen, but I can't see why the *Times* seem to think it quite so important," he said.

"It says here," replied James, "that everything depends on how Austria responds. I mean, it's quite clear that these chaps must have had some support from the Serbian government. Austria won't take that lightly, and they might even choose to invade."

"Quite right too. If somebody had a pop at the prince of Wales, I'd be the first to make merry hell, but this is just a local spat, surely? Austria has every reason to declare war on the blighters, and good luck to them, but we don't need to get involved," said Elliot in an unusually assertive tone.

"I don't know, old chap. My father seems to think that the balance of power and the systems of alliance are so precarious that we might all be for it, as countries take one side or other," explained James.

"I can't see it myself," said Elliot. "I mean, I'm an educated sort of chap, and I've barely heard of Serbia. The public won't wear it if they're asked to fight on either side. It's simply nothing to do with us."

"I hope you're right," said James, setting down his paper and draining the last dregs of the now-cold coffee. "I really do."

Like all pleasures partaken too frequently, flying for James had quickly mutated into addiction. As the lessons progressed, he found that the Boxkite had conquered some part of his subconscious and filled his resting mind with images of graceful glides over sunlit English countryside. He had been delighted to discover that he had genuine talent for flying. A meticulous command of the safety routines complemented a growing sense of the plane's capabilities and his touch as a pilot. After completing seven hours of airtime in the first week, Vaughan, visibly thawing in the face of James' progress, had allowed him to fly in windier conditions than were usually permissible. He had acquitted himself well, maintaining his calm and compensating with use of rudder and stick as the wind buffeted and lifted the plane's lightweight frame.

The second week of training had seen James make his first solo flight and his first stall. The engine had cut out as the plane was climbing away from the aerodrome. Surprising himself with his calm, he had pulled back the stick, cleared the stand at the edge of the Brooklands track, and managed to bring the plane down in a field before all airspeed had completely deserted him. There had been some damage to the tail box of the plane, caused by its catching on a hedgerow as it came to rest, but the ground crew at the Hewlett and Blondeau flying school had quickly repaired that. Vaughan had even congratulated him for not panicking and forgetting the first rule.

By the tail end of the second week, with thirteen hours of airtime behind him, James was certain he could fly. He began venturing further away from Brooklands, taking the machine to higher altitudes and into steeper dives, always careful to pull up before the wing tremor turned into the onset of a spin, something Vaughan called "the nemesis of the fledgling flyer." He began to explore the limitations of the plane, experimenting with banking turns taken at different speeds and altitudes. Too steep a climb could induce a stall, and he became more expert in using gravity to create pressure on the propeller to restart the engine. He also took afternoon lectures from Vaughan on the dark art of navigation and spent his evenings poring over maps of the Surrey countryside, plotting the prominent landmarks on routes to take the following morning. Church spires were a great help, as were rail tracks, substantial roads, towns, and villages. Soon, he found he could navigate anywhere within a ten-mile radius purely by sight.

Elliot was some way behind him in terms of progress, not through any real absence of talent, but because he seemed to lack the same instinctive feel for the plane. Therefore, it took him longer to master the rudiments. Vaughan was remarkably patient with his friend, compensating for the slow curve of his learning by giving him extra tutorial time in the air. By the end of the second week, Elliot had completed his first solo flight, an achievement marred slightly by his tipping the machine onto its nose on landing, breaking the supporting skis and inducing Vaughan to deliver a blistering and colourful assessment of his parentage. James had been forced to pay the mechanics to repair the damage, while a shamefaced Elliot mumbled about tail lift and wind strength.

They met Vaughan as usual at Brooklands just after dawn on the morning of Friday, July 1st, two days after the assassination of the archduke. James was feeling subdued, having received a plaintive letter from his father the previous evening. Godfrey was concerned about the escalating tension on the continent and the ongoing repercussions of the Curragh mutiny in Ulster, which still threatened the stability of the Asquith government, as well as fanning the anger of the Irish Republican and Unionist factions. Godfrey had instructed James to return home as soon as he was able to in order to discuss events. The letter closed with the news that he and Sylvia were planning a lengthy trip to the United States and strongly suggested that James would be wise to join them. If war came, thought James, it seemed that his father was determined to keep him out of it.

The morning was grey and overcast, although the cloud level was high enough for a reasonably skilled pilot to take to the air, and there was no rain yet. James was bemused to note that the airfield was populated by more than the usual handful of mechanics. A mysterious group of four men sat in the trackside seating, one of them wearing a khaki-green uniform emblazoned with a pair of silver wings. Vaughan greeted them with an unusual degree of animation, and James noticed that he seemed to have spruced himself up a little, although he still smelt faintly of alcohol. He was wearing a formal suit of reasonable repair, and his wild, wispy hair was secured under his battered trilby. He was sporting a tie, and the savage excess of his moustache had been clipped into a semblance of good order. If not quite smart, thought James, the man might pass as a gentleman in a darkened room.

"Good morning, gentlemen," said Vaughan, his usual scowl exchanged for twinkling eyes and a light smile. He extended an arm in the direction of the watching men.

"These gentleman are here to witness a test trial for a new version of the AVRO later today," he said, "but I have managed to press gang them into providing objective support for my judgment that you should both now be regarded as competent airmen, a rubber stamp for your ticket in short."

James reddened slightly, while Elliot beamed with pure joy. Vaughan merely gave a tight-lipped smile.

"I would not say that teaching you has been an unmitigated pleasure, but somehow we have contrived to still be here and, more importantly to my employers, Monsieur Blondeau and Mrs. Hewlett, so is the Boxkite. I consider you ready gentlemen, and although there is no formal test of your proficiency, I would like you to demonstrate your meagre skill to those here assembled by way of a final right of passage," he said, waving a hand in the direction of the observers.

"That way," he continued, dropping his voice substantially, "I might just get a few more pupils sent my way, which would come of some relief to Mr. Wheeler, the proprietor of the Bull and Banjo and a lamentably impatient creditor." He laughed.

"Nothing fancy," said Vaughan. "Five turns around the airfield at around eight hundred feet followed by a perfect landing." He poked a finger into Elliot's chest. "A perfect landing Mr. Pearson, so none of your seesawing business."

"Of course," said Elliot, stung by the mild rebuke. "There's no tail wind today. I'll be fine."

"And nor was there on the day you nearly ruined my livelihood," snapped Vaughan, "but no matter. Caulfield, you'll go first. Pearson, help him power up, and then you can join me on the sidelines and watch how it's done!"

Vaughan stalked off to the seating area, doffing his hat to the seated men and then shaking each of their hands in turn before settling down beside them. James donned his goggles and buttoned his flying jacket, climbing into the pilot seat of the waiting Boxkite.

The routines of the engine start-up were second nature now, and he went through the litany quickly and efficiently while Elliot acted as the mechanic. The engine roared into life, and James marvelled at the sense of power as the vibrations thrilled through the struts and wires of the plane. He waited for Elliot to take a seat with the others, made a last check of the runway for any stray mechanics, and then taxied down the landing strip, opening the throttle as he did so. Takeoff was the second most dangerous part of any flight, next to landing, and James focused on the sound of the engine as the plane took to the air, listening for the spluttering signs of an imminent stall. The engine held up though, and James climbed into the grey skies of the July morning, experiencing the unparalleled pleasure of the perfect harmony of man and machine.

He climbed in a slow spiral, reaching the required height within a few minutes and settling into a slight left-banking pattern that took him on a lazy arc around the edge of the Brooklands racetrack. Wisps of grey-white cloud trailed through the open bay of the plane, mixing with the smoke trails of the engine. The wind whipped particles of moisture onto the glass of his goggles, requiring an occasional wipe with the back of his glove. Below him, he could still see the tiny figures of the seated observers and the scampering outlines of mechanics attending the planes and bringing up materials and parts from the hangar. Brooklands itself looked small from this height, like an oversized train set, incongruously scattered with toy planes. Briefly, the sun filtered through the clouds, and the whole vision was tinted with a golden light that seemed to come straight from the hand of God before passing once more into obscurity.

Each circuit only took a few minutes to complete, and before he knew it James had completed the five Vaughan had requested. He turned sharply into the centre of the airfield, hearing the engine strain slightly as he did so. He overflew the landing strip and then executed a one-hundred-and-eighty-degree turn before dipping the nose of the plane and approaching the airfield from the south. He cut back on the throttle slightly and descended quickly, pulling the plane into a more level pattern, forty or fifty feet above the ground. He inched the nose down, adjusting the stick incrementally until he felt the familiar harsh bump of the thin wheels as they hit the concrete of the landing strip. There was a slight bounce, but the wheels took, and James cut the throttle and came to a standstill at almost the exact point at which he had set off. He cut the switches and climbed out of the Boxkite, gratified to receive a small round of applause from the observers gathered at the trackside. Removing his goggles and gloves, James walked over to join them.

Vaughan stood to greet him as he approached and held out his hand. James took it, and they shook hands vigorously.

"Bravo, my boy," said Vaughan still shaking James' hand. "I'm delighted to tell you that the consensus is that you'll do. I'll write to Hendon, and they will issue you with a ticket. Congratulations!"

James extricated himself from Vaughan's grip, who was too excited to notice, and shook hands with Elliot, who was smiling every bit as heartily as the older instructor. Vaughan introduced him to the other four men, Messrs. Hopkins, Appleton, and Carter from the committee of the Royal Aero Club, and Lieutenant Colonel Trenchard, a pilot and an old colleague of Vaughan's from the army. James, who had not known of Vaughan's military past, was astonished to meet such a senior officer.

A tall man at close to six feet, Trenchard looked older than Vaughan, probably somewhere in his late thirties, with slick black hair parted high on the left-hand side. He had sharp, dark brown eyes and a thick, carefully groomed moustache that was turning to white under the nose. He offered his congratulations to James in a deep, rumbling voice, faintly tinged with a West Country accent, as Elliot made his way over to the plane, followed by a mechanic freed from other duties and temporarily available as a starter.

As Elliot took to the air, Trenchard explained that he was attached to the Royal Flying Corps' Central Flying School, where he worked as the school's examiner, amongst other duties.

"You certainly have the edge over me as a pilot, young man," he said to James, his eyes on Elliot's climbing plane. "I was taught at the Sopwith School here at Brooklands, and I'm ashamed to say that I was something of a burden to my teachers." He smiled ruefully.

"Nonsense," interrupted Vaughan. "You were perfectly capable, even with that dodgy eye of yours. It's just that Sopwith couldn't teach a man to boil an egg. Capable designer though, I'll give him that."

Trenchard smiled, still looking at the circling plane above. "I think I may know your father, Mr. Caulfield. The MP, Mr. Godfrey Caulfield of Cavendish Square?" he enquired.

"Yes Sir," acknowledged James.

"A remarkable man, if I may say so, with an excellent command of the military situation for a civilian. He gave me quite a grilling at the war committee a few years ago, alongside that rogue Churchill. Of course, I was still in the infantry then," said Trenchard.

"Thank you, Sir, I will be sure to mention you to my father. If I may be so bold, what made you transfer to the RFC?" asked James.

Trenchard gave a slow, rumbling laugh. "To be quite frank, I have absolutely no idea! A late, lamented friend of mine suggested I might enjoy flying. I got my wings, and, well, here I am."

One of the other men, whom James thought might be Mr. Carter, said, "Good job you did, Hugh. The RFC needs men who can organise them. Rather a joke at the moment, I gather."

Trenchard looked mildly offended, but replied with dignity in the same deep-rumbling bass. "Well, I'd say that was a matter of opinion, Peter, but it is certainly true that nobody at the war office is yet sure what to do with us."

Glancing at James, he added, "The other problem is the acute shortage of decent pilots. If you ever need a billet, young man, I do hope you might consider us."

"I'd be honoured to, Sir, but I'm afraid my father has other plans for my future," James replied courteously.

"Well, the situation being as it is, none of us know what tomorrow may bring," said the older man wistfully. "Should it come to war, I hope you might look at us before the damned cavalry."

"Certainly, Sir, I'd be happy to," said James, thinking regretfully of his father's plans for America.

Vaughan suddenly leapt to his feet, pointing at Elliot's plane as it rounded the opposite side of the Broadlands track. "See that?" he asked the others. "I'm sure I saw a spark from somewhere."

The others dutifully raised their eyes to the sky, with one man, Mr. Hopkirk, removing a pair of antiquated binoculars from a battered leather case at his feet and raising them to his eyes. James looked carefully, but the distance was too great, and he could see nothing useful. Elliot was continuing normally, in the same slow, banking arc. There was a rumble of thunder from somewhere to the west, and James frowned as he realised that the skies had darkened considerably since he had begun talking to Trenchard. For the first time, he noticed how close the day had become, humid and cloying. He loosened his flight jacket, feeling a droplet of sweat prickle onto his brow.

"Good god!" exclaimed Hopkirk, dropping his binoculars. "The fuel pipe has caught! Bring him in, Vaughan, bring him in!"

Vaughan raced into the middle of the landing strip, frantically waving his arms at the plane, which continued to circle nonchalantly around the airfield. Although no flames were visible with the naked eye, Trenchard had picked up the abandoned binoculars and confirmed Hopkins's sighting. Having done so, he rushed to the makeshift canvas hangar at the edge of the field, bellowing for the mechanics to man the fire engine. He returned holding a flare gun and fired it into the sky over the airfield.

As Elliot rounded the circuit to his side of the field, James could now see the telltale orange glow of a small fire, immediately behind the pilot's seat, on top of the propeller mounting and the engine. As long as the fire was confined to that part of the aircraft, it could still fly, but if the flames spread along the stiffened canvas of the wings or the sparse wooden frame of the fuselage, the whole structure would ignite, bringing the plane plummeting to the ground. As he watched, the bright red cloudburst of the flare blossomed into life over the airfield, casting a hellish glow across the uplifted faces of the helpless watchers on the ground. James saw the wings of the Boxkite wobble, presumably as Elliot strained to see what was happening on the ground. He must have spotted the waving arms of the frantic Vaughan and Trenchard as the plane immediately began to descend. All pretence of elegance was forgotten in the frantic rush for the ground. The wooden fire truck had been dragged into place at the side of the landing strip by a team of mechanics and riggers, who stood ready with buckets and a pump-driven hose.

The seconds ticked past as the plane came down. In his haste, Elliot was off course, the plane descending at an angle to the concrete strip and coming in far too steeply. Prudently, Trenchard bawled at them to clear the strip, and there was a rush for the relative safety of the racetrack barrier a few hundred feet away. At last, the plane flew over them, black smoke streaming from a sputtering fire that had caught on the wooden propeller and was licking up the back of the pilot seat and finding purchase in Elliot's hair. Mercifully, the wings were untouched, and the thin wooden struts of the fuselage, although smoke-blackened, still looked stable. The Boxkite bounced once on the hard surface of the concrete, rose a few feet in the air, and then came down again, the tiny wheels gaining purchase and skidding forward across the width of the strip. It slid onto the wide expanse of grass, the greater inertia of the surface slowing the plane until it came to a rest around ten feet away from the metal barrier to the racetrack.

James watched as Elliot, flames curling up the back of his leather flying coat and with his hair full ablaze, paused to cut the engine and then leapt from the plane, running a few feet before throwing himself to the ground, rolling and beating at his head with gloved hands. He rose to his knees, just as the fire truck was hauled into position by two burly riggers. An overall-wearing mechanic began to man the fire pump as his mate rushed across to Elliot and threw a bucket of water over him. The scene was tragicomic as Elliot's face registered surprised indignation and his head and coat began to steam.

It was too late for the plane though. The fire had caught on the upholstery of the pilot's seat and burst into a bright orange flame that stretched several feet in the air. The other rigger ran forward with a bucket of water and threw it over the new blaze, but it barely checked. Just as the water began to trickle from the end of the hand-cranked pump, the tip of the flames caught the top wing, and the fire spread with the speed of toppled dominoes along their length. Within seconds, the entire canvas covering of the wings had been reduced to curling, blackened strips, clinging stubbornly to a smoking wooden frame that threatened to ignite at any moment.

At last, the water began to flow, and the hose was used to douse the engine block and the smouldering frame. As James jumped the track barrier with Vaughan and Trenchard, he could see that the hose was doing its job. The flames were out, and the blackened frame of the aircraft steamed and hissed. It was intact, but looked more like a vast matchstick model than a viable aircraft. It would be a long time, if ever, before it flew again.

Then, as if in celestial salute to the hubris of man, it began to rain.

Two hours later, James was sat with Vaughan in the bar of the Hand and Spear, watching the rain battering the long sash windows, toying with a large brandy and incessantly smoking the instructor's hideously strong Russian cigarettes. In Trenchard's vast Stearn Knight touring car, they had taken Elliot to the small community hospital in Weybridge, where he was quickly sedated and allocated a bed by a hostile nurse clearly irritated by the steady flow of accident victims from Brooklands. The burns on his scalp had been quite severe, his red hair reduced to blackened stubble, with substantial blistering covering the crown of this head and his temples. He had gone into shock, and the weak, tepid tea brought up by the caretaker had been unable to help. He seemed to have no idea what had happened in the air but confirmed that he had only noticed the flames from his engine when he had seen Trenchard's flare. He seemed most anxious about whether he had passed his ticket and was relieved when Vaughan told him that, in the circumstances, he had done superbly. He'd join James on the Hendon lists.

"Jump or burn," said Vaughan morosely, downing a large brandy and indicating to the barman for another.

"What would you do?" he asked James, as the bespectacled barman set a bell glass on the table.

"I don't know. I suppose it depends how high I was flying," said James uncomfortably. "I mean, if I was at six thousand feet and on fire, I'd have no chance of grounding the kite before I burned to death. In that circumstance, I'd probably jump. It's quicker and less painful that way. On the other hand, if I was close to the ground like Elliot," he shuddered at the memory and took a quick sip of brandy, "I'd do what he did. Try to land the thing and get away from it before it blew."

"If only we had parachutes," said Vaughan. "Not that it would have done Pearson much good at that height, but at least they offer some hope when things go wrong."

James nodded. He'd asked Elliot about the same thing in the first few days of their training. Various forms of parachutes had existed since the early days of hot air ballooning in the late eighteenth century, but they had proved utterly unsuitable for jumping from a fast-moving platform. Attempts to experiment with chutes that worked had led to some very public failures, most notably in a series of tests conducted at the Eifel tower in Paris, which had seen numerous people fall to their doom. However, two years earlier, an American pilot had successfully jumped from a fixed-wing aircraft with a parachute bundled in his arms. The problem with that approach, though, was that a pilot had to sit with the chute in his lap, something not thought to be viable in cockpits that required extensive movement of the feet. In 1913, a Slovak inventor had patented a design in the USA that allowed a pilot to wear a parachute in a backpack, which could be opened by a toggle on jumping. Although widely used in the USA, the idea hadn't caught on in Britain, and parachutes were rarely seen except as part of stunt displays at air shows.

"It's the planes, you see," continued Vaughan, idly lighting another stubby, black cigarette. "They are too bloody valuable. The first thing Blondeau said to me on the telephone at Brooklands wasn't, 'How's the pilot?' but 'Can the plane be salvaged?' That says everything."

"I'm not following you," said James. "What does that have to do with parachutes?"

"Well, they'd issue them at flight schools and to pilots at the RFC if it wasn't for the fact that the planes are more valuable than the pilots," said Vaughan bitterly. "Basic supply and demand, I suppose. There are about three ticketed pilots for every plane in Britain, maybe more. Value is assigned by scarcity, ergo the planes are more valuable than the pilots," he said, shaking his head.

"Forgive me, I'm obviously tired, but if a plane is on fire and can't be saved, then what harm in giving a pilot at least a chance to escape?" asked James.

"Well, in that circumstance, I'm sure even the most hard-hearted capitalist would probably agree, but the power of the parachute lies in what it does to the mind of the pilot, and that, my young friend, is why they aren't issued as standard."

Draining his second brandy and nonchalantly raising his finger to the overworked barman, he continued. "You see, if a chap thought he could save himself, he might be tempted to jump out at the first sign of trouble. Look at Pearson. If he had known that some airborne spark had ignited his oil, he'd have been straight over the side, assuming his plane had the right height. Instead, without a parachute, he had no choice but to try to land. The plane was burnt through, but the frame held. It's much cheaper to replace an engine and rig a new set of wings over an existing frame than it is to build a whole new plane. The school owners don't want to encourage a psychology where the emphasis is on the pilot surviving rather than the plane."

"That's monstrous," said James, thinking of the blistered Elliot rocking in his arms on the soaked grass of the airfield.

"It's just economics," shrugged Vaughan. "No worse than sending a man down a mine to scrape out coal in the certain knowledge that he'll die of emphysema somewhere down the line."

"I suppose so," said James uncertainly. He had never thought it through before and was uncomfortable with the notion that a man could be considered a commodity like any other.

"I've had it with the school anyway," said Vaughan, nodding his thanks to the barman as his third brandy arrived. "One too many accidents on my watch, I'm afraid. This is the third plane that's gone up in flames in the last two years: one man dead, two burned. Monsieur Blondeau was very clear that my future as an instructor with his school is to come to a premature end."

"What will you do?" asked James.

"Have to do something," said Vaughan bitterly. "Between us, I've run up a few bad debts over the last few years. The booze mainly, but I'm rather too fond of cards for my own good, so I need some kind of income. My parents haven't spoken to me since I joined the army a lifetime ago, so I need a job to keep the wolf from the door."

"Doing what exactly?" said James

"All I can do," smiled Vaughan, "flying. I spoke to Hugh Trenchard. I'm going to apply for a commission in the RFC."

London, July 30, 1914

For a Thursday evening, the streets of London were buzzing with activity as James embarked on the short walk from the house at Cavendish Square to Claridge's Hotel and Restaurant. Conspicuous in full evening dress, he attracted the odd good-natured hoot of derision as he made his way down Harewood Place towards Hanover Square. Although Mayfair was generally renowned as the playground of the well heeled, the proximity of the fleshpots and gin palaces of Soho occasionally led to the incursion of earthier types, attracted by the quieter pubs on Wigmore Street and Cavendish Place. As James passed groups of men idling in the last rays of the evening sunlight, the same words followed him like a catechism, spoken in tones of reverential excitement. "Russia," said the men. "Serbia. Germany. France. Surely we will fight. We must fight. We will fight."

Here and there were colours. The Union Jack draped outside the Phoenix public house. Children waving miniature homemade flags of Saint George outside the Old Explorer, egged on by drunken men bellowing "Land of Hope and Glory." An old tramp stood on the corner of Regent Street and Cavendish Square, babbling in near incomprehensible Glaswegian, incongruously waving a saltire and damning the eyes of the kaiser, to the titters of passing ladies. The flagship of jingoism was afloat on a sea of gin and cheap beer. Not the ideal time to be a foreign visitor, thought James. Although the atmosphere was celebratory, just a hint of a passing Prussian accent and the mob would erupt into the violence it so desperately desired.

The previous month had been a strange time. The Austrian court had reacted to the death of its heir apparent with characteristic belligerence. The *Times* had carried coverage of the Austrian demonization of the Serb patriots as "pestilent rats," and attempts to negotiate a continuing peace seemed tokenistic on both sides, not least due to rumours that an attack on the Austrian legation had been planned with precision in Belgrade. Britain, with the usual introspection of an island nation, had focused on its own problems; further disturbances in Ulster and the progress of the government of Ireland bill through the Commons and the Lords had occupied much of the press throughout July. If a conflagration was anticipated, then Britain's government, in the fine tradition of its greatest admiral, could yet see no ships.

Then, a week earlier, had come the Austrian ultimatum to Serbia—a calculated piece of humiliation so contrived as to guarantee rejection by the proud Balkan state. The Serbs duly did so, and on the 28th of July the Austrian guns had begun to bombard Belgrade, mere minutes after they had issued a declaration of war. The following day, Czar Nicolas II of Russia had ordered a full mobilization of the vast forces of his army in support of little Serbia. Although Germany had yet to react, the dominoes had begun to topple one by one. Full war now seemed inevitable, and although Asquith's government vacillated about British involvement in the coming conflict, the people had begun to vote with their feet.

For James personally, the month had been a return to the tedium of the social whirl. Vaughan had departed for London immediately after their evening in the hotel bar, but James had stayed in Weybridge for a few days, waiting until Elliot was released from the hospital, and then travelling to Farnborough with his friend and ensuring that he was comfortably ensconced in the rather shabby boarding house in which he took his lodgings. Elliot carried scarring on his temples, and there were patches of blackened skin on the crown of his head where it was unlikely that his red hair would again take hold. The damage stopped short of disfigurement though, and a hat, worn low on the forehead, would disguise the worst of it, at least until it had begun to heal more. His spirits were reasonably high; he was revelling in his status as a ticketed pilot and seemed to see the accident as a necessary rite of passage. James had then returned to London and to the dubious pleasures of parental dinner parties and the banalities of the gentleman's club. Aside from a weekend in the family home at Berkhamsted, attending a shooting party given by his father, he had not ventured out from central London. Only the Aero Club license that had arrived at Cavendish Square a few days after his return prevented him from seeing the weeks in Weybridge as a glorious but implausible dream.

James arrived at Claridge's; handed his coat, hat, and cane to a footman; discretely gave his name to the maître d'hôtel; and was politely ushered by a waiter into the opulence of the Reading Room restaurant. The hotel had been rebuilt some fifteen years earlier, and the ordinary redbrick facade of the building concealed a mixture of marble, wood, and brass in the best traditions of Victoriana and the splendid arrogance of a confident empire. The restaurant was crowded with genteel diners of both genders, elegant in their evening finery and chattering of coming cataclysm with a joyous but understated excitement that only marginally differentiated them from the drunks in the streets outside. The waiter led James to a corner table, at which his parents were seated, talking quietly and drinking flutes of champagne.

Godfrey seemed skittish, and James noted that his face was flushed, as if he had been drinking for some time. He sat James next to him, gestured vaguely towards the champagne bucket in the middle of the table, and wordlessly passed him a leather-bound menu of such thickness that James had mistaken it for an abandoned novel. On the other side of the table, Sylvia was her usual mercurial self, welcoming James effusively, commenting on the cut and quality of his evening dress, and recommending the *confit de canard* as a starter.

"I've just come from the House," said Godfrey impatiently, cutting off his wife's meandering speculations on the likely quality of the beef. "The situation is worsening. Germany looks ready to declare, and France is mobilising openly now."

"I know," said James. "On the streets, the people are baying for blood. I don't think we can keep out of it now."

"Asquith won't have the courage to stand up to the mob," agreed Godfrey, taking a greedy swallow of champagne. "The fool would rather take us into a continental war than risk the fall of his government."

James nodded, although he wasn't sure whether Britain could honourably keep out of the coming conflict. They were allied to Russia and France, and when, as now seemed certain, they were attacked by the axis powers, Britain would be obligated to fight or else risk its international standing as a nation that stood by its commitments.

A waiter arrived to take their order, but Godfrey waved him away, telling him to return later, looking briefly annoyed as the man paused to refill their champagne flutes from the bucket on the table.

"We're leaving," said Godfrey flatly as the waiter left them. "We sail for New York tomorrow evening."

The subject of their trip to America had consumed much of his parent's dinner party discourse over the last few weeks, and Godfrey had made it very clear that he expected James to join them. The trip was explained as a necessary business excursion, with James expected to play some sort of nonspecific supporting role for the general improvement of his all-round education. James had persistently demurred, remaining noncommittal and mouthing meaningless platitudes about the need to prepare himself for the Cambridge term that was due to start in a few short months. He realised that further procrastination was no longer feasible, and he cringed inwardly at the thought of having to stand up to his father.

"You must join us, James," added Sylvia. "If there is to be war, I'm sure my people will have the sense to stay out of it. We can travel for a few months until it is all over."

"I rather think my place is here, Mother," said James, with more force than he had intended.

"Why?" said Sylvia petulantly. "You are half American, and your father has extensive business in the country. Surely, nothing could be more natural than visiting your extended family."

"And," added Godfrey, "it is not as if we are at war yet. If we go now, before Britain declares, there can be no implication of desertion or even the slightest taint against our name. I have been preparing the ground all summer. It is simply business as usual. We'll be back by Christmas, and hopefully it'll all be over by then."

James had never previously heard his parents speak so candidly about their reasons for the trip to America, and he suddenly felt angry and ashamed.

"You would have me leave my country when it is on the brink of war in order to save my own skin?" he said, his voice rising in volume and causing Godfrey to glance around to see if anybody had overheard.

"Of course not, my dear," said Sylvia in a placatory tone, stretching her hand across the table to rest on his arm. "We simply want you to be safely and understandably out of the way if the worst were to happen." She smiled imploringly.

James was not mollified. He turned to his father.

"And what about you, Father?" he asked. "Where is your much-vaunted sense of patriotism?"

"Patriotism is the last refuge of the scoundrel," snapped Godfrey, his eyes dancing with anger. "It is a political tool to win the affections of the mob, nothing more than that."

Thinking about the crowds thronging the streets, James considered that if that was true, then it was a tool that could be considered to have done its job.

"Think of it like a small holiday, my dear," said Sylvia. "You won't be running away from anything, just taking a short break before you go up to Cambridge. I'm quite sure that there wouldn't be any scandal."

"I'm not going, Mother. I can't go. I would feel like a coward," he said, his eyes blazing pointedly at his father.

"Better a live coward than a dead hero," said Godfrey bitterly. "You forget yourself, boy. I have been dealing in weaponry all of my adult life. I know something of the reality of modern war, and you are deluded if you think there is any glory to be won on the battlefield. There is no room for valour in the old sense. There will only be mechanistic destruction, with men mown down by machine guns in their thousands and blown sky high by powerful munitions. I do not want my son to be a part of that."

He paused, punishing the remainder of the champagne and rudely gesticulating to the waiter for another bucket. Sylvia looked at him distastefully and sipped her own glass, her hand still resting lightly on James' forearm.

"Although I wouldn't express it quite so crassly, my dear, you have to see that your father is right," said Sylvia. "I'm American, and we understand that what happens overseas is no business of ours. Neither is this Britain's quarrel, but it seems the people think differently." She waved a hand vaguely in the direction of the door. "Come to America, and I'm sure you will feel differently."

"I do understand, Mother, but I'm afraid I can't. Perhaps I am naïve, but I believe that I should stand by my country. That is what I was taught at school, and that is what you have *both* brought me up to believe. Should it come to war, and even now, it might not, my place is here," said James, holding his mother's gaze.

"Then you are a fool, boy," said Godfrey furiously. "This is your chance for an honourable exit. If you don't leave now, you will regret it right up to the moment a German machine gun ends your misery."

"Godfrey!" exclaimed Sylvia. "I realise you are overemotional," she nodded at the empty champagne flute before him, "but that was quite uncalled for. Perhaps we should take pride in the fact that we have raised a son whose idea of honour is not entirely dictated by the exigencies of realpolitik."

"And mine is, I suppose?" shouted Godfrey, all sense of propriety forgotten. "Damn you both. I am trying to do my best for my family, that's all. And this bloody fool," he said, pointing at James, "is intent on throwing his life away for nothing. Nothing!"

"No, Godfrey. You are trying to do your best for yourself, as you always have," said Sylvia with icy disdain. "And if your selfishness means that I will emerge from this horror with a husband intact, then I am grateful for it. But you cannot criticise our son for having a sense of honour. We raised him, and if we are to lose him, then we should take pride that he is, perhaps, a better person that you or I."

The waiter arrived with another champagne bucket and set it down on the table. Politely enquiring if they were ready to order, he was rebuffed by Godfrey with startling aggression, attracting the disapproving glances of the people at nearby tables.

"Perhaps," said Sylvia, looking at Godfrey, "you should return to the house, my dear. I would like to enjoy a quiet meal with my son before we depart for America, and I fear that your current mood is not conducive to that aspiration."

Godfrey looked as if he would argue, but then nodded in defeated acquiescence and rose uncertainly from his chair, staggering slightly.

"I will see you in the morning," he said to Sylvia, with a spitting malevolence. With wild eyes, he turned to James. "I doubt I will ever see you again."

He stalked out of the Reading Room restaurant, the eyes of the assembled diners watching his weaving progress as he made his way to the door. As he reached the threshold of the dining room, he turned and looked back at the table. James was startled to see that there were tears in his eyes before he turned and made his way out of the hotel.

Two weeks later, James passed an eager queue of young men outside a conscription centre at Charing Cross, resounding to the sounds of a brass band and the bawling exhortations of a flamboyant sergeant major. The newspaper he held and had read on the tube detailed the incredible excesses of the German army in its imminent conquest of plucky Belgium. Babies and children had apparently been bayoneted by the savage Teutonic hordes as they rampaged across the lowlands, and some imaginative scribbler had dubbed them Huns in a nod to the ancient nemesis of classical Rome. The word was a clarion call to arms, a folk memory to stir the people to consciousness, and British men responded in their droves. A man may not be able to read, but he could still defend civilisation against the barbarism of the new Attila, Kaiser Wilhelm.

In truth, for most British people, the war remained an abstract. The streets were unchanged, and the people continued as normal, content merely to vilify the Central Powers, volunteer in the thousands, and confidently assume a speedy victory for the noble Allies. The British peacetime army was tiny, and although a token force had been sent to France under Sir John French, with all the pomp and ceremony that a modern imperial power could muster, the hundred thousand men that the force included could hardly compare to the millions that France and Germany could field. It was symbolic war from afar, but still the papers proclaimed that it would be over by Christmas and that a man had to hurry if he was to see any action before that day dawned.

James was hurrying. His parents had departed the day after their ill-fated dinner, and he had tactfully elected to stay at his club that night and for most of the following day, thus successfully avoiding any repetition of the scene in the restaurant. When Asquith declared war in response to Germany's invasion of Belgium, he had returned home as master of the house. Immediately on arrival, he had written to the Imperial Command at Horseguards, requesting a commission in the Royal Flying Corps. Reasoning that if the ground was to be a mechanistic killing zone, as his father had claimed, James had decided he was better off with the uncertainties of the air, where at least he might expect some degree of control over his own fate. He had cited Hugh Trenchard as his referee. Two days later, he had been delighted to receive a letter from Elliot explaining that he had done exactly the same. The day after that, he was invited for an interview with a commissioning board.

Arriving at Horseguards on Whitehall, he was challenged by a small, officious young man wearing the uniform of a corporal. He showed his letter of invitation and was briefly amused as the man began to raise his arm in automatic salute before realising his error and dropping it back to his side. With a gruff, "Follow me," the little corporal led James on a winding path through the labyrinthine corridors of the old building. The internal layout was unfathomable, seemingly consisting of a series of small houses built in a variation of different styles and periods, roughly knocked together and encased in an impressive shell of dressed stone. James walked through a faux baroque corridor, lined with oil paintings showing the campaigns of Marlborough, before taking a set of creaking, dank Georgian stairs where an abandoned mop festered in water that might have been first drawn at the battle of Blenheim. Their progress continued up and down staircases and through courtyards and cloisters until James had lost all sense of direction. Eventually, just as he was convinced that he must be underground, the corporal showed him into an anteroom that appeared from the window to be on the second floor. The room was lined with books and dominated by a grand piano. Six chairs sat against the wall, and in one of them sat an immaculate man in the uniform of a cavalry officer. To the right of him was an imposing set of closed double doors. As the corporal entered, the man started up in alarm, glancing at the doors before seeing James and sitting down again in relief.

"Sorry, old chap, thought it was my time," he explained, as the corporal withdrew with some sotto-voiced pleasantry.

James sat down in a chair next but one to the man. He looked nearly the same age as him, thin with a long neck and sparse black hair that was coated in grease and plastered back. A prominent Adam's apple and a flushed, pale complexion gave James the impression of an elongated turkey in uniform.

"I say, you here for the RFC?" the man said, his hand fluttering nervously in the air.

"For the commissioning board, yes," said James. He held out his hand. "James Caulfield. I'm pleased to meet you." He smiled weakly.

"Arthur Paget-Stanley, glad to meet you too," replied the man.

They sat in studied silence for a few seconds, each appraising the shelves, the carpet, and the ceiling, before turning to each other and speaking simultaneously. They laughed nervously and then spent moments negotiating the minefields of decorum before deciding that James should speak first.

"Are you a flyer then?" he said, gesturing at the smart cavalry uniform.

"Gosh no! I've only seen an aeroplane once. Never been up in one," said Arthur cheerfully.

"Forgive me, but why are you here then? I thought this was a board for RFC officers," asked James.

"Oh it is. I'm good with horses, you see. Been riding since I was a babe in arms. The family has a place in Somerset, and I was always good with the horses." Arthur smiled.

"Horses?" said James incredulously. "But surely, you're already in the cavalry?"

"Oh yes," said Arthur. "Commissioned last year, but I busted my leg riding and had to stay home when the regiment went to France. Confounded nuisance. My CO said that the RFC needed pilots and that good horsemen should apply, and well, here I am."

"Can't you re-join your regiment?" asked James, suddenly suspicious.

"Yes, of course," said Arthur, too quickly, "but I rather fancy an adventure. The 'undiscovered country' and all that, and the CO was ever so convincing. I say, are you a flyer?"

"Yes," said James. "I have my ticket at least. I'm not an expert or anything, but I can fly."

"What's it like?" said Arthur eagerly.

"Dangerous," said James bluntly. "Even in peacetime. It can be fun, but you have to have your wits about you and your eyes on the machine, not the ground."

Arthur nodded thoughtfully. Just then the double doors opened, and he jumped out of his seat and snapped to attention. An infantry officer emerged from the next room, beckoned with his finger, and Arthur marched behind him, pausing only to close the doors behind him on entry. James was left to his own thoughts.

Forty minutes later, James sat on a solitary wooden chair in the middle of the floor in the vast expanse of a spacious office. A desk stood four feet in front of the chair, and behind sat three bored-looking men, all at least fifty. The man in the centre was a full colonel. He had whitening, nineteenth-century side-whiskers and a balding head. He was flanked on either side by near-identical men, marginally younger than the colonel and both with thinning, bootblack-dyed hair and moustaches, each wearing the epaulettes of an army major.

"I am Colonel Everett, and these two are Majors Appleton and Sherwin," said the old man. "We are here to ascertain your suitability for the honour of His Majesty's Commission and for a role in the Royal Flying Corps."

"So, Mr. Caulfield. Where did you school?" he asked.

"Rugby, Sir," replied James swiftly.

"Really?" said the colonel. "I was at Harrow myself, but I have fond memories of our sporting tussles with your chaps," he smiled.

"I assume you have no university education?" asked the major to the left, a pen poised as if to strike.

"No, Sir, I don't, although I do have a place at Cambridge in October, but events have rather taken care of that." James smiled regretfully, but the major merely nodded and wrote a note.

"Do you ride?" asked the colonel, his eyebrows raised in a faint parody of subtlety.

"Yes, Sir" said James. "My father has a seat in Berkshire, and I was blooded as a child," he said, referring to the unpleasant practice of daubing the novice hunter with the blood of the captured fox.

"Good, jolly good," smiled the colonel. "And what of your other sports?"

"Cross-country running, Sir. I won the crick run at Rugby twice. Swimming and fencing too."

"Marvellous," beamed the colonel. "An individualist!" He turned to his left. "Major Sherwin, anything more from you?"

"Yes, Sir," said Sherwin, with a slick smile. "Why the Royal Flying Corps? Is it because you think you can shirk the battle to come in the relative safety of the air?"

As uncomfortably close to the truth as that question was, James managed to eke out an answer.

"No, Sir, it's really only because I can fly, and I was under the impression that the army was short of competent pilots," he said.

"You have flown?" said Sherwin, looking surprised.

"Yes, Sir," said James. "I have an Aero Club ticket."

"Really?" said Sherwin. "Why on earth didn't you mention that in your letter?"

"I believe that a gentleman should prove himself a gentleman before he boasts of his achievements, Sir," said James simply.

"Quite right too," guffawed the old colonel. "The boy has your measure, Sherwin, what!"

"How much time in the air?" asked Sherwin suspiciously.

"More than twenty hours, Sir," said James.

"Where?" said Sherwin sharply.

"At Brooklands, Sir. I engaged a private tutor, a Mr. Vaughan," replied James.

"I see," said Sherwin, carefully noting down the name.

There was a moment of silence before Colonel Everett turned to his right and asked, "Anything from you, Appleton?"

"No, Sir. I think we have seen quite enough."

"Jolly good," said the colonel affably. "I shall show you to the door, Mr. Caulfield," he said, rising creakily from his chair and squeezing his ample frame through the small space behind Major Appleton.

In the empty anteroom, the colonel shook James' hand and said in a quiet tone, "I know your father from old. My apologies for this charade, but Sherwin is some sort of church scholar, not one of us, if you take my meaning, and rather a stickler for the modern way. He does like to make such a fuss, even when it is quite obvious that a chap is a gentleman. But you are a flyer, Sir, and clearly a chap we can trust. Nothing he can get his fangs into there. You'll have to do army training, I'm afraid, but that'll be over swiftly. I'm sure I shall see you in France in a month or two," he said, slapping James weakly on the back and leaving him to struggle through the maze of Horseguards alone.

Near Amiens, France, October 4, 1914

James shivered as he climbed out of the battered and sodden BE2c onto the damp turf of the airfield. He pulled his kitbag from the back seat and shouldered it. A very young and somewhat emaciated mechanic, with an unruly shock of mousey brown hair and wearing the baggy, plain-green uniform of an RFC corporal, placed a pair of wooden blocks under the wheels of the plane and snapped off a salute.

"Any problems on the way over, Sir?" the mechanic asked in a rolling Welsh lilt.

"Nothing substantial. A few squalls over the channel that got a little hairy," said James. "So, I took her up to eight thousand feet and got above the cloud cover. The engine could do with a little attention. It took a few attempts to start her up, and the chap at Andover thinks the magneto is on its way out."

"I have a spare in the hangar, Sir. I'll replace it before you take her out again. I'm Corporal Evans, by the way, Sir." The man smiled, exposing horrifically splintered teeth.

"Lieutenant Caulfield," said James, automatically holding out his hand before remembering his place and dropping it back to his side.

"You'll be wanting the flight commander, Sir," said the man, still smiling his gap-toothed grin. "He's in the flight office in the farmhouse. If you'll leave your bag with me, Sir, I'll find your batman and take it to your quarters."

"Very good, corporal," said James formally, dropping his bag from his shoulder, handing it to Evans, and stalking off in the general direction of the farmhouse buildings, which were clustered in a rambling huddle at the edge of the field.

The past two months had been a whirlwind, and to James, it was something of a relief to finally find himself at the front. He had spent a few anxious days at Cavendish Square, waiting for a letter from the commissioning board. That had finally arrived, and James and the redoubtable Harper had then spent a hectic few days at a selection of military outfitters, procuring the requisite uniforms and supplies. On impulse, he had also invested a substantial sum in a Mauser high-calibre hunting rifle and ammunition. Although the army would issue him with a service revolver, the newspapers were carrying stories about new recruits drilling with sticks and wearing mismatched uniforms due to a chronic equipment shortage. The Mauser was a fine gun, much more accurate than a standard rifle, and gave James some much-needed reassurance. Ironically, it was also German.

In the middle of August, James had left for a makeshift military camp attached to the RFC base at Andover, where he had then spent six miserable weeks endlessly repeating variations of the same marching drill under the deferentially sadistic oversight of a decrepit sergeant major called back from the reserve at the outbreak of war. The training was desultory, seemingly designed to reduce the officer recruits to little more than automaton marionettes, with only the bare minimum of focus on any actual fighting skills. In the entire time, he had only fired a weapon on two occasions. Instead, James had spent his days wheeling, marching, and turning before returning to the damp and cold of his tent at night and collapsing on the weak springs of his camp bed, exhausted. Although he had sometimes seen BE2s flying low over the base from the nearby airfield, he didn't approach or touch a plane the entire time he was at the camp.

That changed after he had passed basic training and had been transferred to the air base at Andover. Having already qualified as a pilot, James was excused from the RFC's formal tuition, but had been granted some orientation time to accustom himself to the BE2 and get in some much-needed flight time ahead of his transfer to France. Such was the value placed on the machines, though, that he was confined to one hour of solo time in the air a day, usually at dawn and only when conditions were absolutely perfect. He found the BE2 to be a solid and dependable plane, stable in the air but with a very slow climb and sluggish in the turns, even compared to the Boxkite he had trained on at Brooklands. Remarkably, given that the country was at war, it carried no weaponry, nor were there plans to introduce any. When James had queried the training squadron's commanding officer about this omission, he was told that the role of the RFC would be confined to reconnaissance. They represented no direct threat to the Germans and would be highly unlikely to need to defend themselves.

Towards the end of September, Elliot joined the training squadron at Andover, and the two friends, with time on their hands, spent a comfortable few days sampling the limited delights of the town, using their newly acquired wings to procure free drinks in pubs and restaurants. Elliot had largely recovered from his accident. His RFC cap hid the bald patches on his scalp, and apart from an angry, red welt just visible next to his right ear, he otherwise appeared his usual self. His confidence was back too; the outbreak of war had given him a new impetus, and James noted that his flying skills had improved too. Unlike James, he had managed to keep working on his flying at Farnborough, where test pilots were always needed, and he took to the BE2 with an easy familiarity.

The news from the continent had not been good in those first few weeks of the war. The British Expeditionary Force, with a handful of supporting aircraft, had embarked for France in an optimistic mood. The prevailing consensus was that the German and Austrian armies would be caught between the hammer of the Anglo-French army in the west and the anvil of the vast Russian army in the east. In fact, the Germans had surprised everyone by the speed of their assault on Belgium and France, harnessing the power of the railway system to move vast numbers of infantry quickly to various weak points and managing to get within eighty miles of Paris. They had been pushed back after the French victory at the Battle of the Marne, but the fighting remained intense, and the British, holding the northern sections of the line, had been slowly pushed back as the Germans looked to loop around their flank and attack the French from the north. The so-called "race to the sea" was on, with the small British army bleeding itself to death in a series of engagements intended to preserve the lifeline of the northern French ports—and the gateway to Britain itself. Despite horrendous British casualties, the German advance was now slowing, and the entrenchments on both sides were solidifying into semipermanent constructions. More British volunteers were being rushed to the front, and it was increasingly clear that a quick conclusion to the war was a rapidly diminishing possibility. The RFC had proved its worth early, however, spotting the German army's wheel towards the sea outside Mons on the 22nd of August, the very first day of active British involvement in the war.

Twenty-four hours earlier, James had been informed that he had been allocated as a replacement pilot to B Flight, part of squadron number 4, and based on farmland near the town of Amiens in the northern French province of Picardy. He was allocated a nearly new BE2c and told to make his way across the channel, refuel at an airfield designated only by a map reference, and then continue on to Amiens. He had set off the following dawn, waved off by Elliot, who had yet to be allocated, and finally landed at the squadron airfield at 3:00 p.m. the same day. He was cold, tired, and irritable as he made his way towards the flight office to report his arrival. But, he considered, at least he was finally there.

The airfield was typical of the camps that James had seen since joining the RFC in September. Sagging tents congregated along temporary streets, adorned with handwritten signs made from discarded wood and bearing the names of various areas of London. James passed along a path, optimistically labelled "Hyde Park," and came to an open space containing an unmanned Lewis Gun emplacement partially surrounded by sandbags. To his left, there was a vast tent, doubling up as a hangar, where a group of uniformed men sat just inside its doorway, brazenly ignoring the tacked-up posters warning them not to smoke near fuel supplies. As they spotted James, they recalled urgent business elsewhere, extinguished their cigarettes, and disappeared into the bowels of the tent, where the outlines of two planes could just be made out in the afternoon gloom.

A few steps away from the hangar stood a hand-pulled fire engine, piled high with buckets of sand and adjacent to an alarm bell roughly secured to a pole and looking suspiciously like it may have been plundered from a church. James came to the farm buildings, a tumbledown collection of nineteenth-century constructions fashioned from undressed grey stone and knocked together to form a semi-coherent whole. A lean-to, built from corrugated iron and bricks, was the only new addition and contained a stacked collection of unopened supply crates, together with a sign reading "DO NOT TOUCH, by order QM RFC." Dilapidated wooden barns surrounded the main buildings and contained more supplies—mainly engine and mechanical parts packed in straw.

Three shabby wooden doors provided access to the main farmhouse. One, leading to what looked like a large stone outhouse, was labelled "The Hilton." The second, leading to a large open room, possibly the original farmhouse kitchen, was "White's Club," and the third, a gateway to some sort of storage room, simply said "B Flight, 4th Squadron, Flight Office."

James approached the last door and tentatively knocked. To his surprise, the door was immediately flung open, and a rotund sergeant in his early thirties poked a jowly face into the afternoon drizzle and squinted at him with obvious suspicion. On seeing his flight coat, he straightened himself and saluted.

"Good afternoon, sir! I am Sergeant Jackson, welcome to B Flight," he said in the nasal monotone of Northwestern England. He moved his ample frame out of the way of the door, and James casually returned his salute and then stepped over the threshold and into the dry of a dishevelled office.

"I am Second Lieutenant Caulfield," said James, glancing around the deserted room. "I believe I am expected. I had hoped to introduce myself to Captain Ladley, but I see he is not here."

"No, Sir. Captain Ladley is currently on a reconnaissance flight. He is due back in an hour or so."

"I see," said James. On the back wall of the office, directly opposite the door, was a large blackboard with a chalked-out grid listing the names of active pilots and their flying activities at key points in the day. The names of Ladley and Stanley were both listed as being on an afternoon reconnaissance, lasting until 4:30 p.m. None of the three other names on the list were currently in the air. The rest of the office was a mess. An untidy desk sat in front of the main window, covered in a mountain of unsorted paper that partially obscured a telephone. A smaller, clear desk stood against the right-hand wall. The room had only two chairs, one at each desk, as well as a large map of northern France pinned up next to the blackboard, with various coloured markings tacked to it using pins. The wooden floor was uncarpeted, and there was seemingly no electricity, judging by the two oil lamps that stood on the corner of the main desk. Nor was there a fireplace. Spartan and utilitarian, the room didn't look like the hub of an efficient fighting machine. Instead, it resembled the study of a rural schoolmaster.

"Where can I wait?" asked James.

"You would probably be most comfortable in the mess, Sir," said Sergeant Jackson. "I'm sure you are in need of refreshment after your flight. Your batman is currently preparing your quarters, and they should be available shortly. I will inform you immediately when Captain Ladley returns, Sir, although you'll almost certainly hear him come in."

"That sounds like just the ticket, Sergeant. Lead on," replied James with an anticipatory smile.

The two men went out into the slow, incessant rain of the afternoon, took the door labelled White's Club, and emerged into the lamp-lit light of a long, stone room. In the corner was a small bar, manned by an airman busy polishing glasses who looked up as the door opened. Around the room were several battered tables, mostly made from converted crates. A random selection of seating littered the room. There were two old but comfortable-looking leather armchairs, three wooden farmhouse chairs, and a row of uneven homemade stools adjacent to the bar. On the walls was a collection of signs, one giving the distance to Paris in kilometres, others advertising the delights of various French goods. Incongruously, there was also a cricket bat, mounted in pride of place behind the bar, and a rowing oar, strung from the high ceiling. There was a large fire underneath a central chimneybreast, and James was delighted to see that it was lit and that the room was comfortably warm. In the corner, opposite the bar, stood a battered wall piano where a young man in a second lieutenant's uniform played idly with his right hand while sipping from a whiskey and soda with his left. As the door closed, he turned to see who had arrived.

"My apologies for interrupting, Sir," said Jackson, addressing the piano-playing officer. "This is Mr. Caulfield, our new pilot. Mr. Caulfield, this is Mr. Henderson, and that," he indicated the barman, "is Airman Bates, the steward to the officers' mess."

"Ah, new blood. Marvellous. Glad to meet you," said Henderson, rising and shaking James' hand with a painfully tight grip. He was a short, bucktoothed young man of perhaps eighteen or nineteen, with prematurely thinning sandy hair and a wispy moustache that looked like it might fall off in a stiff breeze.

"Drink?" continued Henderson. "My shout by way of welcome. What'll it be?" James noticed the single wing on the breast of his uniform. Henderson was an observer then, not a pilot.

"A whiskey would be appreciated, thank you. I could do with warming up. It was cold up there today."

"Bates, whiskey for Mr. Caulfield. My tab."

"Yes, Sir," said Bates, a sallow-faced man in his late forties who, James noticed, moved with a heavy limp as he took a bottle of single malt from the shelf, poured a stiff measure into a surprisingly well-cut glass, and handed it to James.

They took their drinks to the leather armchairs that sat adjacent to the fireplace and sat down. Henderson politely enquired about James' training and his experience as a pilot. He explained that he had been in the RFC since leaving Marlborough School the previous year. He had trained as an observer and been in France since early September.

"Seen much action?" asked James

"From the air, yes," said Henderson. "The Germans pushed hard all along this section, but the French gathered on Amiens down the road from here and held their ground. Both sides are now digging in a few miles to the east and shelling the hell out of each other. For us, though, it's mostly been reconnaissance at height. It's a little strange really. There has been some fierce fighting on the ground, but unless you look down, you'd never know it in the air."

"What about the German planes?" asked James. "I heard at Andover that they had a sizable air force in this area."

"Oh, indubitably," said Henderson, sipping at his whiskey and soda. "The Albatross B2. Better than our BE2, according to the flyers here. They have a quicker rate of climb, are faster in the turn, and have about a third more power from the engine, from what we can gather. They don't bother us though. Courteous chaps in the main, doing the same sort of things as us I imagine, sketching the ground formations and so forth. If we see them, we usually wave."

"Wave?" asked James incredulously.

Henderson chuckled. "Yes, well there's not a lot else we can do at the moment. I take up a rifle with me, but you'd have to be Billy the Kid to hit a plane up there, never mind a pilot, not that I've tried of course. I did hear about a French chap who chucked a brick at an Albatross. Bad form, but I suppose you can forgive the fellow. It is his country being invaded after all," he smiled, and then continued. "One of our chaps over Belgium, Hillings, I think his name is, actually shot a Hun in the air, but he was an NCO, not a proper gentleman. Probably didn't know any better."

James smiled dutifully but was inwardly confused. The ancient art of reconnaissance had always been conducted on horseback, but the nature of modern war had meant that the role of the cavalry had so far been severely restricted in this conflict, horses being fundamentally unsuited to the noise and clamour of mechanised battlefield. The RFC had hoped to step into this vacuum, offering an unrivalled view of the movement of armies from the air. However, it was also willingly allowing the enemy the freedom to do the same, and thus both armies drew no overall advantage. It seemed inconceivable that equal forces of cavalry, engaged in tracking the movements of the enemy, would not attack each other should they meet in the field. James couldn't understand why the RFC wasn't dong the same. He tried to frame his words carefully, eager not to pique the sensibilities of a brother officer.

"It can't go on like that though, surely?" said James thoughtfully. "The chaps at army HQ aren't going to like it if the Germans know all of our positions."

"That's a matter for them," said Henderson. "Chain of command and all that, old cha. I'm sure they know what they're doing."

James left the issue. Clearly, there wasn't yet the impetus to challenge the Germans in the air, although, he thought, that might change if the war of movement that had characterised the first months of battle was already rumoured to be grinding to a halt. Armies were still on the move in the north of France and in parts of Belgium, but even here, in the heart of Picardy, trenches were being dug and emplacements thrown up. Fixed positions meant fixed targets, and the patience of both sides would quickly wear thin if their big guns were constantly exposed to enemy fire. How long would the infantry and the artillery remain patient while the eyes of the enemy roamed over them at will?

The distant drone of an engine suddenly became noticeable in the quiet of the mess room. Henderson downed the rest of his whiskey, went over to the filthy window by the door, and looked up. James joined him and watched as a battered and wobbling BE2 hesitantly approached the airfield, dropped quickly, and then made a bouncing, inelegant landing, coming to rest twenty feet or so away from the first line of tents. A team of airmen stood ready and approached the aircraft as it came to a standstill. He spotted tears in the fabric of the upper and lower wings as the two occupants of the plane began to clamber out.

"Our lord and master, Captain Ladley, and Paget-Stanley, his observer. Another new boy," said Henderson, pointing at the two men.

As the latter removed his leather skullcap and unwound the silk scarf round his neck, James started in recognition. It was the same man from his interview at Horseguards. His black hair was less ordered, and his face was covered in spots of oil, but it was the same bird-like face and long neck that had reminded him of a turkey when they first met. The second man was rather more imposing. Tight auburn curls topped a square-jawed face that carried what looked like a fencing scar on the right-hand side. The man was big, somewhat over six feet, heavyset, but not fat, and walked with an assured self-authority and a long stride, forcing the shorter observer to scuttle in order to keep pace. Although Paget-Stanley kept up what seemed to be an incessant chatter, the man said nothing, content merely to wipe his face on his scarf and make his way to the dry of the farm buildings. James saw Jackson meet him outside with a clipboard, secure his signature on some document, and then watch as he disappeared out of sight, presumably into the scant comfort of the flight office. Paget-Stanley, nonplussed, looked after the disappearing captain before heading for the other door, in the direction of the officers' quarters. He looked shaken and pale underneath the oil spatters, with the wobbling Adam's apple of a man holding back his emotions. He, too, vanished out of sight, and Henderson pointed to the plane.

"That doesn't look good," he said, indicating the tears in the wing fabric. "Wind perhaps, but damage isn't usually that bad. The skipper did well getting that thing back in one piece."

Looking at James, he added, "I'd drink up if I were you, old man. You'll need to report to the captain now that he's back."

James smoothed out the still-damp wool of his uniform and adjusted his cap. He hadn't had time to wash yet, so he used a handkerchief to remove some of the spots of oil that still clung to the contours of his face. Realising that the captain was unlikely to judge him too harshly, given his own recent return from the air, he said a quick farewell to Henderson, stepped outside, and took the short walk to the flight office. The door to the office was open, but he knocked politely and waited until he heard a growled invitation to enter.

In the office, James marched formally to the area in front of the main desk, stood to attention, and saluted. The captain, sitting in the chair behind the larger desk, with his muddy flight boots splayed across its surface, studiously ignored him. He was still wearing his flying coat, and his face was mottled with oil from his flight. At the smaller desk, Sergeant Jackson was writing notes as Captain Ladley dictated.

"Shells bursting at approximately three thousand feet," said Ladley in a languid, upper-class drawl. "Took evasive action and climbed to five thousand, but the shells were ranged higher. Some damage to the wings resulting in a loss of flying stability. Regret to inform that we failed to reach the designated coordinates and were forced to return to base. A second attempt will be made tomorrow. Yours, etcetera, etcetera, you know the rest, Jackson."

Turning to James, he said, "New chap, I presume? Cauliflower?"

James, still standing to attention, replied in a parade ground voice, "Caulfield, Sir, reporting for duty from RFC Andover."

"Stand at ease then, man. We don't do ceremony here," he waved his arm at Jackson. "Sergeant, have the report sent to corps, and get out of my sight for a while. Give Mr. Caulfield your chair."

The chubby sergeant spent a moment resentfully tidying his papers and then dragged his chair into a position by James before leaving the room. Captain Ladley waved at him to sit down, took his own foot off the table with an audible groan, and then leaned forward, resting his chin on arched interlocking fingers.

Eyes following the departing sergeant, Ladley muttered, "Bloody desk-wallahs. Still, the good sergeant saves me from having to read most of this bloody guff," he said, looking at the mountain of paper on the desk with a shudder.

"Well, they tell me you can fly at least," he continued, indicating a folder balanced precariously on the edge of the desk. "How many hours in the BE2?" he asked.

James made a quick mental calculation. "Just over nineteen, sir, including the flight over. Around twenty on the Boxkite in training before that."

"Better than most," nodded Ladley. "I know of a chap at 3rd Squadron who arrived with less than ten in total. Needless to say, he didn't last long. Engine failed over the German lines, and he's not been seen since."

"Crate intact?" asked Ladley, with the intense look of a schoolmaster about to hear an implausible excuse. "No silly accidents to report on the crossing?"

"No, Sir," said James. "There was an issue with the magneto, but Corporal Evans said he would replace it before morning."

"Mmm," replied Ladley, picking up the folder and opening it, fingers flicking idly through the pages. "Good man, Evans. He built a working tractor as a small boy, so he tells me. Knows his way around a plane too, and we don't have too many like that. Methodist apparently, doesn't take a drink. But then, he is Welsh. Always something of the hills about those chaps."

James, unsure what to say, smiled blankly and kept silent.

"Rugby, I see," said Ladley, tapping his finger on an open page. "Running and swimming. Why they persist in sending me this rubbish, I'll never know." He snapped the folder shut and threw it casually across the room to land on Jackson's desk.

He stood up abruptly and wandered over to the map pinned to the wall at the side of his desk.

"This," he said pointing to an area plastered in red and black flags, "is our sector. I'll get Jackson to drop a map to your quarters. Learn it this evening, because I will expect you to be able to find your way to any point within a thirty-mile radius by dawn, and you'll know how damned difficult it is to read a map in the air, even with the new clipboards Corps has seen fit to send us."

He didn't wait for a reply. "The black markers indicate enemy artillery positions. The red are our guns, French mainly," he said with a hint of distaste. "Our job is two-fold. One," he held up a single finger, "to map the position of enemy emplacements and track major troop movements. Two," he raised a second digit, "to assist our artillery in ranging their shot. Questions?" he barked.

"How do we communicate with the artillery, Sir?" asked James.

"By a series of ridiculous methods, dreamed up by fools who have never been in a plane," barked Ladley.

He pointed to a pile of lamps in the corner of the office before continuing. "The current method is to use these shuttered lamps to indicate to the gunners how to correct their aim. Your observer will handle it, but you will need to be low to the ground in order to be seen. We've tried various other things—dropping notes, flags, that sort of thing, but nothing works well. Until they come up with a method at Farnborough to communicate with the ground, we are stuck with it."

"Thank you, Sir," said James.

Ladley looked at him sceptically.

"You won't be thanking me when you are low to the ground and the shelling starts," he said sharply. "Now that their advance is slowing, the Germans are sometimes using their big guns to fire delayed shell bursts into the air. Corps aren't yet sure how they work, but they detonate in the air and can be set to burst at various heights. It might be some sort of igniferious fuse cut to length or maybe even clockwork, but they can adjust quickly to different flying heights. If you see a cloud of pink smoke anywhere near your plane, then you are being fired upon. Climb or dive immediately. Otherwise, you can lose bits of your wing like I did this afternoon," he said with a shake of his head.

"I'll bear that in mind, Sir," said James. He had read about the new phenomena of antiaircraft fire in *Flight* magazine some months earlier. At Andover, one or two of the trainee pilots had come to refer to this kind of fire as "Archie."

"As to an observer," continued Ladley, "I follow the practice of putting my most inexperienced men in with the most experienced. As the newest pilot, you'll fly with Henderson, who is a regular, a damn fine navigator, and a cool head. He has overall command when you are in the air. I'll introduce you to the rest of the officers at dinner in the mess tonight."

Ladley sat back down on his chair and put his feet back on the table. "As I said, we don't stand on ceremony here, but you are an officer, and as such, you will carry yourself with appropriate dignity in front of the men. You will attend all evening flight briefings, which take place at 8:00 p.m. in the hangar. You will also take your turn inspecting the B Flight guard. We have regular inspections at 6:00

p.m. every night and ad hoc inspections of any aspect of the airfield at the whim of the officer of the day. The rota is indicated on the flight chart, which doubtless you have already seen. I'll add your name tonight, but you will be flying first thing tomorrow, so make sure you get your batman to wake you in good time. Any further questions?" he asked, obviously eager to end the brief interview.

"Only one, Sir. May I take my own rifle in the plane with me?"

"Yes, providing you only use it on those that fire at you," replied Ladley. "I'm not anxious to start an arms race with the German Air Corps, so you will observe the peace for the moment. If you can take a pop at a German gunner, do so, but never risk your aircraft in the attempt." He smiled briefly, and the softening effect on his rough features was quite startling. "I'm afraid to say that your plane is rather more valuable than you are. You will do all you can to preserve it, short of allowing the enemy to capture the thing. If you are ever forced to land, your observer carries grenades with which to destroy the machine. If you land somewhere other than this airfield on our side of the lines, then find a telephone and call in. Depending on how stupid you have been, we may come and pick you up, or we may make you walk back. If that's all, I will see you at evening briefing, after which we shall take dinner."

"Thank you, Sir," said James.

"Be gone then, and learn that bloody map!"

James stood to attention, saluted, and marched towards the door before he heard Ladley call after him.

"Caulfield," he drawled. "I told you about ceremony. Leave that business for the men on the parade ground. We are all flyers, and, in here and in the mess, I am merely *primus inter pares*. You went to Rugby, I assume you have Latin."

Somewhere Over the Somme, France, November 2, 1914

The shell burst with an audible pop, and the pressure of the explosive charge pushed the plane momentarily off course until James was able to wrestle back control. In the front seat, Henderson pointed a hand to starboard, and James banked the machine in that direction as a cloud of pink acrid smoke rolled over them like a wave. Secondary shells burst off to their left. For the moment, at least, they were safe.

Aside from the dangers of antiaircraft fire, James had found adapting to flying at the front relatively straightforward. The problems were virtually identical to those he had experienced at Brooklands, and he had become adept at listening for the telltale hiccups in engine noise that anticipated a stall. He had been forced down twice with mechanical problems and both times had landed on farmland well within the allied lines. He had struck up a rapport with Henderson and found that he respected his unflappable demeanour in the air and his remarkable ability to navigate even at high altitudes, where cloud obscured the ground. His only real problem had been the intensity of the cold in the air, especially now as autumn was slowly giving way to winter. Long periods in the air froze his fingers through the thin leather of his gloves, and his complexion was wind-reddened and raw, like that of a fishermen or an aficionado of the bottle.

The work was easy, in truth. Captain Ladley had obviously decided to ease him in gently, and although he had flown every day, he had not been given the tougher artillery coordination jobs and was instead focused purely on reconnaissance, flying to a location and then circling while Henderson sketched what he could see on the ground. These scraps of information were collated by Sergeant Jackson and then forwarded onto Corps HQ before being eventually passed onto Army Command. Someone somewhere obviously thought it valuable, because the orders kept coming, and the squadron was kept busy. The Germans presented little aerial threat, and after his first few nervous encounters with enemy planes, James had realised that there was little purpose to carrying his weapon when airborne.

He had settled well into life on the airfield too. He had been allocated a sparse room to himself, with two single beds, a small chest of drawers, and a single chair. He had also been given an elderly batman called Davies, a retired infantryman who had volunteered for the RFC in August and who claimed to have fought in the expedition to relieve Khartoum thirty years earlier. He was a dry husk of a man, completely bald, with a stooping, shuffling gait, which he complained was aggravated by having to live in a damp tent. He was capable though, looking after James' effects with a quiet efficiency and never failing to wake him in ample time for the dawn patrol. If his grumbling was an occasional irritant, for James it was offset by the respect he deserved for volunteering for service in France at an age when most men would be thinking of a quiet retirement and a cottage by the sea.

The atmosphere in the mess was convivial and surprisingly informal. Aside from Henderson, Stanley, and Ladley, there were two other officers in the flight, both pilots and both regulars that had first come over at the tail end of August and been involved in some of the earliest reconnaissance flights over Mons. Moore was a blonde, broad-shouldered, earthy Southern Rhodesian, with a crude sense of humour and a rampant hostility towards the Germans, inspired in part by their imperial expansion into East Africa. Cooper was his antithesis, a spry pale donnish man, already into his thirties, who tended to abhor the jingoism of the war and preferred to bury his head in books rather than join in the camaraderie of the mess. And there was camaraderie. The alcohol flowed freely, with the locally sourced wine and pastis supplemented by the private stocks of spirits sent out by the families of the pilots. Bates, the phlegmatic mess steward who owed his limp to a Boer bullet to the knee taken at the Battle of Ladysmith, served them with an unobtrusive discretion that was worthy of the best London gentleman's club. The food was tolerable too, as the base was surrounded by farmland. Luxuries either came from Amiens or were shipped from England. As at least three members of the squadron had substantial private means, there was no absence of the little comforts that made life tolerable. The pilots drank fine teas, ate biscuits from Fortnum and Mason, and occasionally received homemade cakes, packed in tins and sent in the post by enterprising mothers, sisters, and servants.

James, given the manner of his departure, had not been able to contribute to the frenzy of domestic consumption in the mess, although his brother officers were too polite to ever mention it. Talk of home was distinctly discouraged in the mess by Captain Ladley in any case, as was any "shop talk" and religious or political discussion. The only word from home that James had received in his six weeks at the front had been a cursory note from Harper about the progress of some decorating work commissioned by his mother before her departure and a steady stream of letters from Elliot, bemoaning his position. He had eventually been allocated as a trainer to the school at Andover and was now spending his days bumping over Hertfordshire fields in Boxkites piloted by heavy-handed ex-cavalry officers. His letters revealed a deep frustration and were full of questions about life at the front, which James responded to with circumspection. Although officers' letters were not censored like the men's, there was an obvious need to ensure that letters did not reveal too much valuable military detail, even via the relatively secure channel of the military post.

The only source of regret for James was the absence of female company. He'd been somewhat surprised by that. After all, he had attended an all-boys school from the age of eight. However, it was the complete absence of the female sex from the front that he found eerie, the peripheral people that he had scarcely noticed back at home—shop assistants, housewives in the streets, servants, and maids—that formed the backdrop to life in an English home. Such was the scarcity of women that the daily arrival of the milk cart from a local farm, driven by the farmer's daughter, saw groups of the men congregating near the main gate of the airfield and casting surreptitious glances at her unremarkable beauty. Officers were not immune to this wistful longing for the delights of the gentler sex, and

James had sometimes unconsciously found himself in the vicinity, engaged with some unnecessary task.

Still, he thought, as he settled the aircraft back into a straight course, there was always Amiens. After thirty consecutive days of flying, he was entitled to a twenty-four-hour leave pass, and he and Henderson were going to head into the town that evening to sample whatever delights the town had to offer. From the discrete chatter he had picked up in the mess, it sounded like the place certainly had its merits.

From the front seat of the plane, Henderson extended an arm upwards, pointing a finger directly towards a cloudbank. James looked and could just make out a speck flitting through the thick cloud. He squinted and saw a plane emerge. He couldn't see its markings, but the speed with which it was moving meant it couldn't be British. French perhaps, but over this side of the lines, it was far more likely to be German. Henderson made a circling motion with his hand, indicating that they had reached the identified map sector and should commence circling. James descended below the light cloud cover and began to circle in a tight pattern, while Henderson sketched the lines of trenches as best he could in the buffeting wind of the open cockpit. Antiaircraft shells burst above them, having failed to account for the plane's descent. From experience, James knew that he had approximately two minutes before the German guns recalibrated their shot and were able to get a lock on their position.

James watched the ground with a mixture of anxiety and wonder. Seen from two thousand feet, the pattern of German trenches resembled a child's train set, with the pieces thrown haphazardly, as if in pique. Most were laid end to end, with the odd branch line leading to support positions and key storage facilities. Tiny men could be seen in the trenches, packed in perfect alignment, like boxed toy soldiers fresh from the shop. Here and there, sandbagged machine-gun emplacements jutted out along the line, with groups of men congregating around them, alert for any sign of movement from the Allied lines. From the air, the scale was overwhelming. There were tens of thousands of men locked down in small patches of ground and exposed to the lazy, arcing shellfire that periodically came from both sides. The population of a small city occupied ground no larger than the average village, with each side intent on the absolute destruction of the other. It was a hellish sight, made bleaker by the few remaining shattered buildings poking like ancient bones from the churned mud of the French countryside. A few resolute souls on the ground took pot shots at the plane as it circled, but the range and distance was too great for the standard rifle, and the bullets didn't trouble them as they made their observations.

From above and behind him, James heard the dull drone of an engine, and he turned in his seat to see the plane he had watched emerge from the cloud minutes earlier. Expecting it to pass overhead on its way to the British side of the lines, he waved briskly at the two German occupants and turned back to check on Henderson. He was surprised by a sharp whistling sound passing right by his ear, followed by a crack as something hit the wooden strut separating the right-hand wing of the plane, showering splinters across the nose. Henderson started in alarm, turned in his seat, and pointed manically at the German plane. James turned too and saw the plane a few hundred feet away, closing quickly. The observer in the forward seat of the plane was standing and pointing a rifle, weaving slightly as the wind shivered the aircraft.

James shrank into his seat, unconsciously trying to minimise the target he presented to the German crew. There was another shot, this time audible, although the bullet sped harmlessly past them. Raising a hand in query to Henderson, he was relieved to be given the order to bank left. He turned as quickly as the BE2 would allow, towards the Allied lines, and cautiously tried to climb. Incredibly, the German plane followed him, taking a parallel course that placed them off the starboard side. James could see that the strut on his plane's wing was nearly cut through, held together by only an inch or two of splintered wood. Any sudden climb or dive would likely snap the strut, causing the wings to collapse and leading to almost certain death for both pilot and observer.

James couldn't understand why the German pilot had not held course on his tail if his intent was pursuit. He glanced across at the Albatross and then realised that, to fire forward from the plane, the German observer had to stand up in order to avoid hitting the propeller. On this parallel course, he was able to sit, giving him a much more stable position and a far wider angle of fire. The gap between the planes was down to about fifty feet, and even allowing for the difficulties of shooting from a moving platform at high speed, the man was almost certain to hit something. Nor could James evade him with manoeuvring. Any sudden movement risked the stability of the wing, and, in any case, the Albatross was a far quicker and more agile plane. They were sitting ducks, and James cringed and lowered himself more into the pilot bay, not that the stiffened canvas of the plane's body offered much protection, but there was some small comfort in not having the majority of his body exposed to the German's fire.

Several quick shots came in. There was a tearing noise from the fuselage of the plane as the bullets tore through the frame, narrowly missing James' legs. Visible holes appeared in the fabric, but as there was no sudden loss of control, all critical systems seemed intact. Henderson was responding now, and he could be heard above the drone of engine and the incessant whipping whistle of the wind, screaming defiance at the German plane. He had searched in the recesses of his seating bay and pulled out a standard issue Webley Mark IV service revolver, with which he began to fire back at the German plane. The gun wasn't ideal for use in the air, and Henderson missed with all six bullets, ducking down to reload.

They were over the British lines now, but the German showed no sign of turning away. The observer in the Albatross calmly reloaded, took aim, and James banked as steeply as he dared, just before the moment of fire. There was a clunk from the nose of the plane, followed by a powerful jet of engine fuel, which shot into the air and covered Henderson, splashing off the fuselage and over James' legs. Immediately, the plane lost power, the propeller continuing to turn but with the engine spluttering like an asthmatic on the edge of collapse. They began to lose height, with James pulling back as hard as could on the stick, trying to fight the sudden fall in an effort to preserve their fragile wings. Above them, the Germans finally veered away, both pilot and observer waving in obvious mockery of the usual salute.

"Damn the bastards," muttered James. Gritting his teeth, he kept his eyes focused on the splintered strut for any further signs of stress.

In the front seat, Henderson pointed towards the ground. They were only around a thousand feet up now, and the detail of the British support trenches was flashing past in a haze of disjointed images. Muddy faces upturned in alarm, sentries aiming rifles at the plane as it sped overheard amidst the dull explosions of distant shells. James followed Henderson's direction and saw what looked like a vehicle park, some two miles behind the forward trenches. The space was open and looked to have some sort of solid surface—concrete or possibly tarmac. It was a better bet than landing in the quagmire and mud of the trenches, and such was their rate of descent that there was no chance of reaching open country and the relative safety of a field.

James pointed the nose of the plane at the distant park, wincing as he watched the strut of the right wing bend alarmingly in protest. They were losing height, and he was pulling back at the stick with all his strength, but he couldn't prevent the plane's steady fall. Slowly, iteratively, they made up the ground. The jumble of trenches turned into makeshift roads, spotted with tents that were probably impromptu dressing stations. There were even one or two buildings left intact, probably sheltering small pockets of infantrymen anxious for a solid wall to give them an illusion of safety. They were close enough to make out individual faces now, and through his panic James was appalled to see the joy on the faces of the French infantrymen as the plane passed overhead. Like accounts of men watching a public execution, they seem viscerally delighted at the imminent death of another. It was to the sound of jeers not cries that they plummeted towards the ground.

And then the ground was upon them. The plane failed to reach the outside edge of the park, instead clipping the edge of the hard, mud roadway, scattering a marching column of infantry as they touched down. The impact was too much for the supporting strut. It snapped, and the wing collapsed, momentarily blinding them as they bumped and bounced along the road. They were slowing now, with the right wings of the plane providing extra drag, and James was able to cut the engine completely. They continued for another twenty or thirty feet before coming to a rest against a burned-out van. Petrol-soaked, half-blind, and scared stiff, they jumped out of the plane and ran to a safe distance in case of sudden fire. Around them, a group of filthy blue uniformed ghosts picked themselves up from the side of the mud road and gave a round of ragged applause. James looked in alarm at the hideously gaunt young men that surrounded him, their faces scarred with the weight of ages. For a moment, he didn't know if he had survived or whether this purgatorial wasteland was real. He was suddenly certain that he walked among the dead.

The hangar that night was more than usually crowded. All of the officers were present at the regular flight briefing, as was Corporal Evans, as the lead mechanic, and Sergeants Jackson and Carswell, the two senior NCOs. As if in silent recrimination, the battered BE2 that James had crash-landed earlier that day loomed in the flickering lamplight of the vast, dark tent. It had arrived on a lorry from Albert early in the evening, battered beyond recognition and completely missing its right wings, which had torn off on landing. The mechanics and riggers thought it would take at least five days to get it airworthy again. As well as the wings, the fuel lines had been severed, and the fuselage was peppered with holes.

Captain Ladley was predictably furious. The Germans had broken the great unwritten rule and attacked a fellow flyer in the air. Worse, they had driven it down and nearly destroyed the plane and its crew. When James and Henderson had returned by car that afternoon, the senior officer had actually described the action as a "declaration of war." James thought it churlish to point out that they had already been at war for several months. Only the RFC seemed intent on ignoring it.

Pointing at the shattered aircraft, Ladley addressed the line of men, standing at ease in front of him.

"As outrageous as this action is, we cannot assume it is an isolated incident," he said, gazing at each man in turn.

"Indeed, reports from Corps indicate that the Germans are switching from reconnoitring our positions and are focusing instead on preventing our own actions over their lines. The attack on Caulfield and Henderson would seem, prima facie, to be part of the same pattern. As I understand it, Henderson, the Germans held a deliberate course in order to secure a prime firing position?"

"Yes, Sir, they did. Initially they were behind us, but when we banked, they switched to a parallel course and then followed us back over to our side of the lines," said Henderson.

"And was there a clear objective on our side of the lines?" barked Ladley.

"No, Sir," said Henderson quickly. "They followed us and then broke off to return to their lines as soon as it was clear we were in trouble."

There was an outbreak of muttering amongst the other officers, and Moore, the burly Southern Rhodesian, said in the flat monotone of colonial Africa, "It sounds like a conscious change in strategy, Sir. It can't have been a fluke encounter."

"I'm inclined to agree," said Ladley, with a frown. He began to pace across the floor of the hangar, his giant shadow leaping jerkily on the canvas of the tent.

Paget-Stanley swallowed and raised a nervous hand. Ladley brusquely turned on him. "This is not the bloody cavalry, man. In this forum, we all speak our minds and any man," he stopped to point out the NCOs standing in the lee of the plane's rudder, "can offer a view without permission and without usual deference to rank."

"Yes, Sir," stammered the boyish young man. "I was only thinking, Sir, how the Germans knew that Caulfield was there?"

"Balloons," said the bookish Cooper, prompting titters from Moore and the NCOs. Cooper frowned at them before continuing. "I mean the observation balloons that the Germans have in the main salient. They can see us from miles away and presumably have the means to signal over distance. Perhaps they can even signal a German airfield?"

"Perhaps," said Ladley doubtfully. "We can't go after balloons in any case, at least not without consent from Corps. So, gentlemen, what other bright ideas do we have?"

"We fight," said James simply. "I mean, they might be faster, but their tactics are simple enough. If they continue to run parallel to us, we fire on them."

Corporal Evans intervened in his distinctive lilting tone. "If I may, Sir," he said, addressing James. "That fight wouldn't be equal. From what I know about the Albatross, and its not as much as I would like, they are lighter planes. Less weight means less wiring. Their field of sight is much greater than ours. That means they have a much better chance of hitting us than we do them, Sir."

James bristled. "I think that would depend on the gun, Corporal. Less field of sight might be compensated for by greater accuracy. I think that Henderson would agree that the Webley was virtually useless," he paused as Henderson nodded, "so the least that we should take up is a rifle or anything better that we can get hold of."

"Agreed," said Ladley. "And I take the general point on accuracy. Jackson, you will set up a shooting range at the edge of the airfield, and from tomorrow, all flying personnel will spend at least half an hour a day in practice. All pilots and observers will carry rifles, to be issued from the armoury, and solo flying will be kept to an absolute minimum. Do not seek a fight, but if a Hun is in range, fire. Clear?"

A mumbled chorus of agreement rose from the assembled men before Ladley moved on.

"Now, onto the latest targets that Corps have specified for tomorrow. Caulfield and Henderson, you may be excused. I believe the bright lights of Amiens beckon," he said, smiling.

James had never thought himself a puritan, but he was shocked by Amiens. Ostensibly, it was a small, typically French regional capital situated on the basin of the River Somme, at a point where it meets with its tributaries, the Selle and the Avre. Once the home of the writer Jules Verne, it had narrow, stone streets that were frequently congested with military traffic on its way to and from the front. A huge, three-tiered gothic cathedral, built on a ridge overlooking the river, dominated the town and provided the almighty with a grandstand seat to the debauchery of a city in wartime.

The population of the city was probably in the region of seventy or eighty thousand people, but at any one time, there were another thirty or forty thousand people in uniform. They staggered down the streets and alleys of the city under the watchful gaze of the pockets of military police, in their distinctive red hats, standing on corners and in the main squares. The economy of the city had been transformed by the war. A stuttering textile industry and an agricultural market town had been transformed into a pleasure capital. The front rooms of many of the stone houses had been hastily converted into cheap eateries and wine shops catering to the steady supply of military personnel on leave or simply passing through. The backrooms hid the baser sorts of pleasures, although here and there lines of shuffling infantrymen indicated the presence of an officially sanctioned brothel.

The pleasure palaces of the bustling city were strictly demarcated between men and officers, and it was to enforce that strict separation, together with a general need to keep the peace, that prompted the presence of the military police. Establishments reserved for officers were congregated around the more salubrious riverside areas, in the shadow of the looming cathedral. Although it was approaching ten o'clock when they arrived, James and Henderson found a pleasant lodging house in the Rue Cormont, left their kitbags, and embarked on a walk along the riverfront. Despite the cold of the late evening, the area was thronged with soldiers of all ranks, some walking arm in arm with ladies of variable levels of repute.

They settled on a little restaurant called "Lumieres" that they found in a side street off the Place Vogel. Sitting down in the window seat at the behest of the egregious owner, they tucked into a very passable meal of oysters and veal, accompanied by two superb bottles of burgundy. Replete and a little woozy from the wine, they were just deciding where to take themselves to next when a face loomed large in the window next to their table. They both jumped from their seats until they realised that it was a British Private, staring at them through the window and gesturing to some men in the shadows behind.

The man was dishevelled and clearly extremely drunk. He was dressed in the green khaki of the infantry, but the uniform was battered and soiled, and his face was twisted in anger. The candlelight of the restaurant cast his face into shadow, making him look somehow monstrous, a spectre at the feast. He was talking now, but his words were inaudible until he began to shout.

"Fucking cowards," he screamed, as two other men came into view behind him. "Leave us to do the dying, while you swan about like lords watching it all from the grandstand."

A few yards from the window, with the barrier of the table between them, James considered what to do. The restaurant's owner had come over from behind the bar and was clearly alarmed for the handful of other customers still finishing off meals. This was gross insubordination, and after the events of the day, James was angry enough to tackle this fool on his own terms. He stalked to the door of the restaurant, threw it open, and faced down the man and his mates.

Up close, it could be seen that he was little more than a boy. A generous estimate might place him at eighteen, but smooth cheeks, a thick mop of black hair, and an unwrinkled brow made him seem much less, perhaps fifteen or sixteen. His mates were older, and one of them, a sergeant sporting outlandish side whiskers, grabbed his arm and tried to pull him back as he turned towards James.

"Come away, son, this won't do you no good," said the sergeant kindly. The boy broke away from his grip and threw himself at James, swinging a fist as he did so. The blow was telegraphed, and James easily evaded it, rocking backwards on his feet and watching dispassionately as the follow-through took the boy to the floor. Henderson had now joined him and was flanking him on his right. Through the window, the restaurant owner looked on anxiously.

The sergeant and another private leant over the boy and pinned his arms and legs to the ground. He struggled briefly against the weight of the bigger men before beginning to sob in a keening, high-pitched wail.

"Bastards, fucking bastards," he screamed, and James was unclear whether this latest abuse was aimed at himself and Henderson or the two soldiers restraining him.

Stepping forwards, he addressed the sergeant. "What is the meaning of this?" he drawled, every inch the young officer.

The sergeant, still crouching, tried to attempt a salute, but as soon as he raised a hand, the boy threatened to break away, so he sighed and gave up. "I'm sorry, Sir, very sorry. The boy has had a hard time up at the line, lost a lot of mates. He can't take his drink, and he's had a belly full tonight 'cause we go back tomorrow, Sir."

"I see," said James. "The man attempted to strike an officer, which last time I looked was a court-martial offence."

"I know, Sir, and I am very sorry for his behaviour. He's a good lad usually, though, never gives us any trouble. I hope you might consider letting this one go, Sir. You can be sure that when he's sober, I'll give him what for," said the sergeant pleadingly.

James looked down at the still-sobbing boy. In tears and pinioned to the ground, he looked even younger. He couldn't report him, but neither could he let the incident go. It was Henderson who came to his rescue.

"Perhaps," said the observer, "you might do us the courtesy, Sergeant, of explaining the boy's issue with us?"

"It's the wings, Sir," said the sergeant, nodding at the design on the breast of their uniforms. "Not 'cause you're officers, Sir, but because you're flyers."

"And what so incites a young man about a pair of wings that he would risk a court-martial to strike at their owner?" asked Henderson, raising an eyebrow.

"Sir, if I may speak freely?" asked the other man, holding the boy's legs.

"Yes, man, get on with it," said Henderson.

"Thank you, Sir," said the private. "Well, obviously a lot of blokes think you are onto a cushy number, Sir, but I know I wouldn't want to go up in one of those things. No, there's bad feeling because of the artillery, Sir. When you lot signal to our guns, you're in the air so long that you give away our positions. You are ranging our guns, Sir, but you are signalling back to the infantry. The Germans see that from their balloons, and then they know where we are, Sir. They blow us to hell. Sometimes, sir, one or two of our lads have got so angry that they've taken a shot at you as you fly past."

Henderson laughed. "Good lord, I never knew that. No wonder the poor sod was so anxious to tear into us. James, if you are content, I suggest we ask these men to pour their colleague back into his bed."

James nodded his consent, and with effusive expressions of gratitude, the two men gave a faltering salute, picked up the still-sobbing boy, and carried him off into the night.

"He was right you know, Caulfield," said Henderson, wine spilling from the corner of his mouth.

"Who was?" slurred James, his eyes on the tight curves of the young women singing at the piano in the smoke-filled bar. It was the middle of the night, but the bar was still lively. Officers lounged around in ones and twos. All were drunk, and some were chatting to the cluster of young ladies who approached the tables with smiles and invitations. One or two couples occasionally peeled off and made their way upstairs, sometimes to the applause of the other men.

"That poor young sod from the infantry. We are cowards by ommission," said Henderson, warming to his theme and jabbing a finger in the air.

"Perhaps," said James. "Although it's not our fault, is it? We have to follow orders, and, until now, those orders have been to refuse engagement. Preserve the plane and all that business."

"Exactly, old man," said Henderson, "but if you're slogging through mud and brains to get at the enemy, it'll hurt to see chaps like us waving at each other in the air, as if we were strolling in the park."

James, who had privately held the same view since he had arrived in France, nodded.

"I've seen this new plane in a copy of *Flight* in the mess," he told Henderson. "Made by Vickers, the FB5, I think it's called. Anyway, it's a pusher plane with the propeller at the back, but it has a fixed machine gun on the nose. You shoot where you point."

Henderson sobered up for a moment and looked at James. "Are they making it?" he asked.

"According to *Flight*, they are," said James. "But the copy of the magazine is months old, so who knows what's happened since then? According to the article, some squadrons in England are testing it. Maybe they'll get here soon."

"A machine gun," murmured Henderson. "That would change everything. Might even be the end of the line for the observer."

He shook his head. "Enough shop. What I need is a girl," he said, standing up and making his way over to the bar. After a brief conversation with the landlady behind the bar, he returned, his buckteeth exposed in a wry grin. He slapped James jovially on the back.

"Don't worry, old chap, I've got one for you too!" he said

James went ashen, and even through the alcoholic fog, Henderson immediately noticed. He laughed uproariously and slapped his hand to his head in exaggerated surprise.

"You don't mean to say you haven't been with a woman before?" he said in a loud voice that attracted the amused gaze of a couple of infantry captains, drinking themselves into oblivion at the next table.

"No, as it happens," said James in a hurt tone. "It's not all that surprising surely? I was at an all-boys school, and I'm obviously not married."

Henderson laughed again. "Such innocence is a delight to behold," he said with mock seriousness. "I'm afraid I've never been averse to seeking out what my father always called, the 'negotiated affection' of young ladies. And I've negotiated two this time. Come on," he said, pulling James to his feet. "Duty calls. You can show the girl your officer's sword." He laughed again, and with his arm around James' shoulders, he half-dragged him towards him to the stairs, ignoring his muted, half-hearted protests.

Later that night, as the two men staggered back to their lodging house, through the first grey tendrils of the Amiens dawn, James thought that if a German bullet were to end his life now, at least he would die a man.

Near Amiens, France, December 5, 1914

James ran out of the mess room with Henderson as soon as he saw the plane coming in. Sergeant Jackson was frantically ringing the alarm bell, and everywhere he looked men poured from tents in various states of undress. Ladley, too, had rushed out of the organised chaos of the flight office and stood by Jackson, eyes raised to the heavens, a hand shielding his eyes from the weak morning sun. A light frost covered the ground, and the grass crisped under James' feet as he raced towards Ladley. The fire wagon was already primed, and men stood anxiously waiting, eyes uplifted, reminding James of church and the raising of the host.

The plane was trailing flames from the engine block as it circled inelegantly around the airfield. Moore, the pilot, could be seen beating at his own clothes, while Paget-Stanley, as observer, was standing up in the front seat and waving his arms at the men on the ground. Slowly, painfully, the plane descended. It wobbled at fifty feet, straightened, threatened to land, and then the wings caught in a sudden whoosh of flame. Like a game bird picked off at an August shoot, it plummeted. Flames rushed up the fuselage as it dropped like a stone to the frozen earth, crashing with a crumpled bang as the nose and propeller broke off. James was aware of Ladley shouting something, but he was paralysed in horror as he watched the fire wagon being dragged across the field towards the wreckage of the plane. Moore had been thrown some thirty feet from the plane, and his whole body was ablaze, Henderson standing helplessly a few steps away from him. With the strange dislocation that sometimes comes with exhaustion, James watched himself move jerkily towards the crashed plane. Moore was literally melting, his flight goggles melding into the ravaged raw flesh of his face and his torn clothing showing patches of crisping flesh. The air was pungent with the smell of petrol and cooked meat. He was clearly dead, and James only hoped that he had been killed outright by the crash. To burn like that was the worst of all deaths, a death by inches.

Somewhere James heard a scream. He saw the men pointlessly throwing water over the burning plane, the hand pump cranking, and a weak dribble of liquid spewing forth from the end of the hose. The plane was completely covered in burning fuel, and it would take an age to put out the blaze. The scream sounded again, and James looked down. A few feet away, Paget-Stanley was still alive. Ladley was leaning over him, cradling his head, and speaking in a voice that James could not hear. As if spellbound, he moved towards them and could see the tears falling from Ladley's cheeks as he mouthed meaningless comforts. The young boy on the floor was mewling like a wounded cat, his face stripped of flesh and his lips and eyelids burned completely away. His flying cap was lost, and two blackened holes were all that remained of his ears. He was conscious though, his eyes wild and staring. For a moment, he locked his gaze with James. The eyes of an animal in torment silently pleading with him to end the pain.

Wordlessly, James approached the kneeling Ladley. He removed his service revolver from the holster at his belt and tapped the captain on the shoulder. Ladley looked up, saw the weapon, and angrily slapped it away, causing it to fall to the ground. Standing, he rounded on James.

"Pull yourself together!" he said, in a strangely soft one. "Get a medic out here now, and arrange the transport to hospital. You are an officer, and you will damn well behave like one."

As if waking from sleep, James suddenly felt the harsh cold air of the early December morning and the heat of the weak sun and the burning flames on his skin. His shattered senses reignited, and he turned purposefully back towards the farmhouse. Locating Jackson, he rounded up the two mechanics that doubled as the flight's medics and quickly set them to work. They injected Paget-Stanley with morphine and then carried his recumbent body to the pallet-backed van that served as the airfield's main land transport. He was covered in blankets, and an airman drove him away, with Jackson accompanying Paget-Stanley in the back. James was ashamed at the relief he felt as he watched the van disappear from sight.

Minutes later, after ordering a rigger to prepare a coffin for Moore's body, he was summoned to the flight office. Despite the early hour, the captain was drinking whiskey from a battered tin cup and running a hand obsessively through the tight auburn curls of his hair. His face looked older, more lined, and his hands shook as he waved James to the seat at Jackson's desk, ignoring the younger man's salute.

"War brings enough death, Caulfield, without us giving it a helping hand," he said with sudden intensity. "If there is a repeat of your behaviour this morning, I will not hesitate to court-martial you. Understood?"

James nodded bleakly. "Yes, Sir, understood," he said.

"Good. We will say no more of it now then," he paused to drain his cup. "As horrific as he looked, there is every chance that young Paget-Stanley will survive. The medics tell me that it was only his face that was seriously burned. His vital organs are intact, and although he will certainly be disfigured, he may recover to lead some semblance of a life, unlike poor, bloody Moore."

Ladley stood up wearily, walked over to the map on the sidewall, and stabbed a finger in the region of Arras.

"They were attacked somewhere here, on our side of the lines. We had a telephone call from Corps informing us that the infantry observed them engaged with two German planes. That might be coincidence, but it could also be a deliberate change of strategy to seek out and destroy our planes one by one. "

James shook his head. "I'm not sure that would do them much good, Sir. With rifles, they still wouldn't have that much chance of hitting us, even with two planes in the air. If they flew a parallel course on either side, they would be almost as likely to hit each other as us."

"I agree," said Ladley resuming his seat. "With rifles, they would have to be bloody lucky to down a pilot as canny as Moore, but the infantry subaltern that reported the sighting was convinced that there was machine-gun fire from one of the Albatrosses, perhaps both."

"Machine guns, Sir?" said James, a trickle of fear running down his spine.

"Yes," snapped Ladley. "I have reported it to Corps, who quite rightly tell me that such a thing is impossible on a lightweight craft. A new plane could possibly carry it, like the Gunbus that is in development at Farnborough, but an Albatross shouldn't be able to take the weight. I need visual confirmation from the air."

"Is that where I come in, Sir?" asked James

"Well, with this morning's casualties, we are now woefully short of pilots and especially of observers," said Ladley thoughtfully. "I've already requested replacements, but they won't be here for days. Cooper is on patrol, so that only leaves you, me, and Henderson. My suggestion is that we take the remaining BE2s, Henderson flying with you, and begin to scout the area between Albert and St. Quentin, well within sight of the Hun balloons. Whatever mechanism they have to communicate, we might be able to flush out the Albatross and assess its armaments. If you spot a machine gun, run. I will do the same. Understood?"

"Yes, Sir. When do we go?" asked James

"As soon as Cooper returns from patrol. He might have more information for us."

Cooper returned an hour later in fine spirits. He had spent a pleasantly calm morning hand-sketching gun emplacements near Noyon, unmolested by either antiaircraft fire or German planes. He was shaken from his quiet reflections on the beauty of a frosted landscape seen from the air by the devastating news of Moore and Paget-Stanley and immediately volunteered to accompany James and Ladley on their reconnaissance mission. Ladley refused, pointing out that Cooper had already spent four hours airborne and that his plane was in need of attention. A further offer to fly as Ladley's observer was summarily dismissed, and Cooper was dispatched with a book to the mess, there to mourn the passing of his close friend, Moore.

James and Henderson climbed into their BE2 and began the litany of the start-up, with Corporal Evans taking the propeller. They had armed themselves to the teeth. James carried his Mauser hunting rifle in his seat bay and a service revolver at his hip. Henderson had two rifles jammed between his legs and a service revolver. Spare ammunition was carried in a small bag in the front of the plane, where usually resided the sketchpads and clipboards used on aerial reconnaissance. Ladley too, although flying alone, was well stocked with weapons.

James could see the barrels of at least three rifles in the empty observer seat, and the captain rarely went anywhere without a service revolver at his hip.

They took off into grey clouds, bumping across the scorched, frosty ground of the airfield. The physical residue of the crash had been removed to the hangars for the sifting and scavenging of parts, but the air was still heavy with the smell of petrol. That passed as the two planes climbed into the cold December air, prompting them to wrap their scarves tighter and huddle down into the scant protection of the seat bays. Ladley was in the lead, with James holding a pattern twelve yards off his starboard wing and a short distance behind. Climbing to three thousand feet, they turned north towards Arras, staying on the Allied side of the lines until they could see the dim outline of the gothic belfry tower on the town hall. They banked to starboard and began to fly over the sprawling new trench systems. They grew all the time, spreading across the landscape like cracks in a pane of glass. The growing stasis of the war was perfectly illustrated by the ever-deepening trenches and the proliferation of more solid semi-submerged emplacements and buildings.

Here, the gap between the lines was only a few hundred yards, but the wasteland of contested ground bore all the detritus of the slow attrition of modern ground war. Rolls of barbed wire were scattered like poacher's snares, and in some of them the bodies of men were trapped, caught on nocturnal patrol and butchered where they stood. Shell holes pockmarked the ground and in the weak grey light of the day, handfuls of men could be seen lying in them, perhaps injured or simply caught outside of the trenches with the coming of the dawn light. There was a smattering of fire from the ground, its source indistinguishable at this height and of little account to pilots moving at speed. It got worse as they rolled over the German lines, and a machine gun could be heard barking, but the bullets, if aimed at them, passed them by.

A few miles ahead could be seen the weirdly nautical outline of the German observation balloon. Well aware that these tended to be heavily defended by antiaircraft guns, James was pleased to see that Ladley was beginning to climb. They had done their best to be noticed in their flight over the trench systems, but there was little point in getting to this point only to fall victim to antiaircraft fire before the Germans had launched their planes. Ladley began a circular climb, in full view of both the trench systems and the principal observation balloon, with

James following his pattern as closely as he could. The BE2 was a slow climber in the best of conditions, and the twenty minutes it took to reach a height of eight thousand feet was a nervous time as the Germans calibrated their guns and began to fire their aerial shells at the planes. Despite the fixed pattern of their flight, the German gunners were unable to effectively gauge their height against the grey December skies. The shells all fell short, and soon a layer of wispy, pink cloud trailed a few hundred feet below them.

James was watching the horizon near the observation balloon when, in the front seat, Henderson extended his arm and pointed downwards, pumping his hand forward and back to indicate an enemy sighting. James looked down and could see two planes climbing towards them through the clouds, still a few thousand feet below. At the angle they were flying, he couldn't see whether the planes mounted any weaponry, so with a brief wave to Ladley to check that he had seen them, he banked slightly and began to lose height, trying to bisect their course and present the side of his plane to their nose. He lost sight of the planes as they plunged into cloud, but he held his course, trusting that Ladley would have seen their direction and followed.

The cloud was thick, and it seemed to take an age until they had a view of more than a few yards in any direction. James looked around methodically, spotting Ladley above him on the port side. He couldn't see the planes until he heard a shot from Ladley's plane. The captain was firing over the top of James' plane, and with horror, he realised that he had dropped too low, underestimating the Albatross's celebrated speed of climb. The Germans were above him. In confirmation, Henderson pointed upwards, and James raised his head to see the planes, on a level with Ladley. Henderson had pulled his rifle, but the span of wings and wire prevented him from firing upwards.

James climbed in a steep, banking circle and heard the engine strain as it came close to stalling. He focused and could just make out the staccato fire of rifles above and behind him. It took several minutes to regain his height, and by that time Ladley was engaged at close quarters with the two planes. One of them had drawn parallel to him, only around thirty feet off his port side and matching his speed, whilst the other trailed in his wake, ready to move alongside should he attempt to manoeuvre away. In front of him, Henderson turned in his seat, shouting something that James couldn't hear over the rasping drone of the engine. Henderson pointed vigorously to the plane behind Ladley, and James suddenly saw why he was so unusually animated. On the side of the rear plane, there was a wooden mounting by the observer seat and the distinctive muzzle of a machine gun. James quickly looked over the plane on the parallel course and saw that it was unarmed, save for the observer, who was stood up in the front seat and firing at Ladley's plane with a hand gun.

His orders were to leave immediately, but to do so would be to abandon Ladley to the mercy of the two German machines. He didn't break away, instead approaching the rear German plane from above and on a parallel course, gaining a position within fifty yards or so. Intent on their prey, neither German seemed to have noticed them, so he picked up his Mauser and let the BE2 level off. It was a stable plane, and if the stick was left in position, she would continue to fly in a straight line until she ran out of fuel. Henderson, too, had levelled his rifle, and both of them aimed at the German craft. *Focus*, thought James, as he sighted the gun. There would likely be only one chance, for the enemy would break away in their faster machines as soon as they spotted him. He aimed the gun at the engine block, hoping to cripple the engine and force them to land. Then a memory of Paget-Stanley's charred face caused him to pause, and he switched his aim to the pilot, in the rear seat of the plane.

Henderson shot first, and the bullet missed completely, his aim ruined as the plane hit an updraft of wind and lifted slightly. James shot before the pilot reacted and saw his bullet hit the man somewhere around the shoulders or the base of the neck. There was a little visible spurt of blood, and the man slumped forward in his seat. His plane immediately began to dive, his observer turning in his seat, screaming, and frantically striking at his colleague with his fist. They began to spin out of control and then disappeared into the cloud layer.

The other German plane, outnumbered and without the advantage of a machine gun, banked sharply to port and began to climb away, quickly getting out of reach of the slower BE2s. James replaced his gun, elated and sickened at what he had just done, and pulled up parallel to Ladley, who have him a quick thumbs-up before waving his hand to indicate that they should return home.

Later, James could remember nothing of the flight back to base. He kept dwelling on the face of the observer as he realised that his pilot was dead. Without parachutes, the German would have had nearly a minute fully aware that he was going to his death. The thought was appalling. He wondered whether he had prayed, what he had said as he fell, whether he had family that would grieve for him back at home. James realised that he had taken a life, that war had made him a killer, and that eventually he would be judged for what he had done that day.

The mess was raucous that evening. Ladley, like a Dickensian patriarch at Christmas, presided over a feast of roast beef, roast potatoes, and fresh vegetables, supplemented by a case of the best claret that Bates could procure at short notice from Amiens. The usual rules of the mess had been relaxed, and the boastful talk was of the gladiatorial nature of the air war. James' achievement was celebrated in toast after toast, and Sergeant Jackson had popped through with a telephoned note of personal congratulation from Corps Command.

Inebriated as they were, there was an edge of desperation to their jollity. The memory of the morning's events lingered in the shadows of the flickering oil lamps, and the empty seats at the jury-rigged dining table taunted them with silent accusation. Their drinking, especially Henderson's, had a panicked frenzy to it, like the atmosphere of a besieged city the night before the barbarians scaled the walls. Death and mutilation awaited them with the coming of the sun. Wine and celebration offered only a stay of execution, not the promise of reprieve.

"To us," said Cooper, raising his wine glass. "'We happy few, we band of brothers.'" he quoted.

"Agincourt," slurred Henderson, slumped forward on the table and wagging a finger in admonishment at Cooper. "That was the French, you dolt, not the Germans."

"Unlike you, I've read the play," said Cooper prissily. "I merely point out that due to the chivalric heroism of our brother officers," he tipped his glass to Ladley,

Henderson, and James in turn, "we can now regard ourselves as soldiers in this war, rather than just glorified voyeurs."

"Amen to that, Mr. Cooper," said Ladley, his face flushed and glistening in the half-light of the mess.

"Although," said Cooper, "we may yet need to 'close the wall up with our English dead.'" His eyes were moist as he looked at the empty chairs flanking him.

"Moore was Rhodesian," said James pedantically, "and Paget-Stanley is still alive. Jackson told me when I reported back."

"Both needless sacrifices to the honour of plucky, bloody Belgium," said Henderson bitterly.

"Mr. Henderson," said Ladley sternly. "It is unbecoming to impugn an ally, however indirectly, and especially one that has fought bravely against insurmountable odds."

There were sage nods of agreement from James and Cooper, and, chastised, Henderson straightened in his seat.

"My apologies, Sir. I'm sure it's the wine talking," said Henderson.

"He has a point though, Sir," interrupted the bookish Cooper, motioning for Bates to refill his glass. "The reality is that Belgium has fallen, the bits of it that aren't given over to trenches and battlefields anyway. Belgium has been raped, either figuratively or literally, depending on whether we can believe the newspapers. We have failed in our stated war aims, and now the battle is about the sovereignty of France. I don't know many Englishmen who give a fig for the sovereignty of France."

Ladley sighed and leaned back in his chair. "Mr. Cooper," he said, "your logic is admirable, but we are soldiers and, as such, must fight the battle that is put in front of us. Victory will reinstate Belgian sovereignty, guarantee the integrity of French soil, and put a stop to the barbarous militarism of our enemy. It may not be the fight that we thought we were having, but it is still a fight worth winning. "

"Hear, hear," murmured James. The thought that Moore's death had been in vain was uncomfortable.

"So speaks the tenacious young lion," said Cooper, smiling broadly at James. Looking at Ladley, he said, "I only meant, Sir, that if we fight for Belgium, then we have already lost that battle. If now we fight for France, then we should say so, and we'll see what the flag-wavers back home make of that!"

"It is true that the Francophile tendencies of our own government are probably not shared by the man in the street," Ladley mused, "but although we may be on the back foot, the inning is by no means at an end. I think, gentlemen, it is best if we consider that we are fighting *against* a ruthless tyranny rather than *for* anything specific. The brutalities committed by the German army in Belgium are well known. They are not gentlemen, and they must be stopped, lest our own daughters, wives, and sweethearts should fall victim to the same horrors."

James nodded, although he thought the stories that had been printed in the aftermath of the conquest of Belgium to be exaggerated. It was inconceivable that a professional army, as disciplined as the Germans seemed to be, would be allowed to ruthlessly ransack and pillage their way across a European country. This wasn't Africa, after all.

"I see," said Cooper, smiling impishly. "Then we are engaged in the business of fighting oppression and tyranny. Like modern versions of the Gracchi, I suppose?"

"We're not all bloody classicists, Cooper," growled Henderson, his eyes bloodshot.

"My apologies, Mr. Henderson," said Cooper, still smiling. "I'm afraid I tend to rather overestimate the quality of education in our public schools." He paused to sip at his freshly topped up glass. "The Gracchi, Gaius and Tiberius, were tribunes of ancient Rome, who tried to reallocate the land of the wealthy to the poor. They were both killed in their efforts to do so."

"I don't follow you," grumbled Henderson. "The fellows sound like socialists. We're not damned socialists."

"I think," said James carefully, "that Mr. Cooper is making a point about the essence of tyranny. The Gracchi thought the inequity in land distribution was tyrannical, whereas the modern English gentleman might take the opposite view and regard the populism of the Gracchi to be tyrannical. Tyranny cannot be defined without reference to a broader viewpoint."

"Touché," smiled Cooper. "We shall make a scholar of you yet, Mr. Caulfield."

"I still don't get it," muttered Henderson. "What has some ancient socialist got to do with us?"

"For God's sake, the point is simple enough," snapped Ladley. He was clipping the end of a large cigar using a penknife and, as he looked up, anger deepened the flush in his cheeks.

"Mr. Cooper," he continued, "like most of his ilk, is engaging in academic navel-gazing. He is trying to suggest that fighting against tyranny and oppression cannot be an absolute rationale for war. As each nation defines tyranny on their own terms, by definition any enemy can safely be labelled with the same tag."

"Correct," said Cooper. "Although my point is more pragmatic than you seem to think, Sir." He took a long draught of wine, sighed contentedly, and then continued. "If we fight the Hun because they represent a tyrannical expansionism, then surely we are obligated to pursue the same values in all our dealings with other nations?"

"I think I see," said James. "If we fight one oppressor, then surely we have to fight them all?"

"Exactly, Mr. Caulfield," beamed Cooper. "Your acuity knows no bounds this evening. Personally, I don't think we can regard our gallant allies in Russia to be entirely free of the stain of tyranny."

"Backward lot, the Russians," slurred Henderson, holding an empty glass to the passing Bates. "Still have serfs, I believe. They could probably do with a good thrashing."

"Mr. Henderson!" thundered Ladley, as Henderson raised his hands in apology.

"And it is the Germans who will give it to them," said Cooper quickly. "Were I a Russian serf, I think I'd probably look at the Germans as liberators of sorts. Oppression rather depends on where you stand."

"Yes, yes," said Ladley, calmer now. "We are going in circles. Perhaps, Mr. Cooper, I should rephrase my argument."

Cooper nodded courteously over the rim of his wineglass and waved at his captain to continue.

"I will speak plainly, as befits a soldier," said Ladley. "If the question before the table is, 'What are we fighting for?' then I would answer that we are fighting because we have to. Our elected government believes this war to be a necessity, and whether we personally agree with that position or not is utterly immaterial. We are soldiers, and we go where we are sent, and we fight until we are told to stop or until we are dead." He nodded at the empty chairs. "That is our duty, gentlemen, and if we fail in it, we will lose all honour. In short, we fight because better minds than ours have deemed it so. Ours is not to reason why." He stopped and looked steadily at Cooper.

Cooper, unmoved, raised his glass in mock salute and finished the quotation, "Ours is but to do or die."

"Damn you, Cooper," growled Ladley. "But yes. That's about the size of it."

An oil lamp guttered in the corner of the mess, casting the table into gloom. Despite the roaring fire, James shivered with a sudden chill. Henderson, his head cradled in his arms on the table, stirred slightly.

"And they said it'd be over by Christmas," he said plaintively.

The following evening, James dashed across to the hangar. Due to the scarcity of viable planes, he had been excused flying duties that day and had spent a tedious afternoon drilling the airfield's small guard and inspecting kit. He detested these more routine duties and found it distasteful to have to punish a man for the crime of having a button missing from a well-worn uniform. The impossibility of maintaining standards while living under canvas in a sodden French field seemed not to have occurred to the compilers of military regulations, but rules remained rules, no matter how ridiculous they may seem. The unfortunate fellow, an ill-fed urchin by the name of Marlow, had taken the extra latrine duty with good grace, although it still irked James that the men were given no more latitude than they would get at Horseguards.

It was with an ill temper, then, that James arrived at the hangar for the evening briefing. The meeting had already begun, and Ladley pointedly looked at his watch as James took his place alongside the other officers. A small team of mechanics and riggers stood with Corporal Evans in the lee of

Ladley's BE2, still bearing the bullet marks of the fighting from the previous day.

"For the benefit of the tardy Mr. Caulfield, I shall take the unusual step of repeating myself," said Ladley.

"Corps has informed me that we will shortly have two new additions to the flight, with the promise of more to follow. Both are pilots," he said, looking down at the clipboard he was holding. "Messrs. Brooks and Pearson. Apparently both requested transfer to this flight from their current positions as instructors, which says something for their courage if not their intelligence."

James, who had not received a letter from Elliot for some weeks, was momentarily elated, until he considered that it could well be another Pearson. He raised his hand.

"It is one thing to be late, Mr. Caulfield, but quite another to disturb the flow of my sparkling rhetoric with questions," said Ladley. "What is it?"

"Erm, would that be a Mr. Elliot Pearson, Sir?" James asked.

Ladley consulted his clipboard again. "Yes, do you know the fellow?"

"Yes, Sir. We were at school together," said James with a broad smile.

"God help us," said Ladley. "Another paladin of Rugby to shame us old stalwarts," he said, to the titters of the NCOs huddled in the shadow of the plane.

"Next," continued Ladley, "Corps has finally accepted that we are not suffering from some kind of collective delusion and has agreed that it is likely the Hun has found a way to mount a machine gun to the side of the Albatross. It is going to be some months until the Vickers's FB5 is ready for use in France, so, in order to give us some semblance of a chance in the air, they have agreed that we may experiment with solutions of our own."

Waving an arm at the officers, he said, "As you lot are gentlemen, I don't expect you to understand the slightest thing about how your aircrafts actually work, so I have invited Corporal Evans and his team to suggest some options, which you, Mr. Caulfield, and you, Mr. Cooper, will then test for us. You will be excused patrols during the testing period, and I, with the two new pilots, will substitute for you. Corporal Jones."

Jones saluted and walked over to Captain Ladley's side. He was covered in engine oil, as usual, and his unruly brown hair stuck up in clumps at the side of his head. He looked more like a miner than a soldier.

"Thank you, Sir. Me and the lads have been talking this through, and we're not sure whether it can be done," he said in his distinctive musical lilt. "The Lewis Gun is heavy, Sir, and the BE2 is not very robust. If we mount it on the side of the plane, then there will be yaw in the air towards the side it is mounted."

"So mount two guns man, or use ballast" said Ladley. "It's just like a man carrying a heavy bag. You overbalance with one bag, but with two, equally weighted, you remain on your feet. Simple."

Jones shook his head. "Won't do, Sir," he said with an air of regret. "The frame wouldn't take two guns. It's much too lightweight. Even if it didn't actually crush the frame, I doubt that the plane could take off."

"So we have to wait for the FB5 then?" said Ladley, in an exasperated tone.

"Perhaps not, Sir," smiled Evans. "Obviously, we can't mount the gun on the nose, because the firing line would cut the propeller to pieces. That leaves one spot, on the top wing. We have done some testing on Mr. Ladley's BE2 here, and we think the wings would take the weight, but only if there is no observer in the plane."

"I say, that's a bit thick!" interrupted Henderson.

"It is an experiment, Mr. Henderson, nothing more at this stage," admonished Ladley before indicating to Jones that he should continue.

"If the wings take the weight and the gun stays steady, the pilot would need some sort of remote firing mechanism from his seat at the back of the plane," said Evans, pointing at the distance between the wing and the pilot bay. "The only way that could be done quickly would be to rig up a wire to the trigger of the gun, which the pilot could then pull when needed."

"What about reloading?" said James.

"You can't, Sir," said Evans ruefully. "Same if the gun jams. You can't repair it or reload when in the air, so effectively you'll only have one magazine."

"Better than nothing, I suppose," said Cooper.

"Indeed," said Ladley. "Mount the gun, Evans. We begin testing in the morning."

The plane limped off the ground into overcast skies. The stick was fully back, but the rate of climb was abysmal, significantly reduced from the BE2's underwhelming best and barely giving enough altitude to clear the trees at the edge of the airfield. It was slower too, and the engine whined with the extra weight of the gun.

It took nearly twenty minutes, in a slow circling climb, to get to a height of a thousand feet, and James calculated that a fighting height of seven to eight thousand feet would be impossible to attain before the fuel began to run out. Worse, the handling was seriously impaired. Turns took longer to execute, and all but the most basic manoeuvrability was lost.

Sighing, James levelled off within sight of the airfield, where he knew Cooper, Ladley, and Corporal Evans were observing the painstaking flight through binoculars. He delved around the confines of the pilot bay and retrieved a loop of wire hanging down somewhere by his knees. The wire ran through a series of retainer pins, along the external edge of the fuselage, up the wing struts, then to the firing pin of the machine gun itself. The whole setup looked ramshackle, lacking in precision, and prone to any number of problems.

He pulled the wire sharply, and it bit into the leather finger of his flying glove. Nothing happened initially, but then an angry burst of bullets spewed out of the nozzle of the gun. The plane recoiled from the bullets, and the nose began to drop. He immediately released the wire, and the gun silenced, but it was some seconds before he could level off the plane. He noticed that he had dropped at least two hundred feet in height.

He banked and climbed in a tight upward circle, regaining his height and fixing his position above the airfield. This time he straightened the alignment of the wings and then put himself into a slow upward climb before pulling the wire again. The recoil was less pronounced, although he again lost some height, and he was sure he heard something snap in the vicinity of the top wing. Warily standing in the cockpit, he looked over the wings and could see nothing amiss. He pulled the wire again, and this time, the gun just repeatedly clicked. It was clearly jammed, and there was nothing that could be done in the air. James sighed again, banked, and began to descend.

The effect of the small movement was dramatic. The extra weight of the gun pulled the plane downwards much more sharply than normal, and James was forced to pull back on the stick in order to arrest the rate of descent. A straight dive for the ground was out of the question, and he had to make his way back to the airfield in small, incremental hops. Push the nose down, level off, circle round, and then drop again. It took nearly a quarter of an hour to cover a distance that the plane could normally manage in seconds. Faced with an enemy aircraft, he would be a sitting duck.

On the ground, the others shared his despondency. The plan couldn't be made to work with this aircraft. The sole advantage of the BE2 was its inherent stability, and that was impeded by the addition of substantial weight. The risk to the wings was immense, and the crack James had heard proved to be a splintered support strut. The plane was slowed to a point where it was less than half the speed of an Albatross, and the inability to dive or climb at any speed meant that even the most naive of enemy pilots would be able to manoeuvre away from the forward-firing gun before it could do any substantial damage, leaving the BE2 unable to follow. Overall, the gun was more of a danger to the British than it was to the Germans. A shamefaced Evans was instructed by Ladley to remove it and keep thinking about the problem. Until someone somewhere had a better idea, the squadron would remain at the mercy of a superior enemy plane.

Over Saint-Quentin, January 7, 1915

The planes came from the sun just as James and Ladley had completed their reconnaissance and turned for home. There were three of them, and they pounced on the British machines with the slavering ferocity of hounds cornering a fox. There was an explosion of bullets, which tore though the wings of James' plane, leaving tattered holes in the canvas but mercifully missing both him and the engine block. He dived as planned and rolled to imitate a spin. One Albatross, scenting a ruse, peeled away and followed. The other two manoeuvred behind Ladley, trying to get a firing angle for their observers. Elliot, acting as Ladley's observer while Henderson was laid low with a virus, began a desultory fire with a service rifle that threatened little.

Elliot had arrived a month earlier, only a few hours after the news that the other pilot, Brooks, had been lost somewhere on his flight over the channel. In characteristically flamboyant fashion and unaware of the death of his colleague, Elliot had flown low over the airfield, executed a perfect barrel roll, circled, and landed, leaping from his plane like a victorious jockey jumping from a horse. Fortunately for him, Ladley had been on patrol, and it was James who greeted his old friend outside the mess. They swapped news over a series of single malts, and Elliot had given him a clutch of letters from James' parents that he had picked up from the house at Cavendish Square prior to his departure for the front. The letters were a vapid affair, a recitation of small town society life in the colonies, with a pointed absence of any news of any political import. Godfrey, who had, unusually, deigned to write personally, exhorted James to secure a transfer to Britain and join him in a new venture to produce a viable parachute for sale to the Allied air forces, presumably in his spare time. Sylvia was slightly more expressive, hoping for James' safe return, the speedy end of the conflict, and encouraging James to mend fences with his father. She also explained that she and her husband would take up residence in London again in February. James had put the letters away in the wardrobe in his quarters and resolved to write when duty allowed. Somehow, he had yet to get around to it.

Life since Elliot's arrival had been a strange mixture of pleasant social routine and nightmare. At times, ambling through the streets of Amiens or drinking in the mess, it was possible to almost entirely forget the war and to imagine a return to the pleasant summer days spent in Weybridge the previous year. Flying, when discussed over a convivial pastis or in the quiet moments in front of the fire in the officers' mess, became a joy again, a shared bond between two old friends. On alert at the base though, or over the lines, the tension flooded back, and James' sleep was routinely haunted by the burnt and blackened faces of Moore and Paget-Stanley. Fire was the great fear, and James found that he was acutely conscious of even the slightest mechanical fault in his plane. He had been berated twice by Ladley for turning back too quickly from patrol before his plane was sufficiently damaged to warrant a landing.

Elliot, on the other hand, changed in the air. The gentle, amusing redhead from their schooldays had mutated into an implacable zealot. His interest in the politics of the war was negligible. He existed only to fly and to hunt, and he routinely pursued better-armed German aircraft, taking potshots with his rifle and pistol, oblivious to the dangers of returned machine-gun fire. Initially, James had thought that this was because Elliot had yet to see the horror of a downed machine, but he was quickly disabused of this notion. He had trained over thirty young pilots in his months at the RFC training school, and four of them had crashed and burned to death. Instead, he argued, his own crash at Weybridge had given him a strong sense of fate. Like the infantryman who believed that there existed a bullet reserved for him, Elliot felt the same. If he was reckless, it was because he believed that this was not his time to die. James wished he had something like the same sense of invulnerability, but he was reticent to discuss this with his friend, lest he take from it some intimation of cowardice.

Ladley, after some initial reservations about the urbane young man, quickly realised that he was an excellent flyer. Less intuitive than James, perhaps, but with a level of practical application to detail that was missing in the other officers. In his spare time, Elliot could be found helping the mechanics in the hangar, tinkering with his own plane, and dreaming up ways by which the power ratio could be upped, to get the maximum possible from the flimsy BE2. Unlike the other officers, he actually understood the plane he flew, something that caused consternation amongst the mechanics that held to the deferential view that gentlemen should not get their hands dirty. The other officers indulged the curious young man, equally puzzled by his mechanical gusto and impressed by his application in the air. In the mess, he was a popular figure, and if he sometimes alienated Cooper with his refusal to join in protracted debates on the conduct of the war, his easy charm and dignity more than compensated for it.

In the weeks since Elliot's arrival, the war had settled into an uneasy stalemate. Both sides had consolidated their positions in an ever-growing series of trench works and fortifications. The German plan to flank the Allied army to the north had been finally turned back, at great cost to the British and French armies, and there was already talk of conscription in the British newspapers in order to raise the men needed to plug the growing gaps in the line. For the first time ever, the British army was almost entirely comprised of amateur volunteers. The small, professional nucleus of the British Expeditionary Force had been decimated by a series of bloody battles over small Belgian towns, which had been costly but largely indecisive. Only on the vast plains of the Eastern Front was the war of movement still in progress. There, great battles were the norm, as the Russians severely pressed the Austrians and even got close to Vienna itself. The Germans, concerned about the resolution of their allies, had already begun to move men from the Western Front to the east. Despite this, paralysis prevailed, and the Allies had been unable to force any kind of breakthrough. So stagnant had the fighting been that tavern gossip in Amiens alleged that there had been a kind of informal truce at Christmas between the German and British infantries. Carols had been sung, and an impromptu game of football had apparently taken place. It was rumour, nothing more than that, but it was symptomatic of a sense that the war had ground to a halt. Men clung to their dugouts, kept their heads down, and hoped that the days of the major offensives were behind them. A negotiated peace became a very real possibility.

In the air, the situation was increasingly hostile but equally inconclusive. The BE2s of the RFC, supported by the superior Nieuports and Farmans of the French, were not a match for the Albatross, but they were much more numerous. Although casualties continued at a slow trickle on both sides, so far neither had been able to gain any tangible advantage. Curiously, the addition of a machine gun to the Albatross, which had so worried Ladley and had the potential to be a decisive game changer, seemed to be a product of local innovation rather than an overall strategic development. Only in some sectors were the machine-gun-enabled planes seen, which rather lessened the urgency of either the French or the British factories to react. Despite the complaints of the squadron commanders, the lethargy of Farnborough continued. The long-promised FB5 was still not in action, and despite optimistic parliamentary talk of new fighting machines, the flyers in France continued to conduct their war in fragile reconnaissance machines ill suited for combat. The only real advance was the promise of photographic equipment to speed the process of reconnaissance patrols, but even this much-trumpeted innovation was yet to arrive. The make do and mend philosophy of the War Ministry and the RFC factory was a source of considerable complaint in the officers' mess at Flight B. The sector between Amiens and Saint Quentin had more than its fair share of Albatrosses carrying side-mounted machine guns.

James faced one now. The German plane was manoeuvring behind him, and he craned his neck to watch it wavering from side to side, trying to present a broadside to the British plane and bring his machine gun into play. The trick, as James had learned quickly, was to anticipate the movement of the enemy plane as closely as possible, always aiming to keep directly in front of or behind it. That equalised the fight, as both observers were reduced to taking pot shots with side arms, which required prodigious skill or incredible luck to inflict any damage. He weaved now, flying whilst looking backwards and waving his pistol in the vague direction of the pursuing plane. Flying without an observer, he was at a serious disadvantage, and he contemplated a steep dive in the direction of the British lines in the hope that the German would refuse to follow him. Above, he could hear the rattle of a machine gun and realised that Ladley and Elliot were being engaged, possibly by both planes. Abandoning them now would only give them an additional opponent. He had to fight.

He looked down at his instruments. He was flying at around seven thousand feet, but in the watery sunlight of the early winter morning, he could clearly see the snaking lines of German support trenches leading to the front, which he estimated to be two or three miles to the west. Below him, small puffs of pink cloud showed that the German antiaircraft batteries had spotted the planes but at this range were unable to tell friend from foe and were seemingly firing indiscriminately. Making a quick decision, he dived to lose height and was pleased to note that the German plane followed him, the sun glinting off the grey-painted wings that carried the distinctive cross emblem.

James levelled off and listened for the barely audible pop of antiaircraft shells around him. He could hear nothing over the thrum of the engine, and so instead he scanned the vicinity for the telltale spots of pink cloud. He saw a sizeable patch a few hundred feet away on the port side, and he banked towards it, every nerve in his body taut for the sounds of shell fragments hitting the plane. The German, intent on the kill and oblivious to everything but the beguiling temptation of his own machine gun, continued to manoeuvre behind him. James abandoned the game of cat and mouse, straightened, and then cut the engine. The BE2 continued to glide in near-perfect silence, broken only by the sound of the engine approaching to his rear and the occasional pop of a nearby shell. The German, considerably quicker on the straight, caught up with him and shot past on the starboard side, travelling too quickly for the observer, who fired off a machine-gun burst as he shot past, only narrowly missing the nose of James' plane.

He dived again, steeply this time. The motion of the air kick-started the propeller, and the engine rumbled into life. He was counting under his breath, calibrating the seconds it took for gun batteries to fire off another shell. Looking above him, he could see the German some eighty or ninety feet away and around a hundred feet above. The observer was leaning over the side of the plane, balancing a rifle precariously on the mounting of the machine gun and taking aim. He had clearly moved out of the field of fire of the machine gun, and James smiled as he watched the German fire wildly, the bullet passing yards above him. There was a tearing sound and a metallic groan, and James looked down the length of his plane in alarm until he saw what looked like a kite falling at the periphery of his vision. Whooping with sheer joy, he realised it was a wing toppling through the sky. The German plane had been hit by shellfire from its own side. He watched the pilot try to right the plane, but it was impossible with the entirety of one lower wing missing. It wavered in the air, like wheat in the wind, before rolling. As the plane began to spin uncontrollably, the pilot waved once, in silent acknowledgement of the ruse that had killed him. There was no terror in his face, just a long-frozen moment of acceptance. James waved back, but it was already too late.

At the airfield, James sat in a deckchair, wrapped in his flying coat and watching the skies. Bates had brought him a tumbler of warmed whiskey, and he nursed it as he watched, his ears straining for any sound of an approaching engine. He had sat there for two hours now and was still covered in the oil and grime from his early-morning flight.

Elliot and Ladley were missing. Their fuel would have run out at least an hour earlier, possibly more, but James felt that he would know somehow if they were dead. Some sense of the passing of a life, a celestial shadow across his soul. He had never really thought about religion before the war, simply taking for granted that his parents and his school both required regular attendance at church. He realised now that he had not attended a single religious service since he had arrived in France, even though an army chaplain regularly visited the flight. Perhaps religion meant more than passive acceptance of societal obligation? Or, perhaps God was just a long way from France. As he sipped his whiskey, James closed his eyes and prayed.

The telephone rang loudly in the flight office. James leapt out of his chair, spilling the dregs of his whiskey down his trousers, and with a mild curse barged through the wooden door. Sergeant Jackson was on the phone. He looked up as James burst into the room and held a finger to his lips.

"Yes, Sir," said Jackson. "I understand. Thank you, Sir, I will inform the officers."

He placed the receiver back in the cradle and, unmindful of James, slumped into Ladley's chair at the main desk. His normally flushed complexion was pale, and despite the cold there was a prickle of sweat visible on his brow. James had never seen him so crushed. Even when Moore and Paget-Stanley had crashed, he had been unflappable, quietly efficient, and so emotionally detached that James attributed his imperturbability to his own safe billet in the flight office. Now the man was visibly shaken.

"They were seen coming down on our lines, Sir," Jackson said at last.

"Where?" asked James, in a daze.

"To the north, Sir, somewhere near Albért. A forward artillery observer spotted them and telephoned it in to the Corps. The plane was badly damaged and appeared shot up, but there were no flames."

"Thank God for that. They might be safe," said James, without much hope.

"Perhaps, Sir, although the information is that they landed somewhere near the front line." Jackson looked to the window. "It'll be dark soon, Sir. If they are all right, they'll have to spend the night in the trenches."

"Surely we can telephone them? Find a subaltern somewhere that's seen them? Get a report?" asked James.

"I'll try, Sir, but the shelling near the front plays havoc with the communications. We'd have to be lucky."

"Try, Sergeant. It's all we can do for the moment. In the morning, I'll go up with Cooper and Henderson and see what we can find. Find me in the mess or in my quarters if there is any news."

James turned on his heel and stalked out of the office. He took a moment outside, leaning against the doorpost and ignoring the stares of a couple of passing airmen. Lighting a cigarette in shaky hands, he decided to walk around the airfield to clear his head.

The field was quiet, with all the planes in for repair. Some men sat outside their tents on canvas stools, muffled in greatcoats, polishing kit and oiling weapons. Most pretended not to notice his passing, but one or two of the newer men attempted a salute before realising he was uninterested and returning to their tasks. The hangar was busier, with a team of riggers repairing the canvas on the wings of James' BE2. Nearby, the engine of Cooper's plane lay on the floor in pieces, poured over by three mechanics overseen by Corporal Evans. There was something comforting in the industry of the men, and James longed for something to do to occupy his mind and stop himself from dwelling on Elliot and Ladley's fate.

He walked on and was briefly amused to see Sergeant Jackson marshalling a team of airmen to unload a small lorry full of provisions for the mess. He watched as crates of beer were placed, almost reverently, onto a handcart and then whisked away in the direction of the tent city that dominated the land outside the main farm. Beer was virtually an unknown commodity in the officers' mess, where spirits and wines were the tipples of choice, so these provisions were being taken to the sergeants' mess, which was housed in a tent at the extreme end of the airfield, as far from the officers as feasible. The corporals, too, had their own mess next door to the sergeants. The men shared a common eating tent, where alcohol was a rarity. James idly wondered if the young airman pushing the handcart would be tempted to trouser a couple of bottles from the open crates before he got to the mess area. *Good luck to him if he did*, thought James. Without alcohol, life at the front would be unbearable.

James meandered around the rest of the field, conducting a casual inspection as he did so. The sentry at the wooden entrance barrier looked bored and cold but snapped to attention as James approached, taking on a veneer of martial alertness. The twelve men of the airfield guard were drilling under the supervision of a new sergeant, a man he was yet to meet and who, he recalled, had recently been transferred from the regular army. He had the regulation moustache and the ramrod military bearing of a man used to the parade ground. The guards sweated and wheezed with the unusually rigorous drill, even in the cold of the January day. James resolved to have a quiet word with Jackson to ask him to tell the new man that the RFC did not have the same expectations with regard to the metronomic routines of the parade ground as was common in the infantry. Men here were expected to think on their feet, not just unconsciously respond to orders. Drill was important for men who were expected to go over the top at a moment's notice, but less so for those whose job it was to keep ramshackle airplanes in the skies. James was tempted to intervene on the spot, but to do so would be to undermine the conventions of rank and risk alienating the new sergeant. As he passed, the guards halted and snapped off a collective salute under the watchful eye of the new man.

James returned the salute laconically and headed back to the relative warmth of the farmhouse.

As he took the stairs to his room, he realised how little he knew of the lives of the men on the base. They lived completely separately from the officers, engaged in a mystifying range of different technical tasks and entirely marshalled by the handful of sergeants, led by the redoubtable Jackson. He had talked to very few of them, with the exception of most of the NCOs and one or two of the better mechanics and riggers, but those conversations had been concerned with repairs to his plane or the brief exchange of words that comprised the starting litany. James wondered if any of them actually knew anything about him. Was he thought of as just another privileged boy who looked down on others? Would they care if he came back from patrol? Did they resent being ordered to scrub the latrines by a man half their age? He wondered why he had never thought like this before, and then realised it was simply because he had never lived in such proximity to people of different backgrounds. Certainly, there had always been servants and shopkeepers, but they were peripheral to his life. He had taken them for granted and ignored them in the same way that one might a familiar piece of furniture. He realised that they were people too, that they must have hopes, aspirations, and desires in the same way that he did. For the first time in his life, he realised they probably hated him. If he were to die, it wouldn't matter, as he would soon be replaced by another faceless product of a good school. For some reason, this thought made him despair.

Reaching his room, he threw off his coat, lay down on the lumpy bed, and called to Davies, the elderly batman that acted as his manservant in the field. The old man came shambling down the corridor from the laundry room, holding a half-polished army boot in his right hand.

"Good afternoon, Sir," said Davies, straightening his bent back and saluting. "How can I help you?"

"You can take my coat to dry please, Davies, but sit down a moment first," said James.

Davies looked worried, but sat down on the only chair, a rickety homemade wooden affair, which was pushed up hard against the window, the better to watch the planes. He turned it around, sat down rigidly, and faced James.

"Have I done something wrong, Sir?" he asked nervously.

"Not at all," said James, sitting up on the bed. "Everything is fine. I just wanted to talk to you."

"Yes, Sir," said Davies nervously, his tired eyes looking suspiciously at James.

"Why did you join up, Davies?" asked James. "I mean, surely you didn't need to at your age?"

"Because the king called, Sir," said Davies amiably. "I mean not himself, obviously, but I read in the paper that everyone was needed. We can't have the Hun having it all their own way, can we, Sir?"

"No, that would never do." James smiled. Davies gave him a frozen grin and looked pointedly at the door.

"What did you do in peacetime, Davies?" asked James, failing to notice the older man's discomfort.

"Well, my dad was a farrier, Sir, with his own place, and I was an apprentice as a younger lad for a while, but then I joined the army. Never really known anything else," said Davies warily.

"When did you leave the army?" asked James.

"After the last lot, Sir, in Africa, ten or twelve year ago now." He made as if to rise until James, looking into the middle distance, started to speak again. The old man sat down abruptly and composed his face in an approximation of patience.

"So what did you do in the meantime, Davies?" enquired James in a neutral tone.

"Nothing dodgy, Sir," said Davies testily. "I worked in a pub for a bit until my back started giving me grief, then I did all sorts. Hop picking, selling matches, whatever I could find, Sir."

James realised that he had embarrassed the man and tried, ineffectually, to apologise. "I'm sorry, Davies, I didn't mean to imply, erm … that is to say. No matter. That'll be all."

Davies leapt to his feet like a man half his age, picked up James' coat, saluted, and walked to the door with visible relief. He stopped and turned as he got into the corridor.

"Is everything all right, sir?" he asked sympathetically.

"I'm not sure, Davies, but there's not a lot either of us can do about it at the moment," replied James, settling back on the bed.

So much for building rapport with the ranks, thought James. *It was as Godfrey had always believed. They want us to keep to our place and not interfere in their world.* Suddenly James felt very lonely.

He had been asleep for around an hour when he heard the familiar drone of an engine over the airfield. He leapt from the bed and ran to the window. The view was only partial, and the window frame was nailed shut, so he threw on an RFC jacket over his vest, put on his gun belt, and ran down the stairs to the field.

Cooper was already there, half-dressed in vest and trousers and drinking something from a battered tin mug, presumably tea. Henderson was sat in the deckchair that James had abandoned, still looking peaky from his recent infection and smoking in between bouts of coughing. Jackson joined them, panting from the short run from the flight office, and some of the mechanics lingered at the edge of the hangar. All of them craned their necks, with hands shielding their eyes, and looked for the first sign of a BE2 coming in low over the trees.

The nose of a plane poked out above the tree line at a height of around two hundred feet, and James gave a start, pointed, and shouted.

"It's them. They're back!"

Something was wrong though. The plane was grey, moving all too quickly and not dipping its nose to land. For an absurd moment, he wondered why Ladley had repainted the plane, then he heard Cooper scream in his ear, "Sound the alarm! It's German!"

Jackson ran to the alarm bell and began to ring it with the fury of a demented campanologist at Christmas. Cooper was past him and shouting "Guard to me" as men rushed from tents, grabbing weapons and aiming upwards at the plane. Henderson had rushed to the machine gun, swearing furiously as he realised that it wasn't loaded. James ran to help him, shouting for ammunition. All around was chaos as men ran all over the field, unsure whether to seek cover or to stand and fire at the aircraft.

Mercifully, the plane didn't have a machine gun. Instead, James could see the observer leaning over the side of the craft, carefully measuring the ground as if intently looking for something in particular. They were so close that he could see that the man had pushed his flight goggles back onto his head and that his face was covered in black spots of oil. It flew level over them, circled, and then came back for a second pass.

The ammunition had arrived now, and James helped Henderson thread the roll of bullets into the machine gun. Henderson immediately began to fire upwards, and tracers arced overhead. At the same time, dozens of men, organised by Cooper into something resembling a line of infantry, began to fire their rifles. The plane wavered overhead, although there seemed to be no visible damage. James drew his own revolver and, standing to the side of the sandbagged machine gun nest, began to blaze away at the quickly moving target.

Henderson was getting closer now, and the pilot was obviously spooked. He waved angrily at his observer, who leaned over the side and dropped something. James saw a flat metallic disk fall from the aircraft, spinning in the air as the plane immediately started to climb away, machine-gun bullets trailing in its wake. A ragged cheer erupted from the men, then the disk hit the ground. There was a flash of light, and then everything went black.

James woke in the darkness, and for a moment he thought he was either dead or blind. He remembered the flash of the explosion and then nothing. He realised he was lying on something soft, and, feeling with his fingers, he concluded that it was a bed. Not the lumpy camp bed at the airfield, but somewhere else. He gave himself a few moments to accustom himself to the gloom, but it did no good. He sat up and felt a wave of nausea rush up from his stomach. He swallowed hard to hold back the vomit that filled his mouth before slumping back to a prone position.

He tried to sense if he was injured, but his body felt numbed. Morphine perhaps, he thought. He moved his hands to his head, examining his face for wounds or burns. He could find neither, although there was a padded bandage on the back of his head, and his fingers came away wet when he touched it. He ran his fingers down his body and was surprised to find that he seemed to be wearing pyjamas. He touched his ribs and cried out in sudden pain, although there was no audible sound. Not morphine then, just shock. He forced himself to continue and found that the entire left side of his chest was in agony. His hips and legs seemed fine, and he waggled his foot experimentally. Although he could see nothing, his feet felt like they were moving normally.

There was a burst of light some yards from the bed, and he winced as it spread into the room. A young woman carrying an oil lamp followed in its wake.

She was wearing a near-floor-length apron, a white hat that covered pinned hair, and a waist-length blue cape across her shoulders. She shone the lamp at the bed, and James cringed away from it, rolling onto his side and recoiling at the sudden agonising pain from his ribs. The woman looked down on him from above, and he could see the shape of her face in the orange glow of the lamp. She was in her mid-twenties, with sharp, intelligent features slightly marred by a long, aquiline nose. Tight brown curls peaked out from under her hat, and she looked at James with large blue eyes, more analytical than sensuous. James found her attractive and realised two things simultaneously: she was a nurse, and he knew her from somewhere.

She opened her mouth as if speaking, but no words came out. She continued for a few moments, with her mouth opening and closing like a fish, before frowning and looking down at James. She tried speaking again, stopped, and pointed a finger at her right ear, accompanying the gesture with an endearingly quizzical look. James realised that he must be deaf, and he attempted a smile as he nodded a reply. The nurse returned the smile, set down the lamp on a wooden bedside table, and retreated out of the room into the brightly lit corridor. James shuffled painfully up on his pillows and looked around the room. The single room was painted plain white, with a highly polished wooden floor and a small window set near the ceiling on the wall behind his head. It contained just the bed, the small cabinet, and a few poorly executed pictures of saints and the Virgin Mary, scattered haphazardly in frames on the wall. The room resembled a monastic cell, and the tendrils of light from the lamp that snaked up the walls revealed ancient, uneven stonework that had been poorly whitewashed.

The nurse returned, carrying a pad and the nub of a pencil. She stood in the shadow of the lamp, licked the end of the pencil, and began to write in a rapid, flowing hand. She handed James the pad, and he read, "You are in the field hospital at Dreuil les Amiens monastery. I am Sister Edith and will be looking after you. You have broken ribs from the accident and have been unconscious for two days. It's now 4:00 a.m. and you should sleep. The blast seems to have deafened you, but that should pass quickly. Try to rest, and call for me if you need anything. Any questions?" The words were written in a florid, spidery hand that verged on being over-elaborate. James thought the script curiously beautiful, despite the mundane nature of the words.

James looked at Edith, who was standing with her head cocked to one side, smiling gently.

"Are you English?" he blurted out, and although he could feel the faint vibration of the words in the back of his throat, he was disconcerted to find that he couldn't hear himself.

Edith smiled and nodded in an exaggerated way as if communicating with an idiot child.

"Was anyone else on the base hurt?" he asked, speaking slowly and enunciating carefully, conscious that his words might not have their usual clarity.

Edith didn't seem to have any trouble interpreting his speech though. She took back the pad from James and quickly scribbled a note. It read: "I don't know. If they were, they weren't brought here." James sighed and settled back into his pillow. Sensing that the questions were at an end for the moment, Edith pointed at the door and mimed leaving the room. James nodded in acceptance, faintly saddened that she had to go so soon. She picked up the lamp and made her way out, but as she reached the door, she turned back as if remembering something, dashed to the pad, wrote something more, and then handed it to James. The note read: "You had a visitor earlier when you were asleep. He'll come back in the morning." James nodded again, and Edith went out to the corridor, gave a small wave, and gently closed the door behind her as she went through.

Plunged back into darkness, James thought about why Edith seemed familiar to him. He mentally scrolled through the few women he was acquainted with from London society and couldn't place either the face or the name. He was sure he would recall her distinctively sharp features had he encountered them across the dinner table or at a ball. For some reason, he vaguely associated her with Rugby. Perhaps she was the sister of a friend or the daughter of a master? Idly, he thought about speech days at school and sifted through his assorted mental snapshots of young women in hats and carrying parasols, standing on the close watching the end-of-term cricket match. Nothing seemed to fit.

Irritated, he lay back on the bed and tried to compose his thoughts. He had been in the hospital for two days. Presumably, he had been taken there by one of the transports from the base. That required organisation, which implied that at least one of the officers on the base had survived the explosion. Henderson had been closest to him but had been protected by the sandbags of the machine gun emplacement. Logic would suggest that he was all right. Cooper had been in the middle of the airfield, some distance away, so, in all likelihood, he wouldn't have been in any danger. James recalled that some of the men had been fairly close to him, firing at the aircraft as the bomb dropped. Davies had been one of them, and he hoped that the old man was all right. Perhaps, mused James, it was Davies who had come to visit him? It couldn't have been Henderson or Cooper, as they were so short of flyers at the base that they couldn't have been spared. James didn't have any friends amongst the other ranks, so he was puzzled as to whom it could be. Oh well. It was a mystery that would wait until morning.

He was just dropping off to sleep, thinking about the fate of Elliot and Ladley, when his subconscious mind offered up the image he had been seeking moments earlier. She had been singing a hymn in the rain of an Oxford Street afternoon. She had led the small meeting of woman that he had watched on his return from Rugby two years earlier. She was a suffragette.

Morning brought a spear of sunlight through the uncurtained window of the room, which woke James and gave him an immediate headache. He found that his hearing had marginally improved overnight, and that he could discern muffled sounds from outside, as if heard from the bottom of a well. A male orderly brought him a cup of tea and a slice of dry, white toast, and wordlessly offered him the use of a bedpan, which James refused.

As he munched on the toast, he realised he was ravenous, having not eaten for at least forty-eight hours. He finished eating and quickly grew bored, staring mindlessly at the rough, white walls and the tawdry pictures of medieval saints. His mind wandered to his parents. They must be back in London by now, and he thought regretfully of the nature of his parting with his father. Lying in a hospital bed lent an added poignancy to Godfrey's final words, and for the first time James thought that it really was possible that he wouldn't see the old man again. At the time, James had believed himself impervious to the risks of the war. He wasn't going to be slogging through mud and charging into machine-gun fire. He had thought the risk containable, confined mainly to the normal problems of flying an aircraft. At worst, he had foreseen a knightly duel, a contest of wills between gentleman aviators, not the appalling carnage of machine guns and bombs. He realised now that Godfrey had been right. Nobody was immune to the ravages of war, not even those flying above the battlefield. With sudden, grim certainty, he knew that he had volunteered for death and that it would likely come with pain and fire. He had dismissed Godfrey's warnings as cowardice, but he now understood that his father had merely been trying to protect his son from his own youthful arrogance. If the end were to come, he wanted the chance to explain to his father that he understood the gesture for what it was. He needed to acknowledge the mistake that had led him to a hospital bed and the death of his friends. There was no turning back now, but at the least he should be able to face his end without the sense that he despised his father for his protective instinct. He resolved to write.

He took up the pad that Nurse Edith had left by his bedside and began to compose a letter. The words did not flow as he would have liked, and he found that language could not adequately convey his own sense of contrition. The first draft seemed like the ramblings of a frightened young boy, and he angrily balled it up and threw it onto the wooden floor. The second was better, but it seemed too cavalier, too martial—a young man gallantly defying the odds without fear, rather than a pragmatist coming to terms with the appalling risks he faced. He tore that up too, and then, in a moment of epiphany, he simply decided to be honest. He wrote:

"Dear Mother and Father,

"I have been slightly wounded in a German attack on our base but will quickly recover. I may be entitled to some brief home leave to recuperate, and if that is a possibility, I would like to take the opportunity to visit you. I am sorry I have not been in contact with you for some time and have failed to respond to your letters. As you can probably imagine, life is rather hectic over here, but that is really little more than an excuse. The truth is that I did not know what to say to you, as my home world seems so far removed from the life I live here. I do miss you both, and I truly regret the manner of my departure. I should have listened to Father, but perhaps all of us sometimes have cause to regret the impetuosity of youth. I hope this finds you well, and I hope to see you soon."

Written down, the simple words had a cathartic clarity. He felt cleansed somehow, as he imagined a Catholic might feel after the confessional. He would post it, hope to get some leave, and then build the bridges he needed to. Perhaps then he might be able to face the fear that seemed to grip him. When his maternal grandfather had passed away during James' childhood, his mother had taken comfort from the fact that his affairs were in order. The old man had suffered from a prolonged illness but had taken the time to make a comprehensive will and to write long letters of farewell to his children, full of advice and the sentiment that was usually denied men of his era. Perhaps, mused James, the time was right to set his own affairs in order, to face the reality of his own mortality, and to try to assure the comfort of those he would leave behind. Maybe it was only with the certainty that nothing remained to be resolved that a man could face death with fortitude.

He sensed rather than heard a knock at the door, and Nurse Edith bustled into the room, precariously balancing a tray in one hand. She nodded at him as she set the tray down, and James saw that it carried a selection of nondescript white pills, a steaming mug of muddy brown tea, and a curling sandwich. She reached for the pad, but James put a hand out to stop her, and, for a moment, his fingers brushed the back of her hand. He lingered too long, and she snatched her hand back, her face registering a frisson of anger before it composed itself into a professional mask.

"I'm sorry," said James, his voice sounding like an echo off a cave wall to his damaged ears. "I didn't mean to startle you. It's just that I can hear a little better. If you speak loudly, I'm sure I'll be able to understand." He smiled reassuringly but was mortified that she might think he had behaved inappropriately.

To his pleasure, she relented slightly and gave him a brief smile. With the same exaggerated manner she had deployed the previous day, she held his gaze and enunciated each word slowly and carefully like an English traveller talking to a particularly belligerent foreign waiter.

"These are your medications, please take them now. They are just for the pain, as I'm afraid the doctor feels that we can't do anything for your ribs except prescribe rest. If your hearing is returning, that is a very good sign. You should find that it normalises over the next day or two. The doctor will be in later today, and should your visitor return I'll show him in. I'm afraid you are confined to bed for at least forty-eight hours, but after that you may walk in the grounds of the monastery or visit the recreation room."

James caught around half the words, but understood enough to reach out a hand for the painkillers, and he swallowed the selection of pills with a sip of scolding hot tea. He spluttered slightly, and Edith laughed. The sound was muffled to James, but it was still beautifully melodic, like a tinkling piano scale, high on the treble clef. He realised that he would like to make this woman laugh again, even if in doing so he made himself look foolish.

He grinned and wiped dribbles of tea off his mouth with the back of his hand.

"You know," he said. "I've seen you before."

Edith looked suspicious, arched an eyebrow, and said loudly, "Oh? And where was that?"

"I watched you lead a suffragette meeting in Oxford Street a couple of years ago. I live nearby, you see, and I was rather impressed with your bravery, not to mention your singing voice."

"Bravery is not the exclusive preserve of men, you know," she scowled briefly before her face relaxed and she smiled. "Anymore than singing is."

James chuckled and gasped at the stabbing pain in his ribs. He desperately wanted to maintain the conversation, but he felt shorn of his usual eloquence. For some reason, the woman made him feel like a little boy trying to impress his nanny.

"It's probably best that I don't laugh," he said weakly. "That hurt."

"Captain Samuels, the duty doctor here, usually says that laughter is the best medicine, but in your case that might not be true," she smiled again. "Anyway, how is the patient this morning? Comfortable?"

"I'm better for seeing you," said James and immediately regretted it as a dark cloud of irritation once again passed over her face. "That is to say," he continued quickly, "that I'm a bit sore but otherwise all right. My hearing is getting better by the hour, and it's a joy to sleep in a bed that doesn't feel like someone has stuffed a football under the mattress."

"Good," said Edith briskly. "In that case, I'll leave you to your food. Its not the Ritz, but the charcuterie nearby gives us some decent cuts of ham. Bon appétit."

"Hang on," said James desperately. "Can I ask you a question?"

Edith paused halfway to the door. "You may, although I do have other patients to see."

"How did you come to be here? As a nurse, I mean? It seems an unlikely place to find a suffragette."

Edith snorted in derision. "Hardly—there are thousands of us out here now. I was a nurse in peacetime, and the army needs nurses, so I volunteered. If you men insist on shooting at each other, then someone has to pick up the pieces. Anyway, surely you read that the suffragettes have suspended campaigning until the peace is won? What else should a woman of conscience do when her country is at war?"

James, who vaguely recalled reading something of the sort in one of the old newspapers that periodically turned up in the mess, blushed. "I'm very sorry, I thought you were pacifists, like the Quakers," he said lamely.

Edith walked the few steps back to the bed and her face took on a mildly contemptuous look that reminded James of his Latin master at school when he had made a particularly stupid mistake.

"You really don't read much, do you?" she said scornfully. "The suffragettes aren't a religious sect, however people may paint us. We are people first and foremost and, like all people, have our disagreements. Some people, like Sylvia Pankhurst, are pacifists, and they argued vocally that we should denounce the war. They lost the debate, though, and left the movement when the leadership endorsed the war. Have you heard of the white feather campaign?"

James nodded, remembering Elliot telling him of women handing out white feathers to men in the street who were not in uniform, as a sign of their cowardice.

"I've not seen it myself. I've been here too long," he replied. "But some of the chaps in the mess have told me about it."

"Well," said Edith patiently, "that's a suffragette campaign. We feel that the best way to achieve our aims is to show you men that we can do the everyday things just as well as you, while you are off fighting the war. We can drive, nurse, make armaments, and mine coal. We can do anything you can. If we demonstrate to you that we are your equals in every way, when the peace comes you will have to recognise that simple fact and stop treating us like chattels to be bought and sold. It is in our best interests that the war be won quickly, and hence why we encourage men to stop dallying at home and come over here and fight for the victory. I'm a long way from a pacifist, as much as I sincerely regret all of the suffering."

She paused, her face flushed and her eyes angry. James felt very small in the face of her passion and wished he could stand up instead of lying prone.

"I support votes for women," he said, trying to muster some semblance of dignity.

"Really?" said Edith, her face a picture of utter contempt. "I'm sure we are all very grateful to you."

She turned away and strode out, slamming the door as she did so.

"Well, that might have gone better," said James, with a wistful smile. Despite feeling battered and mentally bruised by the encounter, he realised that an angry Edith was infinitely better than no Edith at all.

James ate sparingly and then spent an uncomfortable couple of hours trying to sleep. He was prevented from doing so by the nagging suspicion that he had said something deeply wrong, which had resulted in Edith's apparent anger. Try as he might, he couldn't see where he had been at fault. Growing up with his mother, Sylvia, he was used to forthright women, although, he admitted to himself, he had always attributed her outspoken nature to her nationality rather than her gender. Nevertheless, he had never truly believed in the absolute male hegemony peddled as truth by most politicians and religious leaders and had always thought that girls were every bit as intellectually capable as boys. Surely that counted for something, he thought resentfully.

The worst thing was that Edith had acutely made him feel his own ignorance. The localised air war had become all-consuming, and he barely had a concept of what was happening twenty or thirty miles away, never mind in the wider war. His awareness of the situation in England had been gleaned from snatched conversations with new arrivals from home and from the occasional perusal of an out-of-date newspaper or magazine. Even his knowledge of aeronautics had deteriorated badly. At home, he had been a regular subscriber to *Flight* magazine, but at the front the only available copies were those shipped from home. They were usually weeks or months out of date, and he had quickly realised that they bore absolutely no reflection to the true state of the war in the air. The last editorial he had read had focused on the ongoing debate about the use of a parachute in warplanes, and the venerable editor had predictably concluded that they were bad for morale. Worse, he had argued that competent pilots would almost always be able to safely down an aircraft in the event of an engine failure, conveniently ignoring the fact that most damage to an aircraft resulted directly from the actions of the enemy. James had thrown it away in disgust and since then had confined his reading to the odd battered copy of penny dreadful novels that seemed to accumulate in the darker corners of the mess.

It was possible, thought James, that people at home just didn't realise the reality of the war in France. The newspapers he had seen portrayed a picture of stoic British soldiers gamely facing the hazards of modern warfare. The papers presented very little coverage of living conditions in the trenches, and small actions were analysed in far greater detail than they merited. It was almost as if there wasn't a public awareness of the almost total paralysis of the war on the ground. The activities of the Royal Flying Corps were almost completely ignored, save as an adjunct to jingoistic accounts of small-scale infantry actions. What accounts there had been of the war in the air tended to emphasise the majesty of flight rather than the grim realities of grappling with the enemy in poorly equipped, flimsy machines almost totally unsuited for warfare.

And yet, if the people at home were ignorant, then their ambivalence was mirrored by the men of the army in France. There simply wasn't an appetite for general, impersonalised news from home, possibly because it prompted feelings of homesickness. James had only the vaguest notion of the role of women in the war, assuming blindly that things were simply going on as normal. Now that he thought about it, he supposed that somebody had to take the places of the hundreds of thousands of British men that now found themselves in France. As a volunteer army, there was some inevitable grumbling about "shirkers" who stayed at home taking plum jobs and profiteering from the actions of others, but there had been very little discussion of the role of women. The casualty rate had been astounding in the early months of the war, and doubtless some of those men were increasingly being pressured to join up, either by the scathing looks of their friends and family or by the suffragettes with their white feathers. When they had gone, who else would society turn to but the untapped labour force? Women must be taking on some of the burden, and perhaps that explained Edith's anger. It wasn't any perceived misogyny that she was reacting to, but his abject ignorance of her cause and the importance of the role that those of her gender had in the conflict.

James sighed and gave up the pretence of trying to sleep. He sat up carefully and listened to the sounds coming from the window. They were sharper now, less muffled, and he felt better for that, as if emerging slowly from a cocoon. He was startled to hear, rather than feel, a knock on the door. Before he could say anything, it flew open, and Edith's head popped into view.

"Your visitor is here," she said, with the same slow precision. She ducked quickly out of sight, and through the door walked an officer in the uniform of a lieutenant of the RFC.

"Hallo, old chap," said a smiling Elliot.

James was momentarily incredulous. He started off the bed, felt a fiery agony in his chest, and slumped back against his pillows, groaning in agony.

"Don't get up!" said Elliot, walking across the room and perching on the small side unit. He put a hand on James' shoulder and scrutinised him carefully.

"Well, I must say, it's rather a joy to be visiting you in the hospital, rather than the other way round," he drawled, taking out a cigarette and lighting it. He offered the packet to James, who refused with a wave of the hand.

"I thought you were dead," said James, tears welling up in his eyes.

"Cease your unmanly blubbing. It seems that despite the apparent fragility of my pale, poetical soul, I am rather harder to kill than might be thought," said Elliot, smiling. Looking at him closely, James thought he looked well. There were a few scratches on his face, but no sign of any serious injury. He looked perfectly relaxed, and there was colour in his freckled cheeks. Even his unruly red hair had been combed, and he looked every inch the dashing young officer, if on the short side. Only his eyes hinted at whatever torments he had gone through. They looked haunted, like the eyes of a man who had seen things that he thought only existed in nightmares.

"What happened to you?" asked James breathlessly. "Jackson said you and Ladley had gone down over the trenches."

"You wound me, old friend," said Elliot, with a hint of his old mischief. "Surely, I deserve a little small talk, a careful verbal dance to avoid the elephant in the room?" He smiled. "No, I can see it is not to be. You are like a bloodhound, old chap, and I'm happy to oblige you, but are you sure you are quite well enough?"

"I'm fine," said James. "Just a few broken ribs and blocked ears. I'll be on my feet in a day or two."

"And back to dear old blighty for a spot of decent tucker and a taste of the good life, no doubt?" said Elliot.

"Possibly," agreed James, "although that would depend on Ladley."

Elliot's face darkened, his good cheer vanishing like the light of a snuffed candle. "I'm afraid it won't, old chap," he said. "Ladley is dead. Cooper has temporary command."

"Oh God, I'm sorry," said James. "How did it happen?"

"No need for sorrow." said Elliot in a subdued tone. "That won't help the old bear now. Perhaps it's best if I tell you from the beginning."

James nodded while Elliot composed himself, crushing his cigarette under his heel and kicking the stub under the bed.

"The last we saw of you was when you went tearing off with that Albatross on your tail. That was a neat piece of flying, by the way. I heard you got the blighter too. Congratulations." Elliot touched his hand to his RFC cap in mock salute. James stifled his impatience and remained silent.

"We had two of the buggers following us," continued Elliot. "Mercifully, only one of them had a machine gun, but we were rather in the soup. One of them kept behind us and took potshots at us with a pistol, while the other tried to manoeuvre around the side." Elliot gesticulated with his hands to show the respective positions of the planes.

"Ladley kept banking, and the chap with the machine gun couldn't get us in his sights, and it went on like that for a few minutes, with me taking pops at the chap behind us whenever there was any hope of doing so without hitting the skipper."

Visualising the plane, James could see the difficulty of shooting backwards from the forward position, over the shoulder of the pilot behind.

"Then Ladley made a mistake. He tried to climb, probably hoping to give me a better angle of fire. In the event, all that happened was that the Albatross with the machine gun was able to climb faster. You know how much faster those things are." Elliot looked at him, and James nodded.

"They got off a burst and raked the wings. One of the struts was almost completely shot through, and there were holes everywhere in the canvas. I had to hold the strut to stop it breaking up, so we lost any chance of being able to fire back, as my hands were full. Sadly, our late captain didn't have your ability to fly and shoot." Elliot smiled weakly at the poor jest.

"We had to dive and risk the wings breaking up, so that's what we did. We banked hard and dived and then kept going until we were only a few hundred feet up. We were somewhere over the German lines, and the Albatross pilots must have thought we had had it, because they left us alone and buggered off to get a schnapps and a bratwurst or whatever foreign muck they indulge in." Elliot smiled again, but James could see the pinprick of tears in the corner of his blue eyes. He reached out a hand and gripped his arm, but Elliot didn't seem to notice, his eyes far away from the small hospital room.

"We came in low over their support trenches, and it was like the charge of the bloody light brigade. The volume of ground fire was incredible. Every German with a rifle was shooting at us, and the range was next to nothing. Bullets kept coming through the undercarriage. I felt one brush my leg and whistle past my face. I really thought we were for it." Elliot stopped, took out another cigarette, and lit it with shaking hands.

"I heard Ladley shout something behind me, and when I turned around, he was holding up a hand that was covered in blood. At first I thought he had been shot in the hand, but the way he was wriggling around, I could tell that he must have been shot in the arse, right through the plane's seat. I tell you, if I ever get back to Farnborough I'm going to put a metal seat in the BE2. It's a scandal that a man should have to risk his balls as well as his life." He inhaled deeply, blew a smoke ring towards the ceiling, and as the early afternoon light caught his face, James could see the tears starting to trickle down his cheeks.

"Anyway, the old man somehow kept control of the kite. The bullets started to peter out as we got over no man's land. At that point in the lines, the gap between the trenches is pretty big, perhaps a mile or so. I could see every detail. There were men cowering in shell holes, Allies and krauts, abandoned bodies, and you know what I noticed most?" Elliot asked rhetorically, turning ancient, tear-filled eyes back to James, who shook his head.

"The emptiness," said Elliot. "There wasn't a tree left standing, not a blade of grass or a bird. There was nothing but mud and misery and the haggard scarecrows that clung to their holes." His voice faltered, and he took a moment to compose himself.

"I thought we might make it when I saw our forward trenches. I could see men pointing from the firing step, and I thought we were home." He stopped again, openly weeping now.

"We weren't home though. They fired at us. An entire bloody *Allied* battalion fired at us. One of the bullets hit poor Ladley in the head." Elliot shuddered, took a last gasp of his cigarette, and dropped it to the floor.

"He must have slumped forward, because we came down so fast that I nearly fell out of the cockpit. I let go of the strut, and it just snapped in two. The wings collapsed, and that's the last thing I remember, that awful dead ground rushing up to swallow me and the terrible sound of screaming. I think that was me."

He stopped, and James stretched out a hand to his shoulder. Words wouldn't help now. Elliot grasped the hand, and they stayed like that for several moments, each lost in their own misery.

James and Elliot spent the afternoon talking. Like men in the winter of their days, they reminisced about the joys and tribulations of youth in an effort to stave off the bleak reality of the present. They laughed as they recalled the glory of past triumphs, and they consoled each other on the injustice of their occasional schoolboy defeats. In confessional tones, James talked of his night in the brothel in Amiens, and Elliot reciprocated by cheerfully admitting that he had been visiting ladies of ill repute since well before he had left Rugby. They reminded each other that they were alive, and they took comfort in the fact that they had known a happy, shared life once, even though it felt dreamlike and intangible now.

As the light in the small room began to wane, Elliot finished his story. He had woken hours after the crash in complete darkness. Delirious with shock, he'd lit a match to look at his surroundings. He had time to see that he was in some kind of deep hole before the match burnt down, to be followed by an immediate and massive burst of gunfire, which he could hear whistling above his head. He concluded he was in a shell hole somewhere between the lines and that his match had attracted the attention of sentries, although from which side he couldn't tell. Without water, without food, and with little protection against the elements, he had crawled around the hole, feeling with his hands to see if he could find anything useful. He soon came across the bodies of two infantrymen rotting in the pooled water at the bottom of the hole. He searched their backpacks and found a pair of battered water cans, which he drank eagerly despite the foul, brackish taste. He'd also relieved one corpse of a greatcoat and sat hunkered down in the watery hole, working out what to do.

After a few hours, he heard the sound of muffled voices approaching his hiding place. Terrified, he strained his ears and was relieved to hear the sound of French voices. He raised his head above the edge of the hole and could just make out a fanned-out group of men, hunched over and walking slowly through the mud of no man's land. The night was cloudy and the light was dim, and Elliot had resolved to call to them when the eerie purple light of a flare burst across the sky, throwing them into stark illumination. The men immediately dropped face down into the mud, and seconds later a burst of machine-gun fire raked their position. Elliot had thrown himself to the ground, but the cries of the men carried, and he surmised that at least a few of them had been hit. As the light faded away, he could see the survivors scrambling, and before he knew it he was confronted by a French corporal, threatening him with a rifle.

"To be honest, old chap," said Elliot, "I never thought I'd be grateful for my schoolboy French. If it hadn't been for Mr. Benfield at Rugby, I'd still be at the bottom of that shell hole now. It took me a while, but once I realised that he understood the word 'aviator,' I was home free."

"He took you back to the lines?" asked James.

"Like a shot," said Elliot, nodding. "I think he was as glad to get out of that shell hole as I was. The others continued on the patrol, but babysitting an idiot English pilot is presumably preferable to being shot at by German sentries, so we crawled back on our bellies and made the French forward trenches."

"What happened then?"

"Well, they gave me some vile gloop in a filthy tin cup for dinner, and then the officer called me into his dugout. It's curious, you know, but even after a few hours in a trench, a beat-up wooden shed ankle deep in water suddenly seems like the height of luxury." Elliot paused, and James noticed that the colour was back in his cheeks, as if the worst was over.

"He asked me about the crash," Elliot continued. "To be honest, he seemed rather put out that I had survived. He kept saying that his men had thought the plane was German, come to strafe the trench. I think he was worried about a court-martial or something."

"He should have been. They'd shot down an ally!" exclaimed James.

"Not sure it would stick, old man," said Elliot, with a hint of regret. "We were flying very low and coming from the east with the sun behind us. It'd be a brave man who'd wait to see the plane's markings before opening fire."

"I suppose so," said James bitterly. "Poor Ladley though—to go out like that"

"Better than burning," said Elliot. "At least it was quick."

James nodded, unwilling to dwell on that horrific possibility. "Did he have any people? Back home I mean?" he asked.

"There's a sister somewhere on the south coast, and his mother is still alive, although apparently she is in some sort of home. Jackson gave me the impression she was rather doolally." Elliot waggled a finger near his temple.

"That's something," said James. "At least there isn't a wife or children."

"I suppose so," agreed Elliot. "You know, I've lived cheek by jowl with the fellow for six weeks, and I only found out his Christian name yesterday, and that was by accident. I happened across Jackson typing up the incident report."

James, who had never heard Ladley referred to by anything except his rank or his surname, registered surprise.

"And what was his name?"

"George," said Elliot in a flat tone. "His name was George."

London, January 24, 1915

Even the first class carriages of the train were overflowing. Officers sat tightly packed and communicated in murmured words, lest attention be drawn to their woeful lack of privacy. Conditions for the men were markedly worse. They were sprawled in the corridors and in the storage racks, and the air was acrid with the smell of sodden wool and cigarette smoke. There'd been no food or water since Dover, and the mood in the train was fractious, a situation only kept in check by the presence of military policemen in all of the second- and third-class carriages. James sat with a kitbag bundled onto his knee, smoked incessantly, and tried to forget that the train had not moved for nearly three hours.

In contrast to his current discomfort, the last few weeks had been idyllic. Within a few days of Elliot's visit to the hospital, Sister Edith had given James permission to get out of bed and take some exercise in the grounds of the converted monastery. He'd been surprised to find a certain Spartan beauty in the medieval buildings. As an urban institution, the grounds were not particularly extensive, but they were well kept, and the gardens and the cloister offered a simple tranquillity where James found he could sit and think. The depression he felt over the deaths of Moore and Ladley began to lift, and he found that he had an urge to re-engage with the wider world. He devoured what newspapers he could find and spent his time writing letters to his family and old school friends. He was particularly delighted to find that he was able to get hold of the English press far more quickly than was the case on the base. A quiet word with Sister Edith led to a two-day-old copy of the *Times* being delivered to his room every morning alongside his breakfast, almost as if he were in a hotel.

The days were cold, so he divided his time between brief walks in the gardens and relaxing in an overstuffed armchair in front of the fire in the recreation room. James imagined that monks must have rather a narrow view of what constituted "recreation," as the room, like the monastery, was ascetic and rather dull. There was a chess set, usually commandeered by two gruff officers from the Scots Guard, a table tennis table utterly ignored by all of the patients and constructed from what was obviously an old dining table, and a handful of old books, mainly adventure stories of the sort familiar to James from his childhood reading of the *Boy's Own Paper*. The room was comfortable though, and the handful of officers that spent time there dozed, read magazines, or chatted in subdued tones, perhaps out of deference to the original purpose of the building.

The other officers were cordial, if not fraternal, and James sensed an undercurrent of hostility whenever anyone spotted the wings on his uniform. He had a few desultory conversations with one or two other patients, but he quickly became embarrassed by the minor nature of his own injuries. Most of the patients had quite serious and obvious wounds, and James felt that his own relatively normal appearance leant weight to the notion that the RFC were a pampered service. He kept to himself and devoted himself to his reading, only vaguely aware that he was doing so in an attempt to impress the much more politicised Nurse Edith.

The news, such as it was reported in the press, was of stalemate and attrition. Casualties were incredibly high in all theatres of the conflict. But, on the Western Front, there was very little tangible change to the lines that had been established in the previous autumn. The news from the east was patchy, compromised by the interrupted lines of communication across the Axis countries. The war there remained fluid, with mobile armies continuing to manoeuvre, but there had been no real breakthrough by either side. Some commentators were already referring to the conflict as the "Great War," whilst others optimistically described it as "the war to end all wars." James had read with some amusement the pithy putdown of the Chancellor of the Exchequer, David Lloyd George, that "this war, like the next war, is a war to end war." There was extensive coverage of the sinking of the battleship **HMS** *Formidable* by torpedoes fired from a German submarine off the coast of Dorset, and James read a selection of related, angry editorials. The men of Fleet Street denounced the German addiction to "underhand" forms of warfare, and James was astonished by the inability of the people at home to grasp the terrifying mechanistic realties of the conflict. In an era of machine guns and aerial bombardment, nobody could expect combatants to fight according to some prescribed rules of fair play.

He also read as much as he could about the suffragettes, ably supported in this pursuit by Edith, who delighted in lending him pamphlets and magazines. He was genuinely intrigued to realise that they were much more than single-issue campaigners and that they had a truly global reach. The movement had started in the USA in the late nineteenth century but had quickly spread around the world. It had been successful in some parts of the world, and James was shocked to read that parts of the Empire, New Zealand, and Southern Australia, in particular, had granted the vote to women in the early years of the twentieth century and that, in this case, it was Europe that was lagging behind. He read about the foundation of the Women's Social and Political Union and the gradual escalation of their campaigns in the prewar years, culminating in some of the more notorious events that he had heard about during his school years. Tales of hunger strikers, attacks on prominent politicians, and the burning of stately homes had scandalised the press. What amazed him most though was the infrastructure associated with the union. The Pankhursts had set up a printing operation to produce propaganda and established a chain of shops around the country to disseminate it. James supposed that the pamphlets and leaflets he had seen from time to time in railway stations and shops had to come from somewhere, but he hadn't really understood the sophistication of the organisation behind it. As he read more, he gradually became more convinced of the justice of the suffragette cause. Women who were capable of organising a political campaign on such a scale and coordinating what amounted to a form of violent struggle could not be stereotyped as "weaker." Although a part of him clung to a notion of the female sex as softer, more caring, and more altruistic than their male counterparts, he realised that this might be a male imposition. Perhaps women displayed those behaviours more readily because they were the only avenues open to them in society? Perhaps, at root, they were as infinitely variable in their ambitions as men? James concluded that this was something that could only be discovered if women were afforded the opportunity to shape the society around them—if they were given the capacity to vote.

His conversion wasn't absolute, and he wasn't sure about the truth of the equalitarian debate. Certainly, women could be the intellectual equals of men, and they could probably do most work comparably well. But there were tangible differences in physical prowess, and surely this was an obstacle to any true equality? He balked at the idea that women could be soldiers, for example. A notional equality of opportunity was fine in principle and, for James, didn't represent any threat to societal stability, but arguing that men and women were simply two sides of the same coin was surely a stretch too far?

Armed with a modicum of new knowledge, he had tentatively returned to his conversation with Edith. Initially sceptical of his clumsy attempts at political philosophy, she slowly came to appreciate his sincerity, the more so as he kept requesting more and more reading material, until she finally confessed that he had seen the lot. What started with snippets of conversation in the recreation room became, within a day or two, lengthy debates as they took a turn around the garden and spent time conversing in the cloister. Displaying all the zealot of a true convert, James' passion began to impress her, and her professional facade began to melt away, replaced by something akin to genuine friendship and affection. As his ribs healed, he was allowed out of the hospital and, discovering a newfound courage, he asked Edith to tea in one of the pavement cafes near the cathedral. To his immense shock, she accepted.

They had sipped weak lemon tea in the fading sunshine of a January afternoon, idly watching people strolling on the riverbank. Edith had dressed fashionably in an understated, dark grey Directoire dress, embellished with a subtle oriental motif. She eschewed the elaborate corsetry of many society women, but the high waist of the dress and her height made her look much more slender and graceful than she usually appeared in the baggy and ill-fitting nurse's uniform. She wore a cape and gloves against the cold but, boldly, chose not to wear a hat. James huddled next to her at the pavement table, wearing full uniform and suppressing an urge to reach out and touch her gloved fingers.

James had half expected her to be accompanied by a chaperone, and when he had asked her if she was comfortable accompanying him on her own, she had merely laughed and said, "The idea that I need protection presupposes ill intent on your behalf. I assume, Mr. Caulfield, that you would protest that you had no such intent?"

James had blushed and said that he hadn't. Edith had held his gaze for a moment and said, "Such conventions belong to another time. I go where I please, and at the moment, it pleases me to be here with you. Of course, if you do turn out to be a brute, I'll kick you where it hurts most!"

James had laughed at that, only half certain that she was joking.

They talked idly for nearly an hour. The politics of gender were forgotten for once, and Edith talked about her upbringing and schooling. Her mother had died as a young girl, and, unusually, she had been brought up by her father, in conjunction with a succession of nannies, whom she referred to as "unscrupulous harpies." She was an only child and had spent much of her childhood alone, reading and exploring the grounds around their country home. Her father was a local squire, and despite the best attempts of the various harpies and housekeepers of his acquaintance, he had never remarried. He doted on Edith and had educated her as well as was possible, engaging various itinerant schoolmasters over the years. She was well versed in most subjects and excelled at the classics and science. Her ambition had been to go to medical school, and she had got a place at the London School of Medicine for Women, but sadly her father died weeks before she was able to take up her place. Consumed with grief and faced with a mountain of debt from years of her father's poor estate management and gambling habit, Edith had been forced to abandon her plans, sell the family home, and move to London. She had eventually trained as a nurse and had qualified in 1912. She had been living in quarters at the Royal Free Hospital since then, until coming to France at the outbreak of the war.

To James, who had never known the absence of familial wealth, Edith's story was deeply tragic. She appeared completely unmoved though, recounting her tale in a matter-of-fact tone that gave no hint of any deeper regret. She had quickly moved on, talking of her interest in moving pictures. James had never seen one and had rather dismissed them as a fad, but Edith insisted that they offered a truly incredible experience and would one day challenge the theatre and vaudeville as the venue of choice for entertainment. She talked excitedly about the filmed version of *Hamlet* she had watched the previous year at the Cambridge Circus Cinematograph Theatre and blushed charmingly when talking of seeing an older science fiction film called "Aerial Anarchists." She admitted that she had found that particular adventure, where airships attacked London, overwhelmingly exciting, particularly in one scene where a train could be seen leaping across a chasm. Despite his obvious lack of expertise, she had asked James how such a thing might be done.

Perhaps it was the film, but Edith was also fascinated by flight. She quizzed James on his background and what it was like to fly, and despite not wishing to talk about the war, he found himself opening up to her in a way he had only ever done with Elliot. He talked of his love of the air, of its challenges and its majesty, and he waxed poetic as he described his halcyon days floating above the fields of Kent while he was learning to be a pilot. Edith was sensitive enough to avoid discussion of the intricate details of the air war, but she could barely contain her excitement about general aviation and kept pressing for more and more detail. When she mentioned that she had a few days home leave scheduled for the end of the month, James acted on impulse and invited her flying, on the assumption that their leave would overlap. The look of joy on her face as she accepted was one of the happiest moments James had experienced in a long time.

He had walked her back to the monastery, and there, in the lee of the gatekeeper's lodge, he took her hand for the first time and asked to see her again. She smiled brightly, threw her arms around him, and kissed him passionately, her gloved hands holding the back of his head. When they had disengaged and were walking hand in hand down the leaf-covered path to the monastery, James realised that he was falling in love.

They had met twice more for tea over the next few days, and James experienced the same electric sense of excitement that he had at their first meeting, together with the sheer physical thrill of kissing her. Edith was tantalising, and he began to find small excuses to seek her out in the hospital, just to see her face. Then, one morning, his travel papers arrived. He was summarily discharged from the hospital and packed off to the station in Amiens, bound for England and a one-week furlough before returning to duty. He only had time to leave a short note for Edith with details of his parent's phone number and the fervent, scrawled hope that she would call.

Now, stuck somewhere outside Victoria station, the memory of those few days sustained him. Although he had only been travelling for twenty-four hours, the journey already seemed to have taken on Homeric proportions. Wartime train travel was a mixture of tedium and horror. Packed like cattle into wagons, ablebodied officers and men picked their way through corridors covered with stretcher-bound casualties. Most of the injured were sedated, but delays meant that medical staff couldn't get to them, and the periods of relative calm were interrupted by the screams of those in pain. For James, unused to the ravages of the trenches, the level of mutilation was appalling. Men had limbs, eyes, and ears missing. Burns were common, and the sickly sweet smell of decay lingered in the air wherever large parties of the injured were deposited. He was glad of the relative comfort of the officers' carriages, where physical injury was less common. A young subaltern of the fusiliers told him that was because officers tended to get killed outright—picked off by snipers or mowed down by targeted machine-gun fire as they led a charge from a trench. Their swords and epaulettes marked them out as targets.

The train lurched into life, and there was a halfhearted cheer from the men further down the train. James looked out of the grimy window and watched the last of the Kent countryside slowly passing by, slightly obscured by the steam from the train. The sky was darkening now, the day passing from the battleship grey of English winter to the purple hues of a polluted night sky. There was a frost in the air, and, without heating, the train was cold. Hardened by months of flying in freezing conditions, James hardly felt it, but he noticed his brother officers unconsciously shrink further into their greatcoats, like tramps sleeping in doorways. *The conquering heroes return*, thought James, looking at the pale sick faces illuminated in the flickering electrical light of the carriage. He thought back to the scenes he had witnessed the previous summer. Had these men marched jubilantly down to the recruitment stations in the certain hope of martial glory? Had they envisaged returning home shattered and scarred to the ambivalent arms of a public frustrated by the stalemate? As the train limped into south London, James knew there would be no brass bands to welcome them, no fanfare, and no celebration. They were the embodiment of a far away war, forgotten until they brought home the victory or until a black bordered telegram told their relatives that they had made the ultimate sacrifice. The injured and the mentally scarred were just an unwelcome reminder of a victory yet to be won. Shuffling, haunted scarecrows that raised the possibility of defeat.

James arrived at Cavendish Square in time for the cocktail hour. He was met at the door by the egregious Harper, who permitted himself a small smile as he took James' greatcoat and advised him to meet his parents and their guests in the library. Sniffing rather obviously at James' soiled uniform, Harper informed him that he would have a bath drawn upstairs and clothes laid out for dinner. He regretted that he wasn't able to provide a footman in lieu of a valet because "all the young gentlemen have left us to do their duty." Such was the solemnity of his expression as he said this that James thought Harper could hardly have been more impressed if they had personally challenged the kaiser to a duel.

He bathed and dutifully struggled into constrictive evening dress, fumbling with his bow tie with hands that were sorely out of practice. He walked down to the library, feeling rather like an exhibit at a zoo, as the various maids of the house melted into the shadows at his approach. He could hear giggles and whispers in his wake as he made his way down the main staircase of the house. Ordinarily that would have annoyed him, but the scarcity of women at the front made the experience mildly thrilling. *A rare visit for a rooster to the henhouse*, James thought, smiling.

He entered the library, taking a drink from the occasional table at the door. Harper hadn't been dissembling. There were no servants in the room, and, shockingly, it seemed the guests were expected to help themselves. Trays of different beverages were located at judicious intervals around the room, and empty glasses lined up along the top of the mantelpiece. The whole impression would have been scandalous before the war, but now, with the casualty rate mounting in France, James guessed that it was a patriotic gesture to be seen selecting one's own G&T.

The room was quite busy. Godfrey stood at the window with his back to the room, talking in hushed tones with a stooped old man with a flowing white beard. Sylvia was animatedly holding court with two uniformed men, both of whom were chuckling at some bon mot of the hostess, as James walked in. Declining to interrupt his father, James approached his mother and was rewarded with a stifled "Oh!" of surprise, followed by a quick peck on the cheek and a broad smile.

"It is delightful to see you looking so well, my dear," she gasped, inclining her glass of amontillado sherry to clink with James. "I think you know our guests?" she added, with a sly smile.

James turned to greet the uniformed men and was surprised to see the weathered face of Hugh Trenchard looking at him, his lips upturned in a smile as he shook James' hand. He wore a tidy if unremarkable RFC dress uniform. The other man was instantly recognisable from recruitment posters on walls everywhere around the country. A huge, dark brown walrus moustache dominated a severe face that seemed set in a permanent grimace. Bushy caterpillar-like eyebrows framed piercing grey-brown eyes, and his tousled brown hair was swept back with an excess of brilliantine. He wore full dress uniform in bright scarlet, complete with epaulettes and rows of coloured bars. This was Herbert Kitchener, first Earl of Kitchener and Secretary of State for War. James shook the man's hand in a daze, ruefully anticipating a long evening.

Godfrey joined the group, beaming at James and clasping his hand in a hearty welcome. The other guest, a Mr. Coutts, was briefly introduced as a "business acquaintance" before making his excuses and departing. Collected around the detritus of glasses on the mantelpiece, the group's conversation was initially hesitant, but Godfrey soon took charge with his customary urbanity, and a lively discussion on hunting with hounds began that saw them though to the sounding of the dinner gong. Sylvia took James' arm as they walked through to the dining room, where the table was set for a full formal dinner. She slowed as they walked through the hall and whispered, "Remember, listen this evening. These men could help you a great deal, and your father has brought them here especially."

James, who had rather expected a cosy if emotional evening with his parents, was feeling disorientated. He was seated in between Kitchener and Trenchard and snatched at a glass of wine as soon as Harper had filled it. Sylvia, catching the movement, frowned slightly.

As the soup arrived, carried by a motley collection of housemaids marshalled closely by Harper, Godfrey broke the uncomfortable silence whilst looking sceptically at the pea-green liquid before him.

"A bad business with the zeppelins, gentlemen," he said, inclining his head towards Kitchener.

"Indeed," rumbled Kitchener. He appeared solemn, although James noticed that his eyes twinkled with an incongruous youthful mischief. "The prime minister is most concerned." He looked knowingly at Trenchard, who blanched and set down his spoon before replying.

"The RFC cannot be everywhere, my lord, and what few planes we have are needed in France. Unfortunately, the protection of East Anglian fishing ports is a somewhat lower priority than taking the fight to the enemy."

"I wonder, though, if the people of Great Yarmouth and Kings Lynn quite appreciate that subtlety?" asked Sylvia in a soft tone.

"Perhaps not, my lady, but we must not let the temporary discomfort of the civilian population dictate the conduct of the war. This is most excellent soup, by the way," said Trenchard.

Sylvia fluttered a hand in graceful acknowledgement but kept to the attack. "I'm not sure that twenty civilian dead can be dismissed as 'discomfort,' *Colonel* Trenchard."

"Quite right too," echoed Kitchener, soup dripping from the tips of his moustache. "It's a scandal, Trenchard. A few dead farmers might not seem a lot in the context of what is happening over the water, but it doesn't do to frighten the natives when we need the nation behind our efforts. Something must be done."

Trenchard sighed wearily, toying with the dregs of his soup. "I quite agree, my lord, which is why I have made many submissions to the war office advocating the production of armed fighters, properly equipped, to meet the aerial threat from the enemy. Indeed, Sir Godfrey here has been most supportive of that effort from the floor of the house. Sadly though, we have been rebuffed."

"Nonsense, man. Only a bad workman blames his tools," said Kitchener. "You have the planes you need, it is simply a case of pointing them in the right direction, and that is towards the enemy!" He emitted a barked rumble, which James interpreted as some sort of laugh. Trenchard reddened but prudently chose not to reply.

The Secretary of State for War finished his soup and turned to James, fixing him with a piercing mesmeric gaze. "You are strangely silent, young man. I understand from your father that you have managed to down several foes, despite still flying the much-maligned BE2. How was that possible, if the aircraft is so fundamentally unsuited to modern warfare?"

James felt uncomfortable under the collective gaze of the table and took a quick sip of wine to hide his confusion. "I'm not really sure, Sir. I suppose I was rather lucky, luckier than some anyway."

Kitchener guffawed again. "The modesty of your boy, Sir Godfrey, is most becoming. But, I suspect that good old-fashioned pluck led him to succeed where others have failed. I'm afraid, Trenchard, that if the RFC had rather more men like this young fellow, we would hear less bleating about the quality of their planes."

Trenchard bristled and glared at the older man. "I would thank you, Sir, not to impugn the honour of the men of the aerial service. As young Mr. Caulfield can tell you, they may face a different kind of war to the ground troops, but they are every bit as assiduous in their pursuit of their duty."

Kitchener held his hands up in mock surrender. "I don't doubt it, Trenchard, but you must admit that you have rather too many cavalry shirkers amongst your ranks. It is those men that I refer to. They thought they could sit out the war a few hundred feet in the air and then come down when it was all over. I imagine it is rather a surprise to them that the Germans have the temerity to actually shoot at them."

Godfrey interrupted before the furious-looking Trenchard could reply. "It is certainly true, my lord, that many gentlemen of the cavalry have transferred to the RFC, but I fear you may have misread their intentions. After all, they are more likely to face a fight in a plane than they would be stuck in stables miles behind the lines. The day of the massed cavalry charge seems finally to have passed."

"Perhaps I'm being uncharitable," said Kitchener, leaning back to allow a housemaid to take away his soup bowl. "I believe my argument stands though. If a subaltern in the infantry refuses to go over the top, then the man is rightly disciplined. If he were then to argue in his defence that his puttees were too tight or his rifle too heavy, then the man would be ridiculed. I see no difference in a pilot blaming his plane for his refusal to take the fight to the Hun."

Although angry, James held his tongue as the bevy of housemaids returned with the main course: salmon-en-croute, served with steaming vegetables. The maids began haphazardly serving the dish, with commendable effort, but without the understated elegant efficiency of trained footmen. In the corner of the room, James saw Harper wince, but the guests didn't seem to notice.

"Marvellous," beamed Kitchener. "Fish. My staff at the War Office seems to have forgotten how to cook fish. Beef is all very well, but a man appreciates a change from time to time." He raised a wine glass in salute to Sylvia and proceeded to tuck in with gusto.

The table ate in silence for a few moments, the only noise being the gentle trickle of wine as Harper refilled the glasses on the table. James took a moment to gulp back half a glass, avoiding his mother's gaze.

"Colonel Trenchard," said Sylvia with a broad smile, "I understand from Godfrey that congratulations are in order. You are for France, I believe?"

Trenchard returned the smile. "In confidence, Lady Sylvia, I am, yes. I am to command a new formation in the field, which will be called the First Wing, with oversight of several squadrons at the front, including this young man's outfit." He nodded at James.

Intrigued, James turned to the senior officer. "Will you be flying yourself, Sir?" he asked.

Trenchard chuckled. "Perhaps from time to time I may get an opportunity, but when you get to my age it seems that we are all condemned to fly a desk. Isn't that so, my lord?" he asked Kitchener.

"Damn right," nodded Kitchener. "And a bloody nuisance it is too. What I'd give to be able to fight alongside our young men, rather than toadying to politicians and filling out forms in triplicate. No offence meant, Sir Godfrey, but diplomacy is vexing to men of action."

Godfrey gave a tight-lipped smile and inclined his head towards Kitchener. "I quite understand, my lord. Even as a politician, I find dealing with my colleagues a challenging business. We are obsessed with finding shades of grey where there is only black and white. It's rather like my parachute venture. It is impossible to get the cabinet to see the sense of it."

"Ah, I had thought you might mention that," said Kitchener. "Time to sing for my supper, I suppose?"

"Not at all, my lord, I had rather hoped for your support though. I know Colonel Trenchard has backed my suggestion, as have Henderson and Ashmore and the other senior men in the RFC."

"I'm afraid you will be disappointed, Sir Godfrey," said Kitchener, looking ruefully at the meal cooling before him. "God knows I don't agree with Lloyd George on much, but, on this issue, I think he has the right of it. In my experience, what allows men to face their fear in battle is the presence of their colleagues. They do not wish to shame themselves in front of their brothers by succumbing to cowardice. The individual is therefore subordinate to the will of the whole, and fear does not unman the soldier. Sadly, despite the presence of the observer, the same cannot be said for pilots. They are individuals and they fight individually. We may disagree about whether some are deliberate shirkers, but the fact remains that there is no one else to police their conduct. I understand the value of the parachute you have licensed from our American cousins, but I say that the thing is simply not practical for deployment in military flight."

"I do understand your view, my Lord," said Godfrey in a placatory tone "but I believe that we could sensibly overcome your objections by the rigorous application of agreed rules of engagement. If, for example, fliers could only use a parachute when their machine is on fire?"

"Wouldn't work, man," snapped Kitchener. "How would the officer commanding know the truth of the matter? We would be entirely reliant on the word of the pilot. It is virtually a mandate for cowardice."

"I wonder, Sir," interrupted James, "if you have seen what happens without a parachute when a plane is on fire? I have known men to spend minutes slowly burning to death. It is a death I would not wish on my worst enemies, Sir."

Sylvia paled, and Kitchener seized on the small gesture. "Now, young man, you are upsetting your mother. There is no need for such detail. My answer, though, is that although I have not seen a man fly in such a condition, I have seen things infinitely worse on the battlefield. It is the risk of soldiering, and pilots must bear the same risks that we expect of all branches of our service. An infantryman cannot throw away his rifle, and neither should a pilot be allowed to throw away his much-more-expensive weapon. It simply won't do."

"Not even if it were to save a man's life?" asked Sylvia quietly.

"Not even then, madam. Sacrifice is part of war, and there lies an end to it." Kitchener picked up his cutlery and began to devour the remaining morsels of salmon on his plate, satisfied that the discussion was at an end. The other diners did the same and polished off the main course in an atmosphere of silent tension.

The desert and cheese courses followed, and perhaps realising that he had come close to offending the venerable old Field Marshall, Godfrey steered the conversation to more congenial subject matters. Politics and the war were left behind, and Sylvia was given rein to lengthily discourse on the problems of securing decent domestic support in wartime. Kitchener and Trenchard breezily discussed the prospects for the summer's hunting, and James was left with the feeling that France and the war inhabited a separate world. A strange academic abstraction to be discussed in the way one might the religious practices of some obscure group of south sea islanders. He sat through the rest of the dinner in absolute silence, drinking heavily and picking at the food on offer. He felt strangely deflated and found himself wishing for the companionship of the officers' mess. Amidst the finery of the Cavendish Square dining room, he felt curiously alien. He was a pauper at the feast, carefully replicating the manners of his superiors before being thrown back to the gutter. Only alcohol provided any solace.

The gong rang to signal the end of dinner, and Sylvia made her farewells as Harper ushered the gentlemen into the drawing room for port and cigars. Kitchener, pleading urgent business, called for his coat and hat and departed in a flurry of handshakes and insincere felicitations. Trenchard, Godfrey, and James settled into armchairs around the fireplace and quietly contemplated the flickering flames.

"I have some news for you, young man," said Trenchard, smiling genially from behind a cloudburst of cigar smoke. "I have read of the depletion of your squadron, and I'm glad to say that you will very shortly be back to a full complement."

James returned the smile and said, "That is good news, Sir. Will that include a new CO? We lost Captain Ladley on the same day that I was injured."

"It will my boy, and I hope you will be pleased with my choice. I have promoted Ben Vaughan to captain, and he will be taking command of Number Five Squadron." He looked at his pocket watch, "any time now. Assuming he hasn't got lost over France."

"Vaughan from Brooklands, Sir?" asked James.

"The very same," smiled Trenchard. "He has been working for me at RFC command, training new chaps, but I need men of his calibre in the field, especially given our recent losses."

Godfrey leaned forward and said, "Always good to have chaps you know around you, eh, my boy?"

"Yes, Father," agreed James, catching the other two men sharing a knowing look. There was clearly more to this appointment than met the eye, but regardless, James still welcomed it. Vaughan was an exceptional pilot, and the squadron was in desperate need.

James' thoughts were interrupted by a gentle knock on the door of the drawing room. Harper entered, apologised for disturbing them, and quietly informed James that there was telephone call for him in the hall.

"A young lady, Sir. A Miss Lannister," he said, with a carefully neutral expression. Godfrey raised his eyebrows, and Trenchard smiled. James stammered an apology and rose to follow Harper. As he was leaving, Trenchard called out.

"Never apologise for speaking to a young lady, my boy. In these times, we must take our pleasures where we may. Take your time, and don't rush back on my account. I'll bid you goodnight and hope our paths cross in France."

Nodding his thanks, James closed the door and made his way to the phone table in the hall. He could feel his heart fluttering, and his mouth was dry. Having just sat through a dinner with the most powerful man in the British military, he was amused to realise that he was far more nervous about talking to a young nurse.

Dawn on a crisp clear north London day. The sun peaked over the horizon and lit up a flawless blue sky. Trailing wisps of cloud clung to the treetops, and the biting cold morning air turned to steam with the breath of the two huddled figures perched precariously on the wire frame of the plane.

James had been forced to turn to his father to secure an aircraft for his jaunt with Edith. Aircraft were scarce, and virtually all of the privately owned machines had been commandeered by the RFC for training purposes. Only a few remained in private hands, with most of those owned by foreign nationals or people too powerful to trouble with such trivialities as military need. It was one of the latter, a choleric earl of Godfrey's acquaintance, that had been prevailed upon to allow James the use of his aging Bristol Boxkite. The machine had been mothballed at Hendon for several months, and James had arrived at the airfield hours earlier to go over it by candlelight with the earl's chauffeur, who doubled as a mechanic. Aside from a little wear to the wing's support struts, it seemed sound enough, although to James' eyes the Boxkite looked incredibly primitive, even when considered next to the BE2.

Edith had no such qualms. She had cooed with delight when she saw the plane standing ready at the edge of the takeoff strip, and, even swaddled in a shapeless ball of overcoat, her twitchy excitement was palpable. As James began the litany with the earl's mechanic, he smiled indulgently at the young woman by his side. Away from the front, she seemed years younger, her eyes smiling easily and twinkling in the pale sunshine of the early morning. James felt a burst of pride that this was a gift few people could give to their loved ones. As the engine rumbled into life, he felt Edith's hand clutch his arm and her head nuzzle against his shoulder. James wanted to shout with happiness as the plane rolled forward and he prepared to show his girl the heavens.

"Hold on," he shouted above the roar of the engine, as the plane bumped across the uneven tarmac of the airfield. Uncharacteristically, Edith squealed as the nose of the plane lifted, and the two were thrown back against the leather of the small bench that made up the cockpit. She held him tighter, and James turned his head to kiss her softly on the cheek as they began to climb.

The flimsy plane, with its minuscule engine, puttered and coughed as it rose into the glorious winter sky, slowly but inexorably gaining height. James was struck at how poor the plane seemed. The climb was painfully slow, with the gentle breeze of the morning buffeting the wings, and he was forced to compensate with precise movements of the rudder. The cold, as they climbed, was biting, and James could feel the tip of his nose, where it poked out over his flying scarf, begin to freeze.

Within a few minutes, they had reached a height of a thousand feet or so, and James banked the plane. He headed north, away from the smoke and grime of London. He would have liked to show Edith the city spread out beneath them, but the Zeppelin scare had alarmed the population, and he was reluctant to add to the growing sense of panic. Instead, they flew over a few suburban streets and isolated factories until they reached the fields and woodlands of open country. He dropped the nose and they plummeted fast, Edith emitting a childlike whoop of sheer exhilaration as they did so. At a few hundred feet, he brought the plane level and then banked in a slow, lazy arc over the farmland of Hertfordshire.

"What do you think?" he shouted to Edith, as the wind whipped through them.

"It's magnificent! I can see so much. Look down there!" She pointed, and James followed the line of her outstretched hand. Below them, an old man was in the process of repairing an old stone wall. He had stopped and was looking open-mouthed at the plane as it soared above him. A pile of stones stood to one side of the man, and James could even make out a knapsack, possibly containing the man's breakfast. The scene was like a flawless miniature, and the man so perfectly still that he added to the ornamental impression. As James and Edith passed overhead, the man waved. Giggling, the pair waved back.

They flew over a copse of trees, where the leaves sparkled with the moisture of early morning dew, and over a small hamlet, where a line of children waited in perfect formation for the long walk to school. They looked like porcelain dolls, dressed in the dull grey fabrics of the poor, until they heard the plane, broke ranks, and waved with a mania and joy that delighted the two flyers as they watched an adult try to shoo them back into line. Edith laughed with pure exaltation as James swooped low over a hay barn, lifting the plane at the last second and clearing it by only a few feet.

As the sun climbed in the sky, James reluctantly pointed the nose back towards the distant spires of London. He kissed Edith as the plane banked for the last time and wondered idly whether his soul would ever know such serenity again.

"We should marry," said James, sipping at a tepid tea in the insalubrious surroundings of Hendon's High Street café.

"Should we now?" said Edith, arching an eyebrow in what would have been a coquettish gesture if it hadn't been for her wind-whipped auburn hair and her mismatched flying clothes. "And what makes you think I want to marry?"

James reddened. Impetuosity had got the better of him, and he realised he should have anticipated Edith's response. Momentarily lost for words, he tried to hide his confusion by lighting a cigarette, but was disconcerted to find Edith staring at him intently when he finally looked up.

"Well?" asked Edith, her eyes amused.

"I don't know," admitted James. "We are getting on so well, it just seems right. I know it's not the right time, but we wouldn't have to do it right away. You could give up your work and come back to London. My family would make sure you were all right. You could make the arrangements with my mother, and then we could do it on my next leave."

"I see," said Edith, suddenly cold. "Why don't you give up your work and make the 'arrangements' with your father?"

James laughed uncomfortably, but Edith held his gaze. "I can't," he said. "I'd get shot for desertion for one thing, and even if I could get a billet back in London, I wouldn't be able to look chaps in the eye."

"Neither would I. Don't you see that?" said Edith, looking sorrowfully over the edge of her chipped teacup as she brought it to her lips.

She drank and screwed up her face as she swallowed the bitter brew. "You might be ever so important to the war effort, but I have my duties too. I can't leave. I'm an experienced nurse, and my patients need me just as much as your squadron needs you. I'm not going to marry you, because you would expect me to play the little woman, and I don't want my wedding ring to be little more than a slave halter. Even were you inclined to make a better fist of a proposal than you just have, I'd still say no."

Angry and embarrassed, James blustered. "That's how it is, is it? I don't understand you. We've been walking out for weeks. I've taken you flying. I've even told my parents about you. I love you, Edith, and I want you to be by my side, is that so much to ask?"

Edith smiled. "You are such a little boy. It'd be sweet if it wasn't so maddening. I love you too, but you have to see that this is my war every bit as much as it is yours. I'll never have an opportunity like this again to show that I can be much more than a wife and mother. I'll not have that taken away because a charming young man deigns to take me up in a borrowed plane."

"I thought you enjoyed it," said James sulkily, crushing his cigarette into the tin ashtray on the table.

"I did," sighed Edith. "It was the greatest experience of my life, but I don't intend to ruin everything by settling down under the wing of your family and waiting forever for you to come home. I deserve my chance too, and pining endlessly for a lost love is not my idea of the modern woman."

"You're impossible," snapped James. "Most women would jump at the chance. I'm offering you security, wealth, and love, and you just spurn me."

"I'm not most women, or hadn't you noticed?" smiled Edith. "I'm not spurning you. I'm happy for things to continue as they are. We can meet in France when we are able to. If we ever get leave together again, I'd be happy to walk out on your arm. I'll even meet your parents. I just don't want marriage, not yet and maybe not ever."

"What about children? If you don't marry, how will you ever have children?" asked James.

Edith burst into peals of laughter, which drew glances from the middle-aged ladies who were the only other customers in the café. "I'll tell you a secret that you might not have learned at your wonderful school. Babies aren't delivered by a stork on production of a wedding ring. They are the by-product of sex, and then only if you're not careful."

James blushed again. Even the prostitutes he had met had never been so forthright. He was ashamed to realise that he was scandalised.

He dropped his voice to just above a whisper. "You shouldn't talk so. It's not decent."

"No," said Edith loudly, looking at the two women at the adjacent table in outright challenge. "What isn't decent is the ridiculous male notion that women shouldn't have sexual thoughts, knowledge, or experience prior to being dragged to some ape's marriage bed. Mentioning sex doesn't make me a harlot, any more than your boasts in the officers' mess make you some sort of Lothario."

"I don't boast," said James sheepishly, desperately trying to keep his voice low.

"Which implies that there is something you are proud not to have boasted about!" smiled Edith, thoroughly enjoying James' discomfort.

"I didn't say that. It's just that it doesn't do to kiss and tell," said James pleadingly.

"Tell me, *Mr.* Caulfield, are you a virgin?" asked Edith. The two ladies at the adjacent table gave a sharp intake of breath and simultaneously got to their feet. Leaving a few coins on the table, they headed for the door, muttering under their breath and staring daggers at Edith, who calmly held their gaze until they were out onto the pavement. "I do so enjoy a scandal," she whispered, as the door closed behind them.

"I don't think you should ask me that. It's just not—"

"Decent? Balderdash. If marriage is such a holy and venerable state, why is it that men so rarely go to the marital bed inexperienced in the arts of love?" asked Edith.

James didn't answer, and Edith triumphantly plucked a cigarette from the pack he had left on the table and lit it.

"I would wager my life's savings that you are not a virgin, Mr. Caulfield," continued Edith, "despite your love of 'decency.' Who was it, some poor deluded servant girl on the family estate or some French peasant in a brothel? Where was your decency then?"

"I don't want to talk about it," said James in a defeated tone. "Suffice to say that you have the measure of me."

"Now we are getting somewhere." Edith smiled and blew smoke up to the grey ceiling of the little café.

"What about you?" asked James, with a sudden sense of dread. "Have you done it before?"

"I've had my moments," said Edith nonchalantly. "I could still wear white at my wedding, if that's what you mean."

"You're incredible," said James with visible relief. "I've never met anyone like you."

"I'm honest. That's all," said Edith, her eyes twinkling with mirth. "In my experience, that makes me nearly unique."

She paused and looked at the thin silver watch on her wrist. "I have just under twenty-four hours until I am due back in Dover. I rather think I'd like to book into a hotel in town, somewhere appropriately expensive, with a fine dining room."

"I'm sure I can stretch to that," said James. "I'll find a telephone and ring ahead to get a couple of rooms."

"My poor little hypocrite, Mr. and Mrs. Caulfield only need one," giggled Edith.

For the third time that day, James blushed to the root of his hair.

Near Amiens, France, April 12, 1915

Vaughan strode into the mess, where the assembled pilots and observers lounged in various states of dress. James started from his chair before remembering that, like Ladley, the new captain didn't insist on any form of protocol when the men weren't present. Around him, the men of the squadron smoked, sipped coffee, yawned, and scratched as easily as if they were in their own parlours.

The squadron had changed beyond all recognition in the three months since Vaughan had arrived to lead it. Cooper, Henderson, and Elliot were the only officers who remained from the old guard—all looking older than the fresher faces that surrounded them. Henderson's receding hair had rolled back almost to the crown of his head, and touches of grey crept in at the temples. He had celebrated his twentieth birthday the week previously, but could pass for at least twice that. Cooper, though, looked positively ancient sitting next to him. His hair had whitened, and the moustache he affected was flecked with grey, giving him the look of a disgruntled badger. He was thirty-two, but his movement and manner made him look like Methuselah in a schoolyard. Even Elliot looked older, although physically he hadn't changed much. It was his eyes that gave him away, haunted and wary, where previously they had sparkled with mischief and mirth. He had the look of a man who understood the danger he was in every time he took to the sky.

The squadron had five new pilots and two new observers, more than doubling the squadron strength from where it had been in the first months of the war. All of them were newly trained pilots, products of the RFC training school at Andover, with no experience prior to that. One of the observers, Simmons, had previously served as a cavalry officer, but the rest were volunteers drawn from the Officer Training Corps at Oxbridge or one of the major public schools. James considered them to be a lighthearted bunch, quick to humour and full of bombastic jingoism, which was marred by their obvious lack of the practical skills needed to stay alive. On his return to the squadron in early February, he had been paired with Simmons and had found him to be courteous to the point of deference. As an observer, he was adequate, but he rarely took the initiative in the air, preferring to rely on James' skills as a pilot rather than any innate ability to sense the presence of the enemy.

Vaughan, too, had changed. Gone was the dissolute maverick that James had known at Brooklands. There was still an edge of raffish disreputability to his manner, but he was clean-shaven, remained largely sober, and commanded through sheer presence and superior expertise, rather than the quirky intimidation he had employed as an instructor. When James had returned to the squadron, Vaughan had been obviously pleased to see him but had shown him no subsequent favours and never gave any public acknowledgement that he had known him or Elliot in a previous life. He ran the squadron with a mixture of carrot and stick, with the emphasis purely on flying. When not in the air, the officers were expected to relax, either in the mess or with the liberal issue of evening passes to visit the delights of Amiens. Inspections, drills, and the routine administration of the air base had been handed over lock, stock, and barrel to Sergeant Jackson, who pursued his new vocation with the exactitude of the born martinet. The only thing that drew Vaughan's ire was the failure to follow a specific instruction or poor judgement that led to unnecessary damage to one of the eight battered BE2s that cluttered the airfield's canvas hangar. Incompetence was not tolerated, and one man had been summarily transferred to the balloon observation corps when it became clear that he was barely capable of landing his plane.

The addition of pilots had made life easier in the last few months. Vaughan employed a complex model of pilot rotation, which, coupled with the inevitable fact that several planes would be out of commission at any one time, meant that it was unusual to have to fly for more than a few hours every day. Patrols consisted of two pairs of planes and were mounted at dawn and in the early afternoon, theoretically meaning that everybody only had to undertake one on a daily basis. The reality was somewhat different, as the demands of the army meant that trench mapping and artillery ranging duties were commonplace and usually required at least two additional planes during daylight hours.

The other great change had come immediately prior to the battle of Neuve Chappelle, which had taken place the previous month and had seen the British break through in the Artois region only to be rebuffed by a strong German counterattack. A team of mechanics had arrived from the Royal Aircraft Factory at Farnborough and fitted several of the BE2s with a new camera system that could be operated by the observer. It was plate-driven and incredibly unwieldy, especially when operated by men forced to wear thick leather gloves to prevent their hands from freezing during flight. The plates had to be swapped by hand, and the cameras were only useful on a steady trajectory and at low height, which heightened the risk from antiaircraft fire and enemy aircraft. The squadron had lost two planes photographing enemy positions prior to the battle, with one dead pilot and Henderson twice consigned to the hospital at Amiens with minor burns. Nevertheless, the quality of the photographs was infinitely superior to the rough, hand-sketched images produced in the early part of the war, and the army was delighted with the results.

Low-flying photographic expeditions aside, since the German attack on the airbase in January, the squadron's casualties had been relatively light. The attack at Neuve Chappelle had forced the enemy to focus its attentions on defence, and air cover in the local sector had been significantly lightened as the Germans were forced to consolidate their forces in preparation for their counter. The Albatross machines with side-mounted guns were increasingly rare, and it was now not unusual for a pilot to go several days without being threatened by anything worse than ground fire. The mood in the squadron had lightened considerably, helped by the influx of new blood, and for a few weeks there was genuine optimism that the RFC might realistically be able to gain complete air ascendency in time. When Hollis, the latest arrival from England, had made this point in the mess, Elliot had wryly replied, "Optimism is what motivates you to stroke a barking dog. Pessimism is what follows when you realise that it really does intend to bite you on the arse. My advice is to avoid the dog unless you have a bloody big stick, and you, my friend, don't."

In the blue tobacco fog of the mess, Vaughan took his customary place in front of the bar and cleared his throat. The low hum of chat subsided, and all eyes turned to the captain, who swept a curtain of dirty blonde hair out of his eyes and consulted the clipboard he held in front of him.

"Worrying rumours, gentlemen," he said, his eyes ranging over the room. "Colonel Trenchard at Wing Command has received reports from the French of a new plane sighted three days ago in the region of Verdun. According to these reports, it downed three Nieuports in less than twenty minutes, and all of these attacks appeared to have come from behind. Unfortunately, there were no survivors, so there is no corroboration from anybody who may have encountered the aircraft in the air, but an observation balloon lieutenant who reported the fight was adamant of the facts. The attacks came from behind, which means what, gentlemen?"

"A forward-fire mechanism, Sir," drawled Elliot, cigarette in hand, with his legs hanging over the arm of his chair.

"Precisely, Mr. Pearson, and given that the plane was a single-seat monoplane with a forward propeller, it seems that some Teutonic genius has found a way to fire a machine gun through the propeller."

"Sir?" asked Elwell, an acne-scarred young pilot who had joined the squadron a few weeks earlier. "If they have a gun at the front, doesn't that make them vulnerable from the side and back? Couldn't we just manoeuvre alongside?"

Elliot laughed, but Vaughan glared at him until he stopped.

"In principle, yes," said Vaughan "but these are monoplanes, Mr. Elwell, and they only have one seat, hence no observer. The Albatross, even with a side-mounted gun, is still faster than us and can climb much more quickly. If the enemy's intent is to fire along the pilot's line of sight, the plane must be built to be as manoeuvrable as possible. God knows the Nieuport is a decent enough crate, and this thing made quick work of three of them. One on one, our BE2s won't have a prayer.

"The colonel is worried, and he doesn't jump at shadows. We have to assume that this is more than just a local prototype and that we will be seeing these planes in our sector imminently. We have to change tactics now in order to avoid us being picked off in small groups. The colonel's idea is to fly in what he calls the 'Big Wing,' all of our operational craft in the air at one time. That way, we can fly in formation and at different heights. If one of these wolves turns up, we all dive on it and have a much better chance of getting an angle of fire at the pilot or engine as he follows one of us. Are there any questions?"

James cleared his throat, and Vaughan indicated that he should speak.

"What about cross fire, Sir? If there are six or seven of us buzzing round a plane, isn't there a chance that we'll hit each other?"

"Yes, Caulfield, there is," replied Vaughan. "However, we don't have machine guns, and as you well know, it'll be a miracle if we hit anything at all. Wing thinks it is a risk worth taking."

"A bloody shambles then," murmured Elliot. "Par for the course."

Vaughan bristled. "Cynicism isn't going to get us anywhere, Pearson. Unless you have any *practical* suggestions, keep your mouth shut."

"My *practical* suggestion, Sir," said Elliot, "is that the only sensible thing to do is to dive and run. We are already outclassed, and if this thing turns up in our sector, we'll be picked off one by one until somebody sends us a better plane."

Vaughan reddened and strode across to Elliot, who was still lounging across his armchair. He raised his voice and waved a finger in the younger man's face.

"I remind you *all* that refusal to engage the enemy is a court-martial offence, and I will not protect any man that does not do his duty. We are all well aware that our planes do not match those of the enemy, but the FB5 has shipped to the northern squadrons, and it won't be long until it is our turn. In the meantime, gentlemen, we will *all* do our best. Understood?"

There was a murmur of assent, and Vaughan walked to the door of the mess. "We start practicing formation flying tomorrow—the old rota will be abandoned, and you will all report at dawn. Patrols will continue as designated for today. Pearson, you will see me in my office in precisely ten minutes. Good day, gentlemen."

He threw open the door, marched out, and slammed it behind him. The officers immediately began talking in low, concerned voices. Bates came back into the mess, and as soon as they saw him they began clamouring for coffee and toast.

Elliot left his seat and approached James. "Sod that, I'm not flying until this evening," he said. "News like this demands whiskey."

"Yes," said James. "If we're going to die, I'd rather we were drunk."

Two days later, the nightmare began.

James was in the mess, sipping whiskey and listening to a scratchy gramophone record that Edith had found for him in a music shop in Amiens. The soprano warbling of Alma Gluck singing "Listen to the Mocking Bird" was not to his taste, nor to that of the other two drinkers, Hollis and Elliot, who sat sour-faced at a table near the piano. He persisted, though, because he felt it was somehow disloyal to turn it off. Edith had given him the record on his last overnight leave two weeks previously, when they had stayed in a small hotel in the Cathedral district of the town. He smiled as he recalled that Edith had booked the room in the name of "Mr. and Mrs. Pankhurst," an innocent deception that was quite lost on the prudish old women who ran the hotel. Things were different in Catholic France, and there was a deep suspicion of couples checking into reputable hotels, especially if one or both parties were in uniform. He'd learned quickly that hotel managers could spot a wedding ring at a hundred paces, and he'd spent an amusing afternoon in the pawnshops of Amiens sourcing a cheap and cheerful gold-plated piece that Edith could take on and off at will. Thus armed, they had tried various different hotels until they finally settled on the dilapidated but peaceful Le Petit Chateau in a quiet back street off the main Cathedral square. Drunken soldiers were barred there, and the only thing that disturbed their trysts was the sound of the bells for morning mass. Edith enjoyed the irony of "sinning in the shadow of salvation," as she put it, while James just enjoyed the luxury of early mornings that didn't involve getting out of bed. Under Vaughan's liberal approach to weekend leave, they had so far managed to meet four times since their return from England, much to the amusement of James' brother officers, who continued to prefer the dubious pleasures of the local brothel.

His reverie was rudely interrupted by Jackson, who bustled into the mess, sweating and visibly agitated. Alma Gluck was reaching her finale, and the sergeant's insalubrious entrance was sound-tracked by a long, piercing note that could have shattered glass. *Gilbert and Sullivan couldn't have done it better*, thought James, as the rotund NCO collected himself into a semblance of respectability.

"My apologies, gentlemen. Captain Vaughan requests that all available pilots meet him in the flight office immediately."

Grumbling, the three men knocked back the remainder of their drinks and made their way outside into the drizzle of a grey April day. They found Vaughan behind his desk, talking to someone on the telephone. He waved them to the two seats across the desk, and as Elliot and Hollis sat down James retrieved Jackson's stool from the corner table and perched on that.

Vaughan was anxious. Aside from the occasional "Yes, Sir," he was listening intently and kept nervously pushing his lank hair back across his scalp. After a few minutes, he replaced the receiver with a curt "Understood," stretched, and walked over to the map in the corner of the room.

"I hope to God you three are sober," he said. "Probably best you don't tell me," he said, holding up a hand as Elliot made to speak.

"Number 2 squadron has reported the loss of two planes. One of them was a new FB5. It's definitely the new monoplane. The Krauts apparently know it as the Eindekker. Anyway, it was last seen heading south, which takes in into our sector. Wing needs to know if there are more, and we are the chaps to tell them."

"Sir," said Elliot. "Half the squadron is in Amiens. There are only four of us here and no observers."

"I know that, Pearson. I signed the bloody leave chits," snapped Vaughan. "It can't be helped. We need to go now. Same principle we practised this morning, but with four rather than eight planes. I will fly at eight thousand feet in a wide arc over the lines. Pearson will fly exactly two hundred feet higher on my starboard side. Caulfield, you will be on my port side at the same height as Pearson. Hollis, follow the three of us, but keep your distance and maintain the same height as Caulfield and Pearson. Take rifles, pistols, bricks, anything you have. I've already instructed the mechanics to remove the cameras to get whatever weight advantage we can. Understood?"

There was a muttered chorus of affirmation, and the men followed Vaughan out to the airfield. The planes were lined up in a row at the edge of the landing strip, and mechanics, sodden in the slow drizzle, stood by the propellers of each plane. From the farmhouse, a flurry of batmen rushed out of the door balancing flying coats, rifles, and leather caps. The venerable Davies also carried James' precious Mauser hunting rifle and a box of ammunition.

Within minutes, muffled against the rain and seated in crammed pilot bays, the four planes were airborne. They followed Vaughan in a steady climbing spiral for several minutes, eventually breaking the greyish-white cloud cover and emerging into a bright blue sky with a suddenness that hurt the eyes. Beneath them, the rolling cotton wool canopy obscured the ground for as far as could be seen. The four planes were alone, cocooned by the wispy trails of moisture that hid them from the watching eyes on the ground. The sun shone brightly at this height, and the rain was a mere memory. The wind was gentle, even in the open cockpit, and for once James didn't feel the misery of the biting aerial cold.

Vaughan levelled off at a thousand feet or so above the cloud layer and turned the nose of his plane towards the east. James peeled off to the right and stationed himself above and slightly off his starboard wing. Elliot, too, took his position, on the port side, and, with the more exaggerated movements of the inexperienced flyer, Hollis swung into place at the back of the formation, veering rhythmically from side to side as he made minor corrections to his course. James, spotting that Hollis was around four hundred feet back, waved at him to close up. The young pilot waved back but could do little about his airspeed and continued to flounder in the wake of the other planes. No matter, thought James, at least back there he couldn't disrupt the tight formation of the three more experienced pilots, and he'd almost certainly have time to manoeuvre if the enemy was spotted.

They continued above the undulating wave of cloud for around ten minutes, taking them well over the German lines. Vaughan signalled a descent with a slow downward movement of his outstretched arm, and the three forward planes manoeuvred into a gentle dive, breaking through the cloud ceiling and back into the murk of driving rain. Visibility was poor, but James could just make out the spire of the church on the ground and, checking the map on his knee, placed it as the German held town of La Fére. He was impressed with Vaughan. Navigating blind across cloud cover was notoriously difficult, and the captain had dropped them directly above where the nearest German airfield was known to be. Glancing behind him, he checked for Hollis, but he had yet to emerge from the clouds. James presumed the young pilot had lost concentration and had missed Vaughan's signal.

"Bloody fool," he muttered, although he couldn't hear himself above the sound of engine and wind.

Vaughan banked and began to circle, still closely flanked by James and Elliot. They were slowly losing height, and all three scanned the ground for any telltale signs of planes taking off. The first pink puff of antiaircraft fire announced itself with a muffled thud a few hundred yards to the right, but the men ignored it, intent on locating their possible prey. James felt a headache prickle behind his eyes, a combination of focus and the whiskey he had been gently consuming since returning from formation practice that morning. Wishing he had remembered to bring his hip flask, he took his eyes off the ground and looked around him. He saw a speck in the far distance, moving quickly and ducking down out of the cloud. A plane, definitely, but whose? He shouted to Vaughan, but the wind whipped away his words, so he tried waving his arms. Elliot spotted him, but Vaughan wasn't looking behind and continued to spiral down towards the town and the airfield.

Waving to Elliot to follow, James broke formation. He banked hard right and flew straight towards the plane that seemed to have set a course directly towards them. Elliot flew parallel to him, off the port wing, and James readied his rifle. A sudden break in the cloud threw a brief shaft of sunlight over the oncoming plane, and the shadow it threw showed it to be a biplane. With a sinking heart, James realised it was Hollis. He had overshot the point at which they dived and emerged from the clouds a mile ahead of them. With a sudden sense of panic, he looked behind him to see Vaughan still spiralling down, but now a shadow was creeping off the ground and rising to meet him.

Without thinking, James dived and banked. Elliot followed him and rushed to make up the gap to Vaughan. The captain had spotted the threat, though, and had levelled off to keep his height advantage on the climbing enemy plane. Even with the airspeed advantage of a dive, the gap was too wide, so James levelled the nose and tried to take the same line as Vaughan. He and Elliot were still a good half-mile behind him though, and James watched in horror as the shadow below formed into the discernable shape of a single-wing plane.

Without warning, Vaughan dived. The plane below was still climbing, although it was doing so incredibly quickly and gaining height by the second. Paralysed by indecision, James held his course and saw the captain plummet recklessly towards his target at an angle that threatened the fragile wings of his plane. To his left, Elliot decided that attack was the only viable form of defence, and, with a shouted, "Tally-ho!" that carried over the gap between them, he dived, brandishing a pistol. Behind James, Hollis limped towards the fray, still some distance away.

James circled, torn between keeping his height, and thus maintaining a slight advantage over the climbing plane, or diving to add his weight to the fight that would break out in moments. His hands hovered over the controls when the unmistakable clatter of machine-gun fire ripped through the skies. A second plane had ducked out of the clouds and emerged almost right on top of Hollis. The decision made for him, James pushed hard down on the rudder and pulled back the stick. He was only a few hundred feet from Hollis, and he could see the man craning round, trying to get sight of the Eindekker that was sitting plum on his tail.

James flew headlong towards Hollis and the German plane at a height that would see him overfly them by about thirty feet. Clamping the stick between his knees, he retrieved the Mauser from the floor of the pilot bay and took aim at the enemy machine as he hurtled towards it. He was bemused to see that Hollis was flying completely straight and not diving or manoeuvring to shake the German from his tale. As he passed over the top of Hollis's plane, he pulled the trigger and saw the bullet rip through the stiffened canvas of the Eindekker's wing, puncturing a hole just by the Iron Cross.

Cursing, James flew straight over the German plane, dropped the Masuer, and banked hard to bring himself up on its tail. As he came back round, the Eindekker fired a quick burst, which ravaged the fuselage of Hollis's plane. The sound of tearing metal was followed by liquid-like jets of flame shooting out of the plane and into the air around. The cockpit was ablaze, and James watched in horror as Hollis's hair ignited. The plane held steady for a few seconds and then the entire structure seemed to crumple inwards, surrounded by a massive fireball. The tail section broke completely away, and the BE2 plummeted like a stone. The last thing James saw was the screaming pilot, with his hair and clothes alight, leaping from the wreckage and tumbling like a rag doll through the skies.

The Eindekker waggled its wings in triumph and, completely ignoring the slower BE2 behind, dived off towards the second engagement several thousand feet below. James, shaken, took a moment to wipe the spatters of engine oil from his flying goggles before he set off in pursuit. Maddeningly, even in a steep dive, he just couldn't match the speed of the Eindekker, and the German plane was soon out of firing range. Craning his neck over the lip of the cockpit, he could see the fight taking place a few thousand feet above the town. One of the British planes, he couldn't tell at this height which, was being closely pursued by the Eindekker. The pilot was manoeuvring left and right, banking suddenly and sharply in an effort to prevent the German plane from getting a clear shot. The second BE2 trailed forlornly behind the German, attempting to get alongside for a clear pistol shot, but the slowness of its movement meant that it was failing to make any headway.

James was overwhelmed with the futility of it all. The second Eindekker would soon be in position, and it was clear that he would simply sit on the tail of the trailing British plane until he could take it out of action with the machine gun. It was hopeless. They were utterly outclassed, and to stand and fight would lead to almost certain death. James was sorely tempted to run back to base to find solace in a bottle of whiskey. It was only the strings of long-term friendship that eventually pulled him towards the fight, all notions of martial honour meaningless in the face of such ridiculous inequality.

James followed at a snail's pace behind the diving German plane. He watched as it straightened and pulled up behind the second British plane. He could see now that it was Elliot, flying level and firing his pistol at the weaving Eindekker in front of him. He hadn't noticed the second plane behind him, and James shouted in useless warning as the German fired his gun, raking the wing and prompting Elliot to immediately bank and dive. The second plane followed.

Vaughan was still under close pursuit, and his plane was badly damaged. There was a trailing plume of black smoke coming from his engine, and there were tears in the canvas of the wing at least a hand's breadth wide. He bobbed and weaved, seemingly at random, although James could tell there was method to his manoeuvring. He couldn't shake the Eindekker, but by varying the length and duration of each turn, he prevented the German pilot from anticipating his movement and thus getting in position to fire a clear burst at the British captain. Taking a quick decision, James opted to follow Elliot, who was now frantically trying to emulate Vaughan's movement and slip the trap the German pilot had caught him in. The skipper would have to look after himself.

The twists and turns of movement slowed the pace of the battle, and James was able to level off and approach the two planes in a banking arc from above. The German plane was now in range, although the line of fire was poor. He had no view of the pilot, due to the angle of approach, and could only aim in the vague direction of the fuselage. Gripping the stick with his knees, he fired two quick shots with the Mauser. Both missed, although the second passed so close to the front of the plane that it momentarily alarmed the pilot. The German lost focus for a moment, and Elliot was able to twist away, gaining a few hundred feet on the German as he did so.

James slowed to avoid overflying the Eindekker and took up a parallel course, slightly above and behind the German plane. At around a hundred feet, the range was perfect, and he was able to fire several shots into the fuselage and wings of the plane. There was no serious damage, but the German pilot was clearly worried and banked away from James, climbing steeply.

"Time to cut and run," murmured James. He spotted Elliot heading west and climbing towards the cloud ceiling. Glancing back, he saw the second Eindekker was circling gently and seemed in no mood to chase the two planes. There was no sign of Vaughan or the other German plane, so James pointed the nose to the west and followed Elliot towards the welcome cover of the clouds. Nobody followed them, but the burning wreck of Hollis's plane in the fields below was clear testimony to the fact that this was a battle lost.

"Pardon my French, old man, but we are royally buggered." Elliot was holding court at the bar in the mess, a decanter of whiskey before him. James stood alongside, swirling the amber liquid in a crystal glass, while Bates polished a glass and did his best to convey the impression that he wasn't actually there. A few of the other pilots had drifted back from Amiens, but had elected to sit outside in the late afternoon sun, keeping an eye on the skies for any sign of Vaughan.

"I've never seen anything so fast," Elliot continued. "We can't catch them, but they'll always be able to catch us."

"They seemed slow in the roll," mused James, knocking back the glass of whiskey and slamming it onto the bar. "Maybe even slower than us, but the pitch and yaw were incredible. They just seem to eat up the air when they climb or dive. When I dived towards you, I lost a deal of distance on the blighter."

"And how do you fight something that will always come from behind you?" asked Elliot. "You can't fly and shoot backwards. Even with an observer, you'd be damn lucky if you didn't shoot through your own tail fin."

Elliot sank his whiskey and poured another two large measures into the two glasses. Bates gave them a speculative glance but went back to polishing glasses when he caught Elliot's eye.

"I read the report you gave to Jackson on Hollis, by the way. Bloody young fool. Why didn't he weave?" asked Elliot.

"I don't know," said James. "Perhaps he didn't know it was there until he fired? Or maybe he thought that if he kept level, I'd have a chance of popping the pilot? When I missed, the poor fellow was a sitting duck."

"Not your fault, old chap," replied Elliot. "You did well to hit the bloody thing at all. I've fired at least thirty rounds today and missed every time. Here's to Hollis, a brave chap and a terrible pilot."

They clinked glasses and downed the whiskey in one long draught. Elliot quickly refilled them, glaring at Bates as if daring him to comment. They lit cigarettes and sipped in silence for a moment, both thinking that Hollis had been with them for barely two weeks. The simple truth was that the boy could hardly fly and should never have been placed in a situation where his plane and his skills were both so massively outclassed.

"So, what do we do next time, Comrade Caulfield?" asked Elliot.

"Cut and run, I suppose," said James. "I don't think Vaughan is going to be coming back, and Corps will have to listen if we lose another captain. We simply can't fight them with these machines."

"It won't wash," said Elliot. "You heard the skipper. They'll have us before a firing squad if we don't try. What I'd give to get one of those HQ generals up there with an Eindekker at close quarters. Then maybe they'd see there is a difference between surrender and tactical withdrawal."

"Grin and bear it then," said James. "Try the 'Big Wing' approach and hope there is safety in numbers. At least you and I can fly a bit. It's the new fellows that will get the brunt of it. Hollis bought it because he couldn't keep to formation. If we stay tight and watch each other's backs, we might hang on long enough to get hold of the FB5 and have a chance."

"The 'Big Wing.' It's absolute tommyrot, James," said Elliot angrily. "There isn't any safety in numbers. We are like a herd of deer being stalked by a wolf. Like wolves, they will circle the herd until they can isolate the weakest one and pick him off. It'll be death by inches. We might survive for a while simply because they're sending out half-trained kids from England these days and those will go first, but we don't have long. The RFC doesn't have long. We need those new planes now, or we're all dead."

The door of the mess flew open, and Henderson rushed in looking exuberant.

"The captain's all right!" he exclaimed. "He ditched his crate in a field somewhere to the south of Amiens. Apparently, the Hun pilot landed behind him and kept shooting, so he was forced to fire the aircraft and make a run for it. He reported to an artillery command post a few minutes ago, and they phoned through to Jackson."

"Good news," said Elliot flatly. "The gallant skipper lives to fight another day, for what that's worth. I don't know about you, gentlemen, but I'll drink to that."

Three weeks later, the sunshine caressed the paving stones of the square, and couples relaxed in the pavement cafés along the riverfront of Amiens. James' hand shook as he poured the water into the glass of pastis, and Edith looked at him with pained eyes.

"You need to cut back on your drinking, darling," she said, as he sipped the aniseed liquid.

"It's the only thing that helps," James replied. "If I'm drunk, I don't think about anything except the next drink."

"Yes, but I bet it's even worse in the morning."

"There is that," admitted James, "at least until I've had a whiskey or two anyway." He smiled weakly. He'd aged in the last few weeks. His cheeks were drawn, and there were bootblack marks under his eyes. His hands shook like those of an arthritic, and there was a haunted, hunted tinge to his eyes that made him look furtive and guilt-ridden.

"Won't you tell me what's wrong?" asked Edith, in a tone so soft that it was almost maternal.

James sighed. *How do you tell someone you love that you suspect you might be a coward? That you were terrified by the death and madness around you? That images of a flaming death haunted you day and night? That the sight of the enemy on the horizon loosened your bowels and made you want to run for home? To talk of it was impossible, for it was to admit to being a lesser man than others.*

"I'm all right," he said quietly. "It's just getting tough at the base. We've lost a lot of people."

"You're not all right," said Edith quickly. "I've watched you these last few weeks, and you are falling apart. It's not just the drinking. Your mind is somewhere else, somewhere up there." She pointed at the sky with a gloved finger. "You can either tell me about it or go back to the base. I don't want to spend time with someone who can't share his worries. And don't give me any guff about secrecy, I hear all sorts at the hospital, and I'm the very soul of discretion when I want to be."

Something snapped inside James, and he felt childlike and small. He felt an almost overwhelming urge to weep, which he gulped back. He watched his hand shaking as he took a cigarette from the packet on the table.

"We've lost six men in the last few weeks," he said, his voice shaking. "Nearly all of the new men have gone, and last week Cooper and Henderson bought it. They were the last of the chaps who had been here since the beginning. There's not one person left from last September."

"Were all of them killed?" asked Edith

James laughed darkly. "No. Henderson was burned beyond recognition but somehow survived to go back to England. He'll live out his days being taunted by small boys and making people ill to look at him. I'd rather be dead than live like that." He shuddered. "The chap they sent us to replace Hollis, a boy called Morrison. He went mad. They call it neurasthenia, but the poor boy was just frightened to death. He had six hours of flight time, and Vaughan sent him up to fight bloody Eindekkers. Three days in, he'd been shot down twice. He woke up one morning and just screamed. We tried everything to calm him down, but he just wouldn't stop. He sat in the mess shaking and crying like a baby. I think Vaughan would have court-martialled the poor chap, but Elliot persuaded him to send for a doctor. He said he was quite mad. He's gone home, but they'll probably just patch him up and ship him back here."

"The poor boy," whispered Edith. "I can't imagine what it must have been like for him."

"I can," said James brutally. "It's hell, Edith. We go up in numbers twice a day, and usually one of us doesn't come back."

Edith took his hand and held it tightly. "It's all right to mourn, you know. You shouldn't believe that you have to hold it all inside. What you are experiencing is horrific, but the worst thing you can do is close yourself off or drown yourself with alcohol. You need to talk about it, darling. You need to get it off your chest."

James sighed and wiped his eyes with the back of his hand. "I can't let myself, Edith. If I talk about them, the lost ones, it's like looking into an abyss. I'm frightened that I'll go the way of Morrison. Go mad with it. I'm one of the only ones capable of keeping the new men alive, with Elliot and Vaughan. We can fly, you see. The new men can't, and they need time to adapt to the situation here. I need to stay strong for them."

"There is a difference between strength and stoicism, James," said Edith. "If you can't talk to them, at least keep talking to me. I may have the body of a weak and feeble woman, but I have the heart and stomach of a king!"

Despite his mood, James smiled. "I think the worst thing is that it is like a horrible déjà vu. Men come in, we welcome them and start to get to know them, and then days later they are dead. Another batch of eager young types turn up, and the process happens all over again. It's like some horrific version of Mr. Ford's assembly line. In come the men, out go the bodies."

"All you can do is your best, James," said Edith. "In the end, it isn't your responsibility. You can only help them as far as you can. Remember, it is the Germans killing them, not you."

"I know, darling, I know. It just feels hopeless. The new boys don't stand a chance."

"There is always hope, darling. When do you get your new planes?"

James gave a hollow laugh. "We've got them. At least we have two of them. Elliot and I have been training in them for the last few days. They are better than the BE2, and they have proper weaponry, but they still don't match what the enemy can field. The idea is that we protect the others in the formation, but with so few of them, I'm not sure how successful that will be. Maybe in time things will change, but right now we are truly in the mire."

"Well, at least there is some improvement, a small spark of hope for the future," said Edith brightly. "Anything has got to be better than shooting at planes with pistols. Things must be changing back home. Perhaps they are finally realising that you need better equipment if you are to make a fight of it. That's good news. Things will surely get better now, darling, and in the meantime, keep your head down and stay safe."

"I'll try, Edith. I owe at least that much to you."

The hangar at dawn had a grim, neglected feel. The dirty white canvas of the tent was streaked with engine oil and mud, and abandoned plane parts littered the ground like bones in an ossuary. The damage to men and machines had been so great that the mechanics were working twenty-four hours a day just to keep the remaining planes in the air. All told, there were six operational machines, four creaking BE2s, so patched up that they barely had an original part left, and the two brand new FB5s, which took pride of place in the centre of the cavernous tent.

Vaughan stroked the nose of the plane fondly as he talked with Elliot and James. Behind the plane, an exhausted-looking mechanic tinkered with the propeller.

"You'll need decent observers," he said. "Caulfield, you can fly with Simmons. He can shoot at least, even if you have to point out where the enemy actually is. The way things are, he is probably the best we have."

The FB5 was a curious-looking machine. The propeller was immediately behind the pilot area, which meant that there was some compromise on performance, especially when climbing or diving. However, that allowed the observer sitting in the front seat to man a nose-mounted Lewis Gun that rotated on a platform. In theory, the observer had a full-forward field of fire and considerable scope for elevating the gun. That meant that the gun could fire upwards at an angle or just straight along the nose. It certainly offered more flying options than the fixed machine gun of the Eindekker, for the plane was capable of attacking an enemy from below or slightly to the side, rather than being confined to simply shooting straight ahead.

"As for you, Pearson, I'm afraid that you'll have to make do with me," continued Vaughan. "The new observer, Jones, has only flown in BE2s and has absolutely no experience manning a machine gun, although he is rather handy with a pistol apparently. I've paired him with Elwell, who at least has some flying time under his belt and might be able to get within shooting range of the Hun. The others will be flying solo."

"Same formation, Sir?" asked Elliot.

"Yes, we can't risk anything too complex with these new chaps," said Vaughan. "The BE2s will fly four abreast, wing to wing. You two are on the flanks, but two hundred feet below the others, and at least four hundred feet behind. Caulfield, take the left; Pearson, the right. That way, we might tempt a lone wolf to attack the sheep, and you can harry them as they try."

"Who do we keep an eye on, Sir?" queried James. Three new pilots had arrived the previous morning, and recent experience showed that they would only have had the absolute minimum of training.

"Hornby is the worst by far," said Vaughan immediately. "I watched his training run last night, and he can barely land the thing. He'll be on your flank, Caulfield. All he has to do is point west and keep straight, but if he strays, stick with him. McCormack and Adams are better, and they'll be in the centre. There's no helping it if they lose each other. Elwell will take the right."

"Babysit Hornby, but otherwise stay back, Sir?" said James.

"Correct. Pearson, are you clear?" asked Vaughan.

"As crystal, Sir."

"Good, let's round up the infants and get this circus in the air."

The group took off into a beautiful clear morning with very little wind. As they sorted themselves into the battle formation, James winced as he watched Hornby struggling to keep his plane level. He kept overcompensating on his stick movement, and he bobbed up and down like a fishing float on a tidal river. The others were better and quickly formed a level line of planes at around seven thousand feet. Hornby eventually attached himself to the left wing and, aside from the occasional small deviation, managed to keep within a wing's length of Adams's plane.

James took his station below and behind the left edge of the formation. Irritatingly, the placement of the pilot bay immediately below the wing in the FB5 meant that he couldn't see clearly upwards, and he was reliant on hand signals from Simmons in the observer's seat to make corrections to his course. He was wondering how to compensate when Elliot's plane broke from his position to the right of the formation and banked towards him. In the observer seat, Vaughan waved at him and pointed upwards. Clearly the skipper hadn't realised how restricted the pilot's view was, and James smiled resignedly as he considered just how ill prepared the RFC sometimes was.

James and Elliot climbed slightly and levelled off in a position about fifty feet above the main formation and a considerable distance behind. It was much easier flying with a view of the convoy, and James amused himself by watching Hornby's wobbling wings as he drifted from side to side. Vaughan had been right—the boy was barely competent. *At least*, thought James, *there was no cloud for the lad to get lost in.*

The formation edged west. Although the FB5 was marginally quicker than the BE2, it was more laborious in the climb, probably due to the extra weight of the machine gun and the placement of the propeller. James was glad to be flying level at just under maximum throttle. The visibility was perfect, and the detail of the trenches and strong points were laid out beneath them like a deranged piece of line art. On cue, as they passed over the lines, pockets of antiaircraft fire burst around them, one or two of them worryingly close. It was too risky with novice pilots to try varying the height, so the formation just ploughed forwards, gambling that they would have passed by the time that the ground gunners had got the range.

Below them, they passed a German observation balloon. James could imagine the binoculars trained on the formation, counting the planes and calculating their probable direction. Within seconds, the artillery observer would be on a phone, alerting the local air squadrons to their presence and giving them detail of their numbers and likely armament. *It won't be long now*, thought James. He leant forward, tapped Simmons on the shoulder, and pointed to the balloon. The observer nodded his understanding with a grim face.

The antiaircraft fire gradually dissipated as the formation reached open country. Vaughan had selected a course that left a buffer of several miles around La Fére. Intelligence from Wing Command estimated there to be at least seven Eindekkers at the airbase near the town, and Vaughan had not wanted to risk drawing large numbers of the aircraft to the fight. Instead, the plan was simply to fly straight into German airspace until they had consumed a third of their fuel supply. When that point was reached, they would turn and fly level for their home base. The hope was that the Germans would not realise that the formation contained any machine guns and would attack in limited numbers. Thinking back to the observation balloon, James wasn't convinced that surprise was still on their side, but it was too late to turn back now. The die was cast.

In the far distance, the perfect summer sky was marred by what looked like an angry black raincloud. James watched idly as the formation moved towards it. Simmons, in the front seat, scrambled for something on the floor of the plane and came up with a pair of binoculars. To James' bemusement, he trained them on the raincloud. He shouted something and turned around in his seat so quickly that he dropped the binoculars over the side of the plane. James couldn't hear him over the whirring sound of propeller immediately behind his seat, but he got the gist, especially when he saw the oncoming cloud fan out into a long line.

"Oh Christ," he muttered. Ahead of him, the British formation wobbled as the pilots realised that there was a horde of oncoming German planes. Adams and McCormack, in the centre, instinctively started to climb, obeying the philosophy that the advantage always lay with whoever was highest. Unfortunately, Hornby and Elwell missed the manoeuvre and became distanced on the flanks of the line. By the time they realised and started to climb, there was a gap of several hundred feet to the planes that should have formed the centre.

Swearing blindly, James realised he had to fill the gap to prevent the two flanking planes from being isolated and picked off. He opened the throttle and began to climb into the cavernous space at the heart of the British line. To his right, he waited for Elliot to do the same, but his friend chose to sweep left across the back of the formation and maintain his distance. He would act as a wicket keeper then, catching anything that made it past the bat of the main British line.

For agonising minutes, the two formations struggled for height. James felt the sheer weight of the FB5 as it inched upwards. The machine gun had only been added at the cost of airlift.

Looking up and blinking into the sun, Simmons manned the machine gun. James could see the caps of the German pilots now, the glass of their goggles throwing glinting reflections as they closed. Suddenly, the noses of the German planes dipped, not quite in unison but in a rippling line, like the shiver of a peaking wave. They dived, and their engines screamed as they attacked the wavering British line. Simmons, sweat pouring from his face like rainwater, adjusted the line of the gun and fired.

James just saw the splintering of a German propeller before his plane was hit by crossfire from two sources. He lost vision and felt viscous moisture on his face. In panic, he wiped his goggles on the back of his glove, convinced that the fuel lines had been cut and the plane was about to go up in flames. The liquid was red though, and it dripped from his fingers in thick globules. In the front seat, Simmons's head was thrown back against the rim of the pilot bay. A hole had been punched in the very top of his skull, and blood streaked along the fuselage ahead of James.

Looking around, James could see that the British formation had been shattered. Behind him, the two German planes that had attacked were banking back towards him. To his left, he could see Hornby flying straight, with a German plane following on his tail and firing. Three planes, two British and one German, were spinning out of control thousands of feet below. Streams of flame followed the British biplanes. To the right, James saw some hope. Elwell and Elliot had managed to retain some kind of organisation and flew in close support of each other, with a trio of German planes circling above them. They were some way off though and could be no help to James, who realised that he was all that remained of the centre of the British line.

He ran. The total hopelessness of his position overcame him with the darkness and cold of a shadow across the sun. Creeping fear overwhelmed him and screamed to some animalistic part of his mind. Intellectually, he knew he should try to join Elliot and Elwell or move to help the floundering Hornby, but his movements were managed by a more basic instinct. He dived straight, covered in blood and unknowingly weeping. Behind him, the two Germans checked and didn't follow. Instead, they broke off and moved off towards the area where the two British planes fought on.

James kept diving steeply, feeling the stress on the struts as he approached the velocity that would cause a spin. He flashed past Hornby, off his port side, and saw the young man wave at him as the German plane behind him opened fire. James kept diving, pulling up only slightly to prevent the plane from going out of control. In the front bay, Simmons's body slumped forward in his seat, his head at a sickening angle.

He heard an explosion above him, but James ignored it. Intent only on gaining distance, he was surprised to see the detail of the ground come into focus. He could pick out individual guns and the traffic of infantry formations on a road. Only then did he bank, turning the plane for home at a height of a few thousand feet.

The sudden calm enveloped him like a blanket. Craning his neck, he could make out a cluster of planes surrounding something, but he could no longer distinguish between the British and German elements. Ahead of him, a fireball plummeted towards the ground. Hornby's plane was at its centre, spinning uncontrollably and throwing a trailing circle of flame that recalled the innocent beauty of a Catherine wheel on fireworks night.

Still weeping, he flew straight for home, only varying his height to allow for the pockets of antiaircraft fire he encountered en route. The fight retreated behind him like the horror of a nightmare receding with the rays of the morning sun. James felt a peace that came with safety.

He lied when it came time to tell his story. He gave his account to Sergeant Jackson in the mess, a decanter of whiskey before him. Through the small window, he could see Simmons's body being carried on a stretcher to the hangar, presumably bound for a coffin and a speedy burial in the industrial graveyards that peppered the rear of the British lines.

"You saw them go down, Sir? All of them?"

"Yes," snapped James, his hand shakily bringing the tumbler of whiskey to his lips. "Adams and McCormack went in the first attack, they were spinning and on fire. Hornby was caught on his own and bought it in the same way. Elwell, Pearson, and the Skipper were jumped by the rest. There were at least six of them left, even after the one I got. They didn't have a chance."

Jackson looked ashen. "You saw them hit, Sir?" he persisted. "What was their condition the last time you saw them?"

James gulped, conscious that this was the moment that could lead to the ignominy of a court-martial. "Yes, *Sergeant*," he said coldly, emphasising the seniority of his rank. "They were both hit and out of control, although I didn't linger to see if they hit the turf. I assume you have heard nothing from our front lines?"

"We have had no sightings, Sir. It's been more than an hour, and they would be out of fuel by now. I'm afraid there are no reports of British planes in our sector coming in from the west except yours. Given your account, Sir, I think we have to assume the worst."

James nodded grimly and scowled as he took a long slug of whiskey. He was numb, and a whirl of emotions fought for precedence in his mind. Waves of self-disgust crashed against the immovable rocks of his fear. His hands shook, and his eyes were hollow. Jackson gave him a pitying look before snapping off a salute and retreating to the door of the mess.

He was left alone, his shaking hands loosely cradling the decanter of whiskey. He realised that the bitter sting of the drink carried a metallic undercurrent. He examined the decanter before him realising, in horror, that his face was still encrusted with blood—Simmons's blood, and the last mark that the young observer had left on the world. James pawed at his face, dislodging coagulated clumps of red-brown matter that drifted lazily down to the table. From somewhere, there came a choking cry of pure despair: a wailing, strangled, inhuman sound of pure primal terror, like the cry of farm animals when the door of the abattoir opens before them.

James didn't realise that it came from him until long after the men came to carry his limp body to bed.

Madness is known by many names. The anchor that held James' mind to his body was cut away by the swirling waters of guilt and self-reproach. For days, he watched himself with the detached impassivity of a critic, as his body seized control and succumbed to howling fits that could only be abated by sleep. He saw the procession of medical staff arrive stage left and came to crave the breaks in performance that followed the injection of sedatives into his broken body. He saw a weeping Edith, gripping his limp hand and looking for a spark of light in the empty chasms that were his eyes. Trenchard, too, came in cameo and stood over his prone form in stoic silence for hours before bellowing orders to the cowering collection of uniformed stagehands that seemed to linger permanently at the edge of his perception. The contortions and screams of the young man at the centre of the performance did not belong to him. Instead, he came slowly to wonder what force had so broken this young man.

It was evening when he came to himself. Davies, the elderly batman, slept uncomfortably next to his bed, hunched forwards in a wooden chair. As James stirred, the old man snapped awake with an oath before cringing back as if expecting a new onslaught of screaming terror. In the dim moonlight of the room, the old man was like a balding marionette whose strings had been sharply tugged by unseen hands. Despite himself, James smiled.

"It's all right, Davies," he said in a cracked dusty voice. "I think my wits are my own."

Davies fumbled for something on the floor before him, and there was the sudden painful flare of a match as he touched it to a candle. James narrowed his eyes as the servant brought the candle closer, his lined craggy face looming unnaturally bright in the purple darkness. James noticed the tufts of grey hair that peppered his face and the pained, almost paternal concern in his eyes.

After a few seconds, the old man sighed, put his candle on the chair, and knelt next to the bed.

"You gave us all quite a turn, Sir," said Davies. "We weren't sure whether you'd come back from this one."

"How long have I been here?" asked James, his voice somewhere between a whisper and a croak.

"Three days, Sir. We were going to move you to the hospital today, if there was no improvement." Davies smiled a gap-toothed grin. "But I knew you'd be all right. Said so to Sergeant Jackson. Lieutenant Caulfield's a fighter, I said, he'll get through this."

"Thank you for your show of faith," smiled James, raising himself onto an elbow. "Any news of Mr. Pearson or Captain Vaughan?"

Davies looked gloomy. "I'm not sure I should say, Sir," he said. "The doctor said not to alarm you."

James felt his heart rate quicken in sudden alarm. He wasn't sure what he wanted to hear, but he knew with a cold certainty that this shuffling, elderly veteran held the key to his fate. Forcing himself to affect calm he did not feel, he said, "I assure you that I am almost myself, Davies. You surely understand that I have to know. Tell me what happened, and please regard that as an order."

The old man sighed and remained silent for seconds that stretched like hours. "Both were killed, so far as anyone can tell, Sir," he said eventually. "Two days back, a German plane flew over the base. We thought it might be another raid, Sir, but they just passed straight over and dropped something over the side. It was a parcel, Sir, containing papers and a few trinkets, a silver cigarette case, and a lighter made from a shell casing. The papers belonged to the skipper and Mr. Pearson, letters home I think. I've seen the captain with the cigarette case before, Sir, and it is definitely his. One or two of the lads think the lighter is Mr. Pearson's."

Vividly reminded of the laughter and sunshine of a far-off Rugby summer's day, James blinked back a tear and was unsure whether it came from relief or sorrow.

"Yes, the lighter belonged to Elliot," he said quietly. "I remember it well."

"I'm sure Mr. Pearson would have liked you to have it, Sir," said Davies kindly. "There was a note too. Sir, in English, but signed by a few German pilots."

"What did it say?"

Davies scrunched up his face as he rummaged through the storehouse of memory. "Something like, 'We salute the fallen as brave adversaries,' and a bit about 'knights of the skies' and 'fields of honour,'" said Davies. "Codswallop really, Sir, but it was decent of the buggers to let us know what happened."

James nodded. Davies's words were lost as he realised with vague shame that the confirmation of the death of his friends brought with it elation, rather than pain. There would be no court-martial, no exposure or disgrace. The men of his flight had sacrificed themselves at the altar of his reputation. Only he would ever know what had truly happened that day. Lacking eyes to discern the tainted husk of his soul, the world would see only a hero. For that questionable victory, men had died. For James, the glorious allure of a life to be lived eclipsed his love for everything and everyone else. With dawning self-awareness, he realised that, although he was now without honour, he was alive. In that moment, he felt an almost spiritual joy. Love, when lost to the cold embrace of death, brought only pain. Life brought hope and the possibilities of tomorrow. His guilt was boxed away at that moment and left to gather dusk in the attic rooms of his subconscious. The box would open again, in the darkness that comes before the dawn. But for now, James was lost to the warm glow of certain reprieve. He sank back against the bed and turned his face from Davies.

In the shadow of the flickering candle, he smiled.

Rugby School, June 26, 1915

James' feet crunched on the gravel outside the headmaster's house, and he felt the contentment that comes with several schooners of sherry and the dappled caress of weak English sunshine. James wore his dress uniform, the shining freshness of the fabric feeling constrictive after months of wearing stretched and faded khaki. Beside him, the austerity of Revd David's clerical attire looked oddly drab, like a pigeon flanked by a peacock.

He had been sent back to England within a few days of his conversation with Davies. The men on the base had proclaimed him a hero, and the new pilots that arrived from England in dribs and drabs made sure to visit him when told of his feats in the battle against the Eindekker. Edith had visited twice and bustled around him in a blur of clinical efficiency that couldn't quite disguise the relief in her eyes. They had talked of futures and possibilities, holding hands in the dusty sunlight of his room, the hum of engines in the distance. Nobody referred to his mental collapse, and the amiable medical officer from HQ had advised a period of rest to "properly recover your spirits," a diagnosis long in tact if short in specificity. He had shared a telephone call with Trenchard and been informed that he was being given leave, followed by an extended posting to a new pilot training school being established in Northamptonshire. The squadron, which in the days of James' illness had been totally paralysed, could gradually be seen to be recovering. Patrols resumed, with more fresh-faced ingenues thrown into the fray. As James had been loading his kit into the lorry that would take him to Calais and then home, Jackson had told him that a new CO was expected that same afternoon. The play would continue, but a whole new cast would now take the stage.

He had spent a pleasant few weeks in London under the careful care of his mother. He spent the time renewing old acquaintances and quickly became used to deflecting the polite enquiries of peers and parents alike, who all wished to know what is was like "over there." Settling into the routines of civilian existence brought his mind back to Elliot, but it was as if his friend belonged to another life, another London, like a peaceful, half-remembered holiday from childhood. There were no ghosts for James, and as the weeks passed he half came to believe the story he had told. His friend had died bravely, beyond his capacity to help him. It was the supreme gesture, but Elliot's sacrifice was subsumed by the admiration reserved for the living. Inexorably, his memory began to slip away, lost in the tumult of the present.

After three weeks of delicious indolence, James was sent to the new RFC training centre near the tiny Northamptonshire village of Crick. Promoted to lieutenant, he spent a few hours each day teaching boys straight out of school to fly a plane in a straight line. The evenings he spent in village pubs, relishing the quiet and anonymity and shunning the company of his brother officers. He could be found sipping pints of bitter, absorbing the trivialities of the local newspapers, and smoking a newly purchased briar pipe. He wasn't quite sure why he had taken up the pipe, but it seemed to suit the rustic calm of his mood far better than the harsh French gaspers he had become accustomed to.

The days passed quickly and easily. The work was hardly challenging, and apart from a daily correspondence with Edith and the occasional dashed line to his parents, James came to find that boredom suited him. The bullish jingoism of his pupils amused rather than irritated him, and he felt unable to dispel the illusions of the optimistic young men in his charge. At the end of May, he received a letter from Revd. David, the headmaster of Rugby, warmly congratulating him on his exploits in France and inviting him to speak to the pupils of the school at the forthcoming speech day. After deliberating for a couple of days, James accepted and agreed by return to deliver a speech on the subject of loyalty and comradeship. He wrote to Edith and invited her to join him, but she had written back to explain the impossibility of securing leave.

Now as he walked, exchanging platitudes and murmured pleasantries with a man that had once caned him, James felt the closing of the circle. Memories of Elliot were sharper here—the laughing mischievous face of his boyhood caught in fleeting glimpses among the shadows in the trees. And yet, even those flickering ghosts were echoes of another life, a time before James came to full consciousness and a world in which the man he was to become was still unknown. He missed Elliot, but only in the way that an old man might recall the endless summer of his youth. As a half dream, a chimera, a memory so achingly perfect that it could not really be true.

Ahead of him, a uniformed man shuffled through the massive wrought-iron gates of the close on his way to the Temple Speech Room. He was limping and leaning heavily on a cane. Even at this distance, James could see that his head was heavily bandaged, another casualty of the charnel house of France. The uniform he wore was plain khaki, although his presence at Rugby made it likely he was an officer. Recently returned from the front then, James thought, and he idly speculated what would bring a man back to his alma mater so soon after being wounded.

He watched the man make his agonising progress across the Barby road and vanish from view down the narrow steps leading to the door of the speech room.

"A straggler, no doubt," said Revd. David, nodding towards the disappearing figure. "Everyone else should be in the hall by now. We should hurry, Lieutenant."

"Yes, of course," said James, omitting the automatic "Sir" only with conscious effort.

The two men quickened their pace, striding along the empty gravel path that ringed the hallowed turf of the Rugby field. They crossed the road and made their way around to the rear of the neo-Gothic building, entered through a small door, and climbed a set of stairs that saw them emerge on to the wings of the stage. Rows of faces stretched before them, like corn in the field, and the clamour of hundreds of conversations was almost deafening. For the first time since his arrival at the school that morning, James felt something like nerves. He had sat through scores of speeches in this room but had never really understood the peculiar stress of holding the attention of a room full of indifferent boys and parents, all equally eager to start their summer. He shuddered slightly as he followed the headmaster on to the stage and took his place on a small wooden chair to the right of the lectern, where Revd. David shuffled a sheaf of handwritten notes produced from some hidden recess in the voluminous folds of his robes.

James scanned the crowd as the measured, monotonous tones of the headmaster calmed the clamour and began the opening lines of his annual peroration. Scrubbed, cherubic boys gave way, row by row, to the stretched limbs and awkward gait of youths on the cusp of manhood. Curiously, all the boys sported the uniform of the school's Combined Cadet Force, and the impression was of a miniature army gathered to hear the clarion call of their general. Towards the back sat phlegmatic fathers, breathing heavily in their woollen suits and flanked by proud mothers, resplendent in wide-brim hats, topped with an assortment of feathers. Here and there was the odd military uniform, and James spotted a naval captain, an infantry colonel, and the curious bandaged man in plain khaki that he had seen shuffling across the Barby road. From here, he could see the man's face, and he was startled to notice that it was horribly disfigured. The skin looked like it had been flayed off, and there were large expanses of raw, red flesh across his cheeks. His nose was ravaged too, the flesh misshapen and flattened, as if it had been spread across his face with a hot knife. Indeed, as if in silent acknowledgement of his own hideousness, the man sat completely alone, surrounded by one of the several sizable gaps in the audience. Revd. David had told him over sherry that at least half of the boys who were of an age had volunteered for France over the course of the academic year, and there would doubtless be scores of fathers engaged in war service of one kind or another and unable to attend.

In that peculiar way that the eye is always drawn towards what it should not be, James watched the strange man as Revd. David meandered through the sporting and academic triumphs of the passing school year. The man seemed rapt, sitting forward with his hands clutched before him, tightly gripping the handle of his grounded cane. His lips were moving as if in prayer, and he watched the stage with an intensity that was unusual in a room full of people itching to be out in the sunlight.

He was so preoccupied with the man that he completely missed the closing sentences of Revd. David's introduction and had to be asked twice to take his place at the lectern. Apologising in a confused flurry of words, he removed his own notes from the buttoned pocket of his RFC jacket, settled himself, and waited for the polite smattering of applause to die down before he began speaking.

In truth, he was not a strong speaker, and the power of his oratory was pretty feeble. He had compensated, though, by personalising his speech. He told anecdotes of himself and Elliot, some of which were still within the recall of the older boys of the school. They nodded in silent affirmation as he referred to the petty misdemeanours and minor achievements of their youth. The point, he said, was that it was through shared experience that bonds of loyalty were forged, that trust was earned. In the air, in the war, those things became a way to survive. It was the trust of comrades that gave men the courage to face risk, and the firmer that trust was, the more likely that each would live to see the victory that would one day come. But, in extremis, it was also comradeship and loyalty that were the bedrock of sacrifice. Loyalty to one's comrades had to be absolute, or a man could not be persuaded to lay down his life in their defence. His school friend had made that sacrifice for him and was lost forever, somewhere in a French field. The nobility behind that action had been conceived on the playing fields of Rugby, and it was right that the school should know that its son had done his duty. He closed with a call for the school to stand and applaud the name of Elliot Pearson.

As one, the crowd rose to its feet, and thunderous applause rolled towards the stage. James paused and looked at the faces. Some of the younger boys were openly weeping, and even the taciturn faces of the fathers looked ready to shed a manly tear. Stepping back from the lectern, he shook hands with Revd. David and resumed his seat on the stage. As the headmaster quietened the room and the audience sat down, James noticed that the injured man remained standing. As Revd. David dashed through his speech of thanks with almost indecent haste the man remained on his feet, leaning heavily to one side, supported by his cane. He was smiling, and something about the eyes forced James to sudden, numbing awareness. The embers of a memory stirred to life, and he saw a young, red-haired man with everything before him laughing under a tree on a summer afternoon.

This was a grotesque parody of that man, but James was coldly certain that it was Elliot.

They talked in the saloon bar of the Three Horseshoes pub. The peculiar combination of the young officer in dress uniform and the mangled veteran in battered and patched service dress presented a welcome object of curiosity to the handful of afternoon drinkers gathered in the bar.

Elliot spoke in hushed tones. His voice rarely rose above a whisper, and when it did, he would gasp and massage his throat. Close up, he looked even worse that he had done in the hall, and even now James struggled to reconcile him with his memory of his friend. The bandage completely covered the top of Elliot's head, and James knew that it disguised a hairline decimated by fire. The flesh on his face was badly burned and, occasionally, tiny globules of blood gathered on his cheeks before being wiped away with a handkerchief. His eyebrows were gone, replaced by an ugly mass of twisted scar tissue, and his nose looked melted, spread obscenely wide across his face in the style of a pugilist long used to losing. His hands were damaged too, burnt and covered in the same snaking scar tissue. He had lost the smallest digit on his right hand, and he scratched the scar obsessively as he talked.

"When we lost you, I knew we were for it," he whispered hoarsely.

James nodded, holding his breath and hardly daring to hope. So far, there had been no hint of recrimination, no accusation, no angry claim of betrayal.

"We were surrounded and cut off. I couldn't see you or Hornby, and suddenly it was just us and Elwell left, with a crowd of them buzzing round us like flies on a honey pot," he said before pausing and glancing at the pipe James had placed on the table. "Light it, would you? I can't smoke, but it doesn't mean I don't still enjoy the smell."

James obliged, packing tobacco into the musty bowl of the briar pipe and lighting it with the shell case lighter he had picked up from Jackson before his return to England.

Spotting it, Elliot smiled. "Keep it," he whispered. "I've no need for it now."

"What happened to Vaughan?" asked James, expelling a cloud of smoke into the air.

"Shot through the neck," said Elliot in a leaden tone. His hand fluttered briefly at his neck. "There were two of them on our tail. There was a long burst, and that was it. One second he was shouting for me to dive, the next there was a spurt of blood and he was gone."

"At least it was quick," said James.

"Yes," murmured Elliot. "So people say. It's funny how death has to have an upside."

"What about Elwell?" prompted James.

"Four of them were on him. The fuel tank blew in the crossfire. The last I saw of him was when he jumped out of the plane."

"Good God. Was he on fire?"

"I don't think so, but you know what it's like. You only see it in fleeting glimpses. I was preoccupied with my own situation."

"Which was?" asked James.

"Bloody appalling, old chap, as you can see by the state of me," said Elliot, somehow mustering a grin. "The fuel lines were damaged in the attack where Vaughan bought it. I was covered in oil, and that ignited when we got hit a second time. I lost power, and there were little pockets of flame all along the fuselage and all over me, I nearly jumped myself, but something stopped me," he paused, sniffing gently at the swirling tobacco smoke hanging over the table between them. "My God, that's good. And speaking of the almighty, I think it was God that saved me. I've never really been one for church, but somehow I knew that it wasn't my time. So, I dived and tried to start the engine, but it wouldn't answer. The krauts left me for dead, they could see the crate was on fire, and I suppose they thought I'd had it. I was burning but I got the thing down in a field, got clear, and then the plane exploded. That's the last I remember for a good couple of weeks."

James looked at his friend, looking for anything in his manner, his demeanour that would tell him that he knew. There was nothing in those weirdly ancient eyes to trouble him though, just an acceptance of fate.

"Some farmers found me," Elliot continued. "I was badly beaten up, as you can no doubt see, but they didn't hand me up to the Germans. They took me to a farm somewhere, and a rather beautiful young girl called Isabelle nursed me. I was in and out of consciousness and in agony. At points, they had to gag me to stop me crying out. No real medicines you see, just soap and water and a lot of prayer. She got me back on my feet after about a month or so."

"How did you get out? How did you get here?" asked James.

"The farmer that took me in hailed from Verdun originally. He had a brother killed in the opening weeks of the war and had no love for the Germans. He risked everything for me. He got me clothing, money, food, a compass, and maps, and then pointed me south. I travelled by night, through the countryside, and slept in woods and barns in the daytime. Somehow I muddled through. The few Germans that I did see mistook me for a beggar. Even krauts are leery of this face. I made it to Switzerland eventually, and the British consulate in Zurich saw me onto a train to Paris. The brass there gave me a month's leave to recover. A boat, a quick visit to your folks in London, and I found out that you were speaking today. I thought I might surprise you and, to be honest, I was interested in what you would say," said Elliot, smiling again.

"But why didn't you write to me? From Paris or Zurich, I mean?" asked James. "You might have told me you were alive."

Elliot's eyes hardened. "I might have done, but then I would have missed my own eulogy, wouldn't I? The nobility of sacrifice, the sacred bond of loyalty, greater love hath no man and all that rubbish. Because it is rubbish, isn't it James?"

James was paralysed by sudden fear. He managed to stammer: "I suppose it is, but it was what they expected to hear."

Elliot's eyes didn't flicker. They bored into James as if tunnelling into his soul. "You left me to die. You *sacrificed* me. I saw you that day, James. I saw you leave all of us. We were probably dead men anyway, but you made sure of it, you yellow-hearted bastard. And then I come home to find that you are the hero, the sole survivor of a great and noble battle. The poor bloody ensign nobly holding the colours as the savages storm the gate."

He stopped, wiped a drop of blood from his cheek, and stared at James, who blanched under the force of his gaze. "Don't worry," he continued. "I won't tell anyone. It isn't done to sneak, is it? I learned that here," He waved a hand in the vague direction of the school. "In the very same place that you learned the importance of loyalty to your comrades. It seems I just learned my lessons a little better than you did."

"I'm sorry," said James in a choked sob, tears pricking his eyes. "I was just so scared. I didn't know what I was doing."

"I would have believed that once," murmured Elliot. "Until today perhaps. All of us are afraid, you see, and sometimes fear makes you do things you thought you would never do otherwise. But you didn't stop running, did you? You never faced what you had done to me. So take a good look now, because you did this, James. My oldest friend did this to me."

James was sobbing silently now, his chest heaving as be fought to control his breath. The pipe lay abandoned and smouldering in the ashtray. "Can you ever forgive me?" he stammered.

"I'll leave that to God, for I never can," said Elliot. "This face is the mirror of your soul, James, twisted and disfigured. Every time you see me, I want you to remember that."

James looked pleadingly at his friend, but he saw no pity left in those eyes. They were dead to him, blazing with a barely controlled fury. Some part of his brain told him that this was the face of divine justice. If honour came with a price, then so too did life, and his price was to be the pain of unrequited contrition. He knew desolation in that moment, his soul steeped in the acrid bile of unimaginable shame. There were no excuses for what he had done, no amends to be made. His life had been bought with the lives of others, and one of the ghosts of the men he had killed had now returned to haunt his waking moments, as well as his nightmares. Guilt manifested and in the form of his oldest friend.

Through tears of self-pity, James watched as Elliot got falteringly to his feet. He manoeuvred carefully around the table, lent down, and brought his mouth to within inches of James' ear.

"You'll see me again in France," he whispered.

Printed in Great Britain
by Amazon.co.uk, Ltd.,
Marston Gate.